Parallel Lies

By

Georgia Rose

A Word of Warning

This book contains a scene of sexual assault and violence which may be triggering to survivors.

*****

1st Edition Published by Three Shires Publishing

ISBN: 978-0-9933318-9-3 (paperback)

Edited by Mark Barry
www.greenwizardpublishing.blogspot.co.uk

Proofread by Julia Gibbs
juliaproofreader@gmail.com

Cover design by Simon Emery
siemery2012@gmail.com

British Library Cataloguing in Publication Data
A CIP catalogue record for this book is available from the British Library.

This book is dedicated to Poppy.
There is a space under my desk where you should
be, and I miss you.

'Everyone sees what you appear to be…

…few really know what you are'

Machiavelli

Chapter 1

He wants to touch me. I can feel it. It's written in the way his body leans towards me as he talks. His arms, as though signalling his intentions, stretch across the fake wood veneer that separates us, and when he gets his chance, he takes it.

The coach pulls into the kerb outside The Snipe and Partridge and there's a slight bump as it comes to a halt, I hear the airbrakes hiss and get up to leave, slinging my bag over my shoulder as I step out into the aisle. He, being the gentleman he is, indicates for me to go first and as I pass there's his hand placed gently in the small of my back, pressing the fabric of my shirt against my skin as though guiding me. It's momentary. I don't acknowledge it and he has to relinquish his touch as he joins me walking towards the exit in the steady stream of fellow travellers. I glance at the bored looking driver as I pass and mumble my thanks to receive only a grunt in response, then I make my way down the steps.

It's late afternoon, the shadows long on the ground but there's a warmth in the air which is welcome after the overly chilled coach. On reaching the footpath I start to walk away though out of politeness I turn to face him, to say goodbye, while continuing to put distance between us with each backward step. He looks disappointed I'm going, and offers me a drink. I could certainly use one and am tempted but not wishing to prolong this exchange any longer I smile, sweetly, of course, excuse myself with the usual 'so much to do' and turn back towards home.

He is Paul, he lives in the next village to mine and is a complete catch, so I'm told. He's older, but not too old, good looking in that slightly pudgy over-indulged rich boy way because naturally in order to be a 'complete catch' he is, of course, rich, a successful professional at something or other and, he's single. Everything a girl could wish for, apparently.

Unfortunately, he is also not my type.

Which is a shame because he's a nice guy, a really nice guy actually, to be honest far too nice. The fact I've used such a lame word three times in one sentence tells you all you need to know but the point I want to make here is, that he is far too good for me.

We've arrived back from an outing organised by the Women's Institute to Danewright House which is situated about forty miles away and there's going to be a quick turnaround before the next scintillating village event, a wine tasting evening. At twenty-four I was the youngest on the trip and as I have my own car and could easily have driven there it begs the question as to why I didn't.

Simple answer, I like to support village activities.

Honest answer, I prefer the camouflage of a crowd.

A similar question could have been levelled at Paul but his intentions were plain and simple. I'd spotted them a while back and his sudden interest in appearing wherever I happened to be made it *bleedin' obvious*, as my mother would have said. I may not have left the failing city centre school I'd occasionally attended with much more than a couple of poor GCSE's and an ingrained despondency about the future but I knew how to read a man. A gift learned at my mother's knee.

As I watch my fellow travellers wander off homeward bound, exhaustion pronounced in every weary step, I doubt many will make the wine tasting later. It had been a long day with plenty of walking, particularly for those who had toured the gardens.

'I'll see you at the wine tasting then,' Paul calls to my back. *Bugger*, I think, amongst all his chatter he hadn't mentioned that little nugget on the journey, but true to my character I turn mid stride, again, call back a chirpy 'okay, see you later' and then carry on walking away. I'm surprised he hasn't got around to asking me out yet, he's not been backward in signalling his interest, leaping into the spare seat opposite me on the coach like an overgrown and enthusiastic puppy, so I guess he's plucking up the nerve. He seems the sort who would need to, and although I hope he never does summon the courage I am ready to parry if necessary. I'll do it kindly though because there's something a little geeky and adorably innocent about him, like only good things have ever happened in his life. One more reason why he doesn't need me in it.

I see Kourtney leaning up against the outside of the pub. She's been working there part-time since she turned sixteen but like most of the kids around here is not averse to socialising there as well. A couple of other girls are close by, although unlike her, because she has a whole darker look going on, they're all lip gloss and lashes, giggling over God knows what and making themselves the centre of attention for a group of boys hanging nearby. As I pass Kourtney glances at me and I'm acknowledged with the barest lift of her chin before she looks away. I'm worried about her, though I don't fully understand why because I barely know her. But there's something, a connection possibly, a recognition, where I see part of me, a younger me, in her and I guess that's where my concern stems from. I suspect she's already running with the local lads and I want to tell her so much that I know I have no right saying.

I walk off down the lane that runs between the church and the pub. On one side is the stone wall that surrounds the churchyard, on the other a small copse which soon gives way to a thick hedge bordering arable land, the fields now dark brown and newly sown following the harvest. Branches laden with blackberries spray out of the hedgerow like fountains, the fruit in various stages of ripening and I know the foragers of the village will be along to pick what they could soon enough. I'd noticed many plants, wild and cultivated, were weighed down with their fruit this year, rosehips, rowans and others, glossy red berries in abundance throughout the countryside. Joe has told me this is an indication of a harsh winter to come. The plants laying in stocks for the birds and I like the thought that nature works like that. On this beautifully warm evening, however, winter seems a long time away.

The road gradually deteriorates the further I travel along it, the surface breaking up into stone and grit around the potholes that have formed. Up ahead I see several sparrows taking a dust bath in a particularly deep one, then taking flight as I approach.

I always enjoy the walk along here, but appreciate it even more today, relishing the peace and quiet after the constant buzz of conversation on the coach, and the strain of having to behave consistently as the lovely girl and good person I'm expected to be, over such a long period of time.

Diane's cottage comes immediately after the churchyard ends and once I'm past that the tarmac peters out completely. My home is another five hundred yards further on down the track, the access to it is unmade but kept in a drivable condition by the farmer who uses it to reach his land that stretches as far as I can see. It is a mystery to me as to why a cottage would have been built this far out but I'm pleased it was, I like the isolation.

When I'd moved here four years ago, I'd rented the cottage from my neighbour, Diane. It was shabby and rundown, a fact that was reflected in the pittance of rent I paid. I guessed Diane was a little short on the readies to get any work done on it herself so I did what was needed to make it dry and warm, decorated it how I liked, and after a couple of years Diane offered to sell it to me. I had never expected to have that opportunity and because of my rather tricky financial situation we came to a mutually beneficial, but, by its very nature, totally non-binding arrangement. I paid Diane in cash which has left her in a considerably better retirement situation that she was expecting and in exchange Diane has left me the cottage in her will. She has shown this to me, not that I needed to see it. Out of necessity I have had to trust her.

I'm sure Diane has been discreet about our arrangement though because villages being what they are I am in no doubt about the chatter there must have been when someone so young was able to buy in this area. If they'd also been aware I'd done so using folding, the speculation would have ratcheted up tenfold. It has never failed to amaze me that people around here have the innate ability to both bemoan the lack of low-cost housing for their offspring while at the same time rejoice in the inexorable rise in their own house prices without reflecting for one moment on their hypocrisy. Because there is nothing, absolutely nothing, that consumes village life around here quite so much as houses, the availability thereof, the price, the location, location, location, the who's buying what where and all that. Well, other than the weather, of course, this is the green and pleasant after all.

The farm track continues straight on past the front of my cottage, which is set in the middle of a garden surrounded by stone walls built to keep out the neighbours that occupy the pastureland that runs up to it on the other three sides. Depending on the time of year this field could be home to cattle or sheep, neither of which I'd seen in real life until I came here. Occasionally horses were turned out in this field too, like at the moment, but I'd seen those before, mostly in times of trouble. Police trained and tough, their legs in padded boots, fluorescent rugs stretching across their backs and visors protecting their faces. Those horses had been intimidating, as was their purpose, but these here were peaceful and contented, grazing with a therapeutic calmness I could watch for hours.

The small wooden gate opens with a squeak, and I leave it to swing closed behind me. Hearing the soft metallic rattle of the catch I enjoy the crunch beneath my feet as I walk up the short gravel path to the front door I've recently repainted a luxuriously rich red like the crimson-licked sole of a Louboutin. This gives an indication of the colour choices for the rest of the cottage because when I walk into the lounge, and mentally correct that to sitting room as that's what people have around here, I'm instantly comforted by the warmth of the colours around me. The cottage is tiny, sitting room and kitchen downstairs, bedroom and bathroom up. Everything I need.

Flicking on the oven, I take a macaroni cheese ready meal out of the fridge, stick it on a shelf to cook, and, ignoring the bottle that calls to me, even from where it stands hidden in a cupboard, I go upstairs to take a shower. After, I dress in a pair of tailored black trousers, a white cotton shirt and court shoes before freshening my makeup. I can smell dinner cooking, crisply caramelising cheese causing me to salivate as hunger makes my stomach growl in anticipation.

I carry the deliciously bubbling container of soft pasta and thick sauce through to the sitting room using a tea towel. Putting the television on to watch the news I sit and eat straight from the dish, blowing on each steaming forkful before trusting it to my mouth, manners dictating that this is something that can only be done in the comfort of my own home. With my stomach satisfied, a few minutes later I check my watch and see that it's already time I was leaving.

Due to my slovenly eating habits it takes mere seconds to clear up from dinner and after putting on my coat I'm soon walking back up the road. I've arranged to call for Diane on the way and as I approach her cottage I can see she's already closing her front door behind her. She waits for me to catch up and asks how the coach trip was.

"Informative," I tell her and smile at the eyebrows that raise at this answer. Diane is probably my closest friend in the village. Actually, scratch that, she's my closest friend anywhere. She has at least forty years on me and would have fitted in well with the age range on the day trip but wild horses wouldn't have dragged her onto that coach filled as it was with 'old people' she'd told me when I'd suggested the idea.

"In what way?" she enquires, and while I'm not about to let on specifically I tell her what I know she will be interested in.

"Paul was on the trip."

"Really? He must be keen." I chuckle, and she carries on, as I knew she would. "I don't understand why you don't go out with him. It's not like you're getting any elsewhere is it?" Unlike any other person I know of her age, or in fact of any age, Diane is very blunt when it comes to sex. She is a highly attractive woman, has never married, telling me she believes it's an unnatural state particularly for women to live in and instead, I gather from the tales she tells, has lived a colourful life and loved a few good men, as well as many bad ones. She appears, at the moment, to be single but I'm not entirely convinced. We have the perfect neighbourly situation as far as I'm concerned and never intrude on each other's space, unless invited to.

"He hasn't actually asked me out, Diane," I clarify, "but if he does I'll be saying no."

"Why would you do that? Might as well get some practice in while you're waiting for Mr Right," she grins, then adds mischievously, "it's not like you've got anyone else parking in your drive at night."

"While I appreciate your concern over my night life, I'm fine, thanks." I laugh, knowing she sees me as some sort of project having voiced her concerns only too often that I was squandering my youth by spending so much of it alone.

We reach the church and pub and carry on up the High Street towards the village hall at the other end. Village events tend to be cyclical and four years ago as a newcomer this had been the first one I'd gone to. When I'd moved here I'd anticipated a life lived happily as a hermit but my aim had been to blend in, and not draw attention which isolating myself away would surely have done, so I'd started socialising. Even now I could easily recall how nervous I'd been, terrified I'd slip up and be spotted as the outsider I was. That side of my life has become easier the more practised I've become but the knowledge that I don't belong here has not entirely gone away.

Unfortunately, on that occasion I'd arrived at the same time as one Letitia Pritchard and not knowing any better had had little chance to get away once she'd pounced on me. Rather disconcertingly, as I was an innocent of village life then, she'd already known where I'd moved into and although I'd introduced myself clearly enough she'd bustled me into the hall

8

and announced me to the assembled throng as Maddy, thereby assuming an intimacy we did not have.

My name is Madeleine, Madeleine Ross. It is a name chosen with thought and because it is classy, and that is what is needed here, so I'd disliked Letitia from that moment on for two reasons. Firstly, for taking the liberty with my name and secondly, because it irritated the hell out of me that I actually liked the shortening, but did not care for the fact she'd been the one to impose it.

All teeth and tits, my mother would have described her as. As Madeleine I try not to be so vulgar but I see her for the trophy wife she is. Only a couple of years older than me, she's all rah, rah, rah and about being seen at the *right* events, wearing the *right* gear and mingling with the *right* people. She and her husband Ben Pritchard, some twenty years older, local property developer, estate agent and all round knob, live in the biggest house in the village, a fact which they hate people to forget, and where the lounge is called the drawing room, at least by her, the second wife, who was once his secretary I am reliably informed. I can't put my finger on precisely what's wrong with them but something is, it's like it's all a front, a fake life played out for appearances' sake, which I realise is a bit rich coming from me.

As we walk into the hall we find we're among the last to arrive and are greeted with friendly enthusiasm by those running the evening. Letitia is there and I'm unable to duck out of the effusive welcome that should surely only be reserved for those who actually like each other.

"Wow!" she says, "I didn't know you were coming," and while I mumble some banal response Diane adds something about not wanting to miss it for the world. She is so much better at dealing with her than I am, she seems to be able to respond on her level whereas I just want to slap her round the face, but I don't, because *that* is not the ladylike thing to do. Fortunately, this time we manage to get away quickly, saved by the entrance of another latecomer behind us.

After saying I'd originally have been happy to have lived in solitude I've found I actually like village life and, on the whole, the people who live here. Many who move to this village do so because they can afford to but they have no desire beyond the advantages of the clean air, the decent frontage and, if they're extra rich, the sweeping gravel drive that country living affords them, to involve themselves any further with village life. I, on the other hand, am happy to immerse myself, finding this a welcome change from the hostile streets I came from. It has given me freedom, moving here, freedom to do what I want, within reason, and I also like to be hidden among many, to be included as one of them rather than being seen as the interloper. You never know when you're going to need to be among people who'd count you as one of their own. Although I appreciate I'm only accepted up to a point and to the real villagers, the originals as it were, an outsider remains just that until they've three generations in the churchyard.

Chapter 2

Chris catches my attention from across the room and gesticulates for us to come over; he's got us a table so we make our way through the gathering towards him. Someone behind me is calling for silence and a hush descends as the village hall chairman announces that we're about to start. We reach our table and Chris greets us with his usual abundance of northern good humour. He's a great friend and although only in his fifties I had high hopes for him and Diane; she loves a younger man, I know, and even though she tells me there's no interest between them I don't get it as they seem perfectly suited to me.

"How did the trip go?" Chris whispers as we get ourselves organised.

"Very good, certainly worth taking a day off work for," I say. Chris loves a day out whenever I can manage to drag him away from his desk where he writes dry as dust academic papers on something that he's told me about before but that I still can't get my head around.

We're going to be trying whites and reds this evening, three of each, only small taster glasses but I know most of this crowd will be rolling out of here later, they can't help themselves. Once those bottles are opened there's no stopping them until every drop is gone. The wine merchant who organises this evening knows this well enough and does a roaring trade though he is far too savvy to actually be seen rubbing his hands in glee.

People are taking their seats and I see Kourtney coming out of the kitchen. I watch as she circulates the room delivering platters of cheese and biscuits to each table. These are provided in an attempt to counteract the intake of alcohol and are a most sensible addition to the event decided upon by the wisest members of the village hall committee a few years ago. This was well before my time and apparently followed a particularly raucous evening which culminated in fisticuffs on the village green after an unfortunate flare up between the then rival committees of the Village Hall and the Playing Field. All differences between the two parties are now done, dusted and relegated to the distant past, I'm told, though you can never be too sure with the fickle nature of village politics.

"Is this seat taken?" I glance over to see Paul, his hand on the back of the chair next to Chris.

Shit.

"No, go ahead," I say, staying true to my character and knowing that was the correct thing to do.

He comes closer and moves in for the kiss. It's what they do here, at least what many do, and I've had to learn the custom although it's always unnerving. Left cheek or right? I think it's meant to be right but there are a few who throw you a curve ball and go for the left then there's that embarrassing near miss with the lips. Others have gone fully European and adopted the two kisses approach and as I understand it the Belgians now do three so it's only a matter of time before that exaggeration arrives over here. Whatever form it takes it's a hazardous business and I'm relieved to get past the moment and sit back down.

"Fancy seeing you here," Diane says to Paul, "it is good of you to come and support another village's events." She's acting all innocent but I can see the wicked twinkle in her eyes as she smiles at him. Chris is suppressing a grin too and I glare across at him.

"I enjoy the company of certain parishioners, Diane," Paul replies.

"Oh, I never knew you cared," and she laughs a laugh which has a faux flirty tinkle to it and I try not to roll my eyes too obviously as I kick her under the table. She ignores me but before she can say anything further the first wine arrives and I realise I need it more than I thought.

I have little interest in wine but listen politely as each is introduced. I drink the whites, because they are there, the reds because I prefer them, and I nibble at the crackers and cheese. I play verbal ping pong with Paul, who because he's driving isn't drinking at all which rather misses the point of the evening, and Diane and Chris assist in keeping the conversation going for which I'm grateful, because after the coach trip I have little left to say to him.

This is a sociable village and as the evening wears on the noise level increases, people mingle, swop tables, chat, laugh and gossip. Over it all though I keep hearing Letitia, that braying laugh of hers that sets my nerves on edge, that high pitched whiny tone to her voice that surely only dogs could hear most of the time, and every sound she makes seems to reverberate louder than anyone else's in the room. Then there's her frequent use of the word 'Wow!' If ever there was a word overused by her it is that one, and it always comes with an exclamation mark. Almost every sentence she utters begins with it and it is her go to for any emotion that needs to be expressed.

I'm on my way to work. Wow!

My dog's died. Wow!

It's going to rain. Wow!

Seriously annoying, and I believe an affectation.

Diane says she behaves like she does because she's insecure, and lacking in self-esteem, but I just don't get it. What the hell has she got to feel insecure about? The big house? The rich husband? Which brings me on to him.

Her other half, Ben, is here tonight and playing to the room. If anyone wants to order any of the wines they've tasted they can. Most do it discreetly, a quiet word at the end of the evening, a slip of paper handed over. Not him. Oh no. He's a pretentious tosser, who's as loud as the peacock blue checked jacket he's wearing (Savile Row you will be told, even if you didn't ask) with his designer jeans. There's a bullish arrogance about him I truly dislike and I suspect he was already pretty drunk when he got here, I've noticed he has been early on at other events, and I hear him now, in fact the whole room hears him as he yells out, "Put me down for three cases of the Barolo."

Dickhead.

Paul asks after my work, about which I'm always deliberately vague, but there's not much about my job with an insurance company that is likely to prolong this direction of conversation and I find it soon causes a glazing over of the eyes. Most people's attention span is so poor, and my job so utterly uninspiring, that when we meet a second time they tend to look puzzled as if they should know, but can't quite remember so end up asking again what it is I do. This suits me and I use it to my advantage as I generally find that not only do people not see what's right in front of them but no one listens to anything anyone else has to say anyway.

I should add that the one anomaly in all this is Chris. He takes everything in. I never think he does but then months after I mention something in passing he'll refer to it again, so I have to be wary when he's close by.

These are good people, I think as I gaze around the room. I regret the fact I lie to them but tell myself I only do it to protect myself. I sometimes think had I been born here with all the advantages that a stable family life bring, I would totally be the lovely likeable person they all think I am. But you can't choose where you're born, or what you're born into and because of this I'm never completely at ease here. This is not familiar territory for me and I know I do not fit in even though it appears as though I do and because of that I can't ever relax, not fully, for fear of letting something slip. Fortunately, I'm good at putting on a front, at covering my nerves and quashing those anxieties which keep me as tightly coiled as a spring and as I sit here, surrounded by friends, neighbours and other villagers, I wonder, and not for the first time, what they would think if they knew what I really was.

I keep an eye on Kourtney. She's delivering glasses, bottles and top ups for the platters before clearing the empties and disappearing back out to the kitchen. She's a hard worker and is kept busy, just like she is when she works at the pub but tonight she's subdued, I can sense it in her, and towards the end of the evening I've had enough to drink and want to find out more. I stand and on the pretext of going to the ladies I pick up a few discarded glasses on the way and head into the kitchen. Kourtney is washing up but looks over when she hears me enter.

"Thanks," she mutters, "put 'em over there," gesticulating with her head to the over-crowded counter to her right.

"You okay?" I ask. She's a pretty girl. Long dark hair that's straightened, pulled back and held in place with an elastic band. Eyes made up in that way that makes them look like they've seen it all, and I hope they haven't.

"Yeah, fine."

"How's school going?"

"I've left." Which was what I'd feared.

"Oh, right!" I say this as if it's a positive thing and try to sound more perky about it than I feel. "What are you planning to do now?"

She shrugs her shoulders. "I dunno." Which is as I could have guessed but I'm heartened by the fact she doesn't sound fatalistic but more, searching, like she doesn't know at the moment but she desperately wants to. This is exactly what I'd expect from her.

I first met Kourtney when she was twelve years old and she turned up at my cottage with the bread I'd ordered from the shop and forgotten to collect. She comes from Oxland Drive at the far end of the village, a small estate where Kourtney and her family live in one of the few properties still in council ownership. Her mother is an 'eight by four' and I suspect number nine is on the way although the latest in the string of feckless men she attracts walked out months ago leaving Kourtney, the oldest of the eight, with a black eye. I'm concerned for her, for her loss of innocence, for her having to grow up so quickly and, for the darkness in her eyes. She's streetwise, considering she's a village kid, resourceful and hard working. A trait she has not inherited from her mother, and I have no idea who her father is. There isn't a business in the village she isn't involved in. Running errands for the shop, waiting on and clearing tables at the pub, cleaning, helping out at the garage and the flower nursery, picking up a few quid here and there babysitting, dog walking, car cleaning. She's an impressive young woman but I still worry about her because of the stage she's at, because of how precarious her life could become with the choices and decisions she will inevitably be making.

I hesitate for a moment then touch her shoulder gently, which stops her as she goes to take the next glass out of the water and she turns her head to look at me. "If I can do anything, Kourtney, help you look for jobs, write a reference, whatever, you only have to ask." She stares at me for a moment as if deciding something, then she says,

"'Ow did you do it?"

"How did I do what?"

"'Ow 'ave you got where you are, owning yer own 'ouse an all when yer so young?"

Oh, sweetheart, you really don't want to know.

I can't tell her the truth but I do wonder if I can help her out.

"Are you busy tomorrow morning?" She shakes her head. "Then pop round, about ten, and we'll have a chat." She visibly brightens, which is great, but right at this moment I haven't the faintest idea what I'm going to tell her. I know I appear as though I'm all grown up and have totally got my shit together but all I'm really doing is pretending. So I guess, like every other day living here, tomorrow will just be another I'm going to have to act my way through.

As I walk back out to the main hall I see everyone is packing up and Paul is looking for me. He sees me emerge from the kitchen and comes over; he's eager and adoring and I know it's time to bring this to an end.

"Can I take you home?" he says.

"Actually, I should walk back with Diane, it's dark down our road, no streetlamps," I explain and hate to see his face fall. I watch him as he hesitates then, checking to make sure that no one can overhear us, he leans closer.

"I could take you both." He really is a nice guy, I think. "But I was hoping to get to speak to you alone." I hold my hand up to stop him from saying anything further.

"Paul, I really value the time we spend together, it's meant a lot to me," and I see in his eyes he knows

17

there's a 'but' coming. "Having recently come out of a serious relationship and being in no position to meet anyone else yet has meant having you as a friend has been wonderful and I really appreciate the fact you're happy with us being just that."

"Oh," he says, and he looks like I've kicked that little puppy spirit in him, but then he nods and, remembering his manners, adds, "I've enjoyed spending time with you too."

"Good. Well we'll leave it at that then," and after bringing an abrupt end to the exchange, and hopefully his ambition, I move on. "I think it's time I should be leaving." We head back towards where we were sitting and he holds my coat as I slip my arms into it. He's such a gentleman, which makes the fact I don't fancy him even more of a shame, I think as we leave with Diane and Chris.

"Would you still like me to drive you back?"

"Thanks, Paul, but I'm sure we'll be fine, it's only a short walk," I smile, as he leans in to peck me on the cheek then gets into his car.

"Why did you turn down his offer of a lift?" Diane asks as we set off down the road. It's colder now and I huddle down into my coat, pulling the collar up around my ears as I tell her of my conversation with Paul.

"I don't get you. A perfectly nice man is wanting to ask you out and you must be well over that last boyfriend by now. He was from before you even moved here, and that was four years ago. You're far too young to be permanently single."

"I have things just as I want them, thanks."

"What things? You live in isolation, socialise with a load of old biddies stuck out in the middle of nowhere and have a very steady job working for an insurance company, frankly it all sounds a bit dull and I can tell you now you're wasting your best years." She's scolding me and I know she has the best of intentions but it makes me laugh inside. If only she knew. I'd thought about confiding in her before but didn't think even my lovely liberal friend Diane would approve.

We say goodnight when we reach her cottage and I hurry along to mine, eager to get home and open a decent bottle.

Later, despite the alcohol, I lie beneath my duvet forcing myself to stretch out, willing each part of my body to relax until eventually I sleep. But the tensions of the lie I live haunt my dreams, the ghosts of my past an unwelcome reminder, and when I wake my body is curled up tight, fists jammed up under my chin, my muscles rigid and aching.

Chapter 3

Kourtney is on my doorstep promptly at ten. I let her in, pleased she's turned up, and offer her coffee.

"I love yer 'ouse," she says gazing around the sitting room as I show her through to the kitchen, "it's really 'omely." I realise the warm colours aren't to everyone's taste but they make me feel comfortable and safe and it pleases me that Kourtney feels the same.

"Thanks, take a seat," and I point to one of only two chairs that fit in each side of a tiny wooden table pushed up against the wall of the kitchen. As I make coffee I get straight to the point. "I hope you don't think I'm interfering but I'm keen on helping you if I can, Kourtney."

"Thanks, but I ain't sure what yer can do."

"Have you applied for any jobs?"

"No. There ain't nothing 'ere an' I can't drive yet, don' turn seventeen till next week, so I can't get out of the village for work, and," she pauses, her eyes downcast, "without a decent job I can't pay for lessons anyway, or a car." It is frustrating because she has a good point there, the public transport around here is shocking so unless she can rely on someone else to drive her she is stuck. I knew her mother didn't drive, not that I thought she'd be up for running Kourtney around even if she could, but all of that meant working out of the village was not an easy option.

"You could always move to where you get a job." She shakes her head.

"Nah, can't leave 'ome at the moment, the kids are too small and mum ain't always of a mind to look after 'em." Her mother drinks and I don't like the fact

Kourtney is taking on that responsibility but rather than air my views on this I move on.

"What about other opportunities in the village?" I open a packet of chocolate cookies and tip them out onto a plate which I place on the table telling her to help herself.

"I'm already takin' all the shifts on offer at the pub, an' the shop, an' saying yes to whatever else anyone asks me to do." I hope that isn't strictly true and wonder how she will take it if I venture into the more private areas of her life but decide to leave that for the moment.

"Okay, so what do you want to do?" She ponders on this a moment while she chews the mouthful of cookie she's just taken.

"I wanna work for meself, I like doing things when I wanna do 'em an' I don' mind doing the dirty work, cleaning an' that, I've done a bit of it." Now we're getting somewhere.

"So why don't you set yourself up in your own little business doing all those jobs the people around here hate?" She's quiet as she thinks about this for a moment, and I carry the mugs of coffee to the table and sit down opposite her.

"I don' know anyfing about runnin' a business." I understand she's wary of what must seem like a big jump and want to reassure her.

"You do exactly what you're doing now, but more of it, offering other services, cleaning, ironing for example but you keep records and organise yourself in a more business-like manner. I'm sure Chris would help you get set up and he's bound to let you use his office to make up some flyers to deliver around the village. I'll have a word with him." I can feel her enthusiasm build as she ponders on what I'd said.

"Would yer? That'd be great." But then her shoulders slump, mirroring her spirits which becomes apparent when she speaks again. "Some people round 'ere think I'm dead common tho', I don't talk posh like you and they won't take me serious."

She is lazy with her speech. There's no reason for her to talk like she does, adults around here don't, mostly, but the youngsters seem to feel the need to dumb down, which is a shame.

"The easy answer is for you to not concern yourself with people who think like that. There will be plenty of others only too happy to take you on." I pause, then decide it's time for me to share, at least a bit. "But just so you know, I didn't always speak like this, Kourtney, I learnt how to, to fit in."

"Where'd you come from then? I always fought you was local." Her brow creases a little with her question and she lifts her mug, wrapping two hands around it before blowing on the contents.

"North London, only when I lived there I called it Norf Landon," and as I lapse easily back to my roots she gasps then giggles, which sounds good.

"Really?" I nod, grinning at her. "I'd never 'av guessed! So 'ow 'd'yer learn?"

"Mostly through old films. My mother watched them all the time and growing up I used to mimic how they spoke. Then when I moved here I kept quiet and listened until I felt confident I could join in without people spotting me for the fraud I was. Don't drop the t's or miss out the h's is a good starting place."

"Okay, so 'ow," and immediately aware she stops herself, "I mean; *how* did ye...you manage to get yer own place?" She speaks deliberately and with too much emphasis on each word but she's a smart cookie and I know if she sets her mind to it she'll soon pick it up. It shouldn't matter but it does and she would have

22

a hard time changing *some* people's perception of her anyway, purely based on her family.

"I saved the money I earned." That was the truth but one that I knew wouldn't wash with someone as sharp as Kourtney. Too few years earning too little money, she could do the maths. I see her disbelief as her eyebrows lift so I tell her the lie. "Okay, so I was left a bit of money so I could put down a decent deposit and make the mortgage affordable."

"Oh, s' no magic answer then."

"I'm afraid not, work hard and save your money is the best I have to offer. I was just fortunate. But I will give you a start and to begin with I'd like to be your first official client, if you'll come and do the cleaning here."

"Really! Thanks," she says as her face brightens, "it won't take long 'cause it's so neat and tidy." I look around trying to view my home through her eyes and I imagine against hers, with all those people squashed into it, it does look pretty organised. I have warm colours throughout, shades of ochre from golden yellows to deep oranges along with rich warming reds and there's not a thing out of place, not that there are many things anyway. I have no plants or pets, nothing that will make a mess or die if I never come back. This is important to me; I don't need the responsibility. I don't have dust-collecting clutter, ornaments or any other crap adorning surfaces and I know where everything is. The house is small, tidy and an easy clean.

"I should think a couple of hours a week would be enough, don't you?"

She nods, telling me she can fit me in first thing on a Tuesday and we agree for her to start the following week. What she says next though makes me realise I was right, she is bright.

"You said 'to begin with'?" She looks at me enquiringly.

"I did indeed, Kourtney. Not much gets past you. The second thing that I want to do is to fund you learning to drive." Her mouth drops open.

"Blimey, thanks, I didn't 'spect tha'." This will mean digging into my now meagre savings but I think she's worth it; however I need her to realise what this is.

"I'm seeing this as an investment in you, Kourtney, it's a loan, and I want you to take it seriously. I will pay for your lessons so that you can save up for a car instead and that way you will get on the road quicker, be able to get more clients by working further afield and be in a position to pay me back earlier."

"Yeah, absolutely, and with interest." I nod. I have no intention of charging her interest but she doesn't need to know that, yet. I feel good doing this. I won't deny the fact that I see a lot of me in her but she is a much better version and wish I'd had someone to help me out when I was her age; how differently things might have turned out.

We talk for a few more minutes about her business ideas and I promise to contact her once I've spoken to Chris. There's a fair bounce in her step when she leaves my place and I smile as I watch her walk off. Once she's gone I change into dark jeans, black trainers and a long-sleeved charcoal top ready for my afternoon out.

Chapter 4

I drive to Oakton, a large village cum small town a few miles away. I'm not sure at what point one becomes the other but Oakton has a high street with a few shops, a couple of pubs and one bank in it. Pricey enough to be filled mostly with the elderly, it apparently has a thriving social life built around carpet bowls, lunch clubs and dog walking.

The latest business to open, a vibrant café going under the rather twee name DelishaBuds, serves wraps, paninis and cupcakes, of course, as well as thirty-two different types of coffee. Its main clientele are those lovely mummies that take their kids to and from the nearby private school and have nothing better to do with their time than to meet, gossip and practise their one-upmanship.

Today, however, I imagine there are some sore heads among those yummy mummies as it was the school ball last night. One of those black tie and posh frock, 'carriages-at-one' types of do.

I leave my car at the end of the road by the church and walk down the cobbled street that runs behind it. Cutting through a narrow pathway between small windowed cottages that prop each other up and have leaned towards those opposite since the Tudor era, I see no one else but, in a place like this, I'm aware that doesn't mean no one sees me. The passageway opens onto an avenue. This is the posh end of town; trees line each side of the road, planted like a row of sentries standing midway across a wide verge. The houses are large, set back and hidden behind evergreen hedges.

My stomach is churning with nerves, which is only to be expected but they are heightened because I don't like doing this so close to home. However, in these days of doing as I'm told sometimes it's unavoidable.

I take a narrow public footpath that's squeezed between the boundaries of two of the houses. Once it reaches the end of the sizeable gardens it branches out to the left and right and becomes a wider track that travels through the outskirts of some woods. I turn right. It's early afternoon and with everyone still focused on lunch no one is out taking the dog for a walk, yet.

No properties overlook this path and I walk for a few hundred metres until I'm where I want to be then, with practised nonchalance, I check that no one's around and take a step to the right, off the path and into the trees that gather either side of this track, disappearing completely from the view of anyone who should now venture this way. I walk with care through the undergrowth, pleased to see there's no evidence of my passing this way before, and after only a hundred metres or so I'm at the property I need. I close in on where the back fence should be, the owners insisting on relying on the line of the woods for their boundary instead. I'm sympathetic and totally understand their preference, of course it's attractive for them to look out on. A large expanse of well-maintained garden edged with nature, what's not to like, but then in their privileged world they have not considered people like me. It's ridiculously easy for me to navigate my way to the corner of their plot, though I stay well back in the trees and I'm careful not to cause any movement that might attract attention. When I get to the vantage point I want I hunker down, my back up against a tree for support. I know I could be here for some time so I get comfortable and watch.

I check on the neighbouring properties, as I've done before, but there have been no changes, no unexpected cutting back of trees or other foliage that would open up the visibility of this garden. From my planning I know there is no CCTV although there is an alarm.

The house I'm viewing is Georgian. On its other side the white glossed windows are stylishly symmetrical around the dark green front door, and at the rear a garden room opens onto the well-tended plot. Today the old fashioned double doors leading out from this room are pinned back giving access to a paved area on which lies a dog that's flat out and absorbing the sun on this fine late September day. It's an old King Charles spaniel and, being on the heavy side of its optimum weight, doesn't pose too much of a challenge. I'm aware he's a bit blind and a little deaf but he's still more than capable of sounding the alarm if needs be. I know that, and I wait.

Shortly after I get into position a boy bounds out through the double doors onto what the people here no doubt describe as a terrace. The dog stirs, lifting his head to check on what has disturbed his slumber then satisfied no action needs to be taken he drops his head back to the ground. The boy, who is eight, is trailed by his sister, six, and he bends to pick up a long stick which he thrusts into the air as he runs across to the elaborate treehouse, with attached climbing frame, that's built between two trees in the opposite corner of the garden to me. He calls to his sister who breaks into a run to join him and I watch them as they play make-believe. I have no experience of what life with a sibling is like but they get on well and I can't help but envy their carefree childhood, one which I'm keen to keep that way.

Time passes and while the kids are active and noisy, calling to each other and occasionally shrieking as they climb and jump, I've become so still and silent, so much part of the environment that nature has come to life around me. There are bugs scurrying around in the natural detritus of the woodland which I try to ignore but then a squirrel runs down the tree next to me and sits on the ground close by. It's inquisitive, raising its nose towards me, interested, but then, not seeing a threat, it moves off slowly remaining constantly alert, its tail twitching behind. While I'm aware of this activity I keep my eye on the garden, not wanting to become distracted. Although it's been dry for a while I can feel the residual damp from the woodland floor seeping up into my jeans. I know I'm stiffening up but not wanting to alarm any creatures nearby and draw attention by frightening them into flight, I tense and relax the muscles through my legs and shoulders and hope I can get moving soon.

I surreptitiously check my watch and know it won't be long, *if* I've done my homework properly. Right on cue a woman appears at the garden room doors and the dog rolls up from his former prone position then heaves himself to his feet, before giving a whole body shake. I silently thank the woman. I always appreciate someone who leads a disciplined and orderly life, it makes mine so much easier.

She calls to the children as she leans down to clip a lead onto the dog's collar. She's elegant. Slim in her casual, but too perfectly fitted not to be expensive, linen dress, she has toned tanned limbs made that way by hours in the gym and an August spent in Provence. To top it off her sleek bob is discreetly streaked and styled to perfection by appointments every six weeks at a hundred quid a time. I note she's wearing pumps, not walking shoes, and this bothers me.

She and the children walk round the side of the house and off down the drive right past the two cars parked there. I'd spotted these already but they didn't tell me much as even if he is away on business he's often picked up by a driver so his car remains. However, the fact that she didn't lock up tells me all I need to know.

They leave at three o'clock.

Moments after they exit via the front gate he walks out of the house and into the garden. I'll be honest, this does put a dent in my plans and I consider aborting my mission. He settles into one of the two sun loungers that are between me and the house and opens up the paper he's carrying. I decide to give it a few minutes, to see if I get an opportunity, so I watch, then smile when shortly after starting to read, his head nods. I give him five minutes, I can't risk any longer, but by this time he's given up on the paper which is now lying on the grass, and his head is back against the cushioned covering of his dozing spot, his eyes closed. I wait until his mouth drops open a little and I rise to my feet.

Sticking to the trees I continue around the perimeter of the garden until I'm at the point where it is the shortest distance between the boundary and the house. He is facing away from me and this is the best chance I have. Checking my surroundings one last time I feel my heartbeat rising as, like the squirrel earlier, I'm alert for any danger. I break cover, moving swiftly on silent feet to the house. I keep my eye on him the whole time but he is sound asleep and I'm past, into the garden room and out of sight before I exhale my held breath. I take a moment as from here on in I'm in unknown territory but I'm also well aware I have no time to waste.

A passage leads directly out the back of the garden room and I can see at the far end of it is the front door. Between the two is a large hall off which there are several doors but out of which rises the staircase. I head for this and, being careful to touch nothing, I leap up it two steps at a time. At the top I pause and look around.

The wide landing spreads out in front of me as well as doubling back around the top of the stairs, and conscious of time pressure I make an educated guess based on where I'd like my bedroom to be, should this be my house.

I choose the last door on the left, which is standing half open and bingo, I choose right. It's a large room dominated by a big double bed prettied up with covers and cushions, a look that I find only those with plenty of time on their hands and considerably more style than me manage to achieve. I take in the overall impression but focusing immediately on what I'm here for, cross to the dressing table, antique, stylish, the polished patina of the gleaming wood dark with warm golden streaks running through it. The top is covered in an array of pots, tubs and tubes containing a multitude of concoctions, creams and moisturisers for treating every inch of pampered skin. Perfumes, expensive, classic scents of the sophisticated are gathered together. Guerlain's L'Heure Bleue, Maroussia, Georgio Armani, Paco Rabanne, Ralph Lauren, Joy by Jean Patou and Chanel No. 5, all Monroe wore to bed. There's makeup galore, palettes of subtle hues, nude lipsticks, bronzers to enhance those cheekbones, all quality, all class, *it's no wonder she looks so good*, I think to myself.

But there, right there in the middle of everything is what I've come for. I'm disappointed because I'd thought some effort might have been made, that it could at least have been put out of sight in a drawer. But no. It's the only thing out of place, the only thing that doesn't fit here, that doesn't belong, and I pick up my prize and drop it into the breast pocket of my shirt. I'm conscious that the time I have available to me is ticking away and I cross to the window which looks out onto the rear garden. The paper still lies on the grass but the sun lounger is no longer occupied.

Uh oh.

I freeze, tense and vigilant, straining for any sound, but I hear nothing.

I tiptoe to the door, thankful that like everything else here the floors are quality, and solid, there are no creaking floorboards to contend with, and I peer out onto the landing. My heart is racing, adrenaline fuelled and pumping hard, the beat sounding in my ears. I'm on full alert.

I check my watch. It's 3:18 and I know I'm short on time. The wife wearing pumps means a short walk today, for whatever reason. It means twenty minutes, perhaps thirty, but no longer. I'd hoped for the usual afternoon hour but I'd taken the chance even though I'd seen the pumps, and now time is running out.

I creep to the top of the stairs and carefully peer over the banister; it's original oak, the spindles ornately carved but I don't touch. Still no one, although I hear his voice. His conversation. He's on the phone and he's telling someone they shouldn't call him here. This is his home, his family, his wife, anyone could have answered, and he's told her not to call. He's annoyed, I can tell, yet he's trying to pacify and he's promising he'll get away, he'll see her soon. He promises, promises, promises and I can tell by his tone she's calming down at the other end and I think, *you utter bastard. You risk blowing this quality life, this quality family apart by your selfish actions. By not being able to keep your dick in your trousers you risk losing all of this*, but while I'm thinking it I also realise he's in the garden room and between me and my planned escape route.

Shit.

I know there's a side door leading out via the kitchen but that is also accessed through the garden room so there's only one alternative. The front door.

It's 3:23 and I'm already on borrowed time. I know from my previous reconnaissance that no other house has a direct view onto the front door of this one but I also know that at any moment the wife and children could turn into the drive and see me coming out of it. And that's going to take some explaining.

But there is no other option, I'm going to have to go for it.

Stealthy and silent, I hurry down the stairs and cross the hall. I've already checked back down the passageway that I can't see him. He's still on the phone, coaxing, flirting and making me nauseous.

One quick glance again and there's still no sign of him, I peer through the peephole in the door and say a silent thank-you for the beauty of the symmetricity of the Georgian design which means I can see straight down the drive. I pull my sleeve down over my hand and turn the key, delighting in the well-oiled bolt that draws back quietly. My covered hand is on the aged brass door knob and I'm about to turn it when I take a final glance out and there in the drive is the wife, the panting dog and the children, running ahead.

I pause, frozen and then look behind me. He has heard his children coming and is trying to end the call. His kisses sicken me. But I'm in a dilemma as I can no longer see her out of the peephole, and I try and gauge how long it will take for her to disappear out of view of the front door and around the side of the house. I give it as long as I dare, as I hear the children squealing towards their father who I can see now standing in the doorway to the garden. His back is to me and he's calling to them asking if they had a good walk and I hate his two-faced deceit.

It's now or never. Before the children reach him and have every chance of seeing me I turn the doorknob, pull open the door to the bare minimum needed and slip out through the gap. I glance around, pull the door closed, being careful not to let it bang and run to the corner. I'm on gravel and the crunch beneath my feet sounds to my ears like a thousand crisp packets being stamped on with every step. But when I peep around the corner I see no one, and taking my chance I run flat out for the woods, disappearing into the cover they provide and getting as far back from the house as I can. My breathing is heavy, caused not by the exertion but by the fear of being caught and I'm annoyed I've not controlled that better. This is not meant to be amateur hour, I tell myself, and it's something to work on.

I stop for a moment and glance back through the trees and across the garden. I see him greet his wife, a peck on the cheek as she reaches him, his hand lingering in the small of her back as they turn and watch their children who are racing over to the climbing frame again. Three of them playing at happy families while the other merely pretends.

I retrace my steps back out of the woods, checking no one is on the main track before I emerge onto it and return to my car.

I resist the urge and wait until I'm home to examine the treasure in my pocket. I've been conscious of it though, from the moment I dropped it in there I've felt it, the weight, hanging next to my breast. But I'm patient and once I'm back in my cottage I withdraw the necklace and spread it out across my palm. There's quality in every stone, every cut, every style is shown here, a host of diamonds, sparkling and twinkling like bright beams of sunlight glinting off the sea, encircle sapphires as darkly blue as a perfect summer night. I carry the necklace up to my bedroom and from my bedside cabinet I take a small, black cloth bag which I drop it into before tightening up the neck with the drawstring. I go to the cupboard that's built into the oddly shaped corner of the room and which serves as my wardrobe, and remove a floorboard from the base by first pressing it down and then sliding it left until the end is released and I drop the bag into the recess below.

My work is done for the day and, fancying a little company, I call a friend.

"Pub?" I say, when he answers.

"Pub." His response before he ends the call.

After the shortest possible English conversation, I slip on a jacket, leather, black, and well used, slide some cash into my pocket and leave.

Chapter 5

As I pass Diane's place I see Joe working in the garden. He stands up straight when I greet him, pushing himself up using the handle of the fork he's been working into the ground. He makes me smile as he comes from an age when a tie was always worn. Today his is rich hazelnut in colour and unobtrusive against his cream and brown checked shirt. His sleeves are rolled up. As usual he is wearing a waistcoat and I know his tweed jacket, its pockets stuffed with a pouch of tobacco and a pipe waiting for a break to be relit and enjoyed, will be hanging over the handle of whatever implement he was using when he discarded it. He's a peaceful man, ageless, gentle and warm. I see him most days, often working in Diane's garden which he tends along with others, including my own, and I can't imagine him ever not being there.

"You alright, Joe?" I enquire over the garden wall.

"Aye, Miss. And you?"

"Fine, thanks. Diane around?"

"Gone out to get in a bit of shopping for supper."

"Oh, okay. Well I'm off to meet Chris for a drink if you or Diane want to join us?"

"Thank you, I'll maybe see you a bit later, and I'll tell Diane." I knew there was no chance of him joining us, there never was, but I always asked. I guessed it was unlikely Diane would make it either, being reluctant to come back out again once she'd got home. I also suspected she would be cooking supper for Joe as well as herself. She had never said as much, but I had an inkling that their relationship stretched further than Joe just being her gardener. He lives at the other end of the village and I've wondered for a while if they

35

had something going on. I'd seen them once, a moment and nothing more. Poring over a seed catalogue together, her hand had rested gently on his arm and there was something so intimate in the gesture the thought had been planted in my mind.

I'd never ask though. Joe is incredibly reserved, his life totally private and I knew if there was anything going on he'd want it to be kept away from the prying eyes of the village. I also knew that Diane would honour whatever he wanted.

After leaving Joe to get back to forking over a flowerbed I carry on up the lane and am soon at the bar of The Birds, as it's known locally.

Josh, behind the bar, is pulling a pint for another punter but says to me, "He's beaten you to it." I smile my thanks at him, turn on my heel and walk off around the fireplace that takes centre stage, and I can see Chris just easing himself into one of the four divided off booths that run along the back wall. He shakes his hand, ridding himself of the drips of beer that have overflowed from the pint he has just set down, then as he looks up he sees me slide into the seat opposite.

"Good evening, Madeleine," I love his formality and the fact he always uses my full name.

"Good evening, Chris." He does not like me to reciprocate.

"I got you a G&T," he states, nodding at the other glass on the table. He's taken a gamble on that, as he does most times we meet, randomly surprising me with different drinks. It was as good as anything else but he was yet to guess what my real drink of choice would be.

"Excellent, thanks," and I raise my glass to clink against his as we say cheers.

"So what have you been doing today?" I ask, "I wasn't sure you'd be up for another outing after last night."

"Been doing a spot of writing actually, but glad to get away from it for a bit. Especially as I need to eat."

"Oh good, I'll join you." I didn't know if we were going to, we don't always, but I'm famished and although it's early I know if we give it another half an hour the place will be heaving with those wanting their once-a-week-night-out-bar-snacks and we will be right down the pecking order.

"Do you know what you want? Or shall I get us a menu?" I say and laugh as he rolls his eyes at me.

"You know what I'm going to order so you might as well just go and put it in. Though *you* might want to take a look at the menu," and he grins.

I return to the bar, wait a moment for Josh to become free then say, "We'll have the usual please."

He shakes his head, a look of despair on his face as he mutters, "You two are like an old married couple," then he turns round to the till to place the order. As I walk back to Chris I ponder on Josh's comment. I imagine to onlookers our friendship may seem a little incongruous. I'm in my mid-twenties and Chris is probably around his mid-fifties, I don't know for sure. That difference in ages might spark some gossip of the 'young enough to be your daughter' type in some quarters and it might well do behind our backs but I couldn't care what people think and I know it would bother Chris even less. In fact, I know even the thought of such a whisper going about would miss him entirely, for he lives much of his life totally unaware of what is going on around him.

After learning a humiliating lesson soon after arriving here I'd recognised the boundaries put in place as our friendship developed and I was happy with those. It's not that I don't find him attractive, because I do, it's more like he's off limits, as if going there would spoil what we have and I suspect Chris feels the same way. There has never been the slightest indication from either of us that one is attracted to the other, we purely enjoy each other's company. I can be relaxed with him because there's no flirtation, no suggestion, and I know there's not going to be a 'is this leading somewhere' moment because I trust him and that puts me at ease.

I know he writes and he tells me it's non-fiction academic stuff but I do wonder sometimes if he's telling the truth. He's so often lost in his thoughts and when we're together he can appear far away, and I imagine he's deep in another world that he has created in his mind and I'll sit and be quite content just to be in his presence. We have no problem with that, the silence, and the times that it sits between us are comfortable.

I look at him now and it appears as if at my call he simply got up from his desk and came here. His glasses have been pushed up towards the top of his head but not quite as far as his slightly receding hairline and he's in need of a trip to the barbers, which I know will be low on his list of priorities. He's wearing a faded once-black tee-shirt and, leaning on his elbows, his hands meet at the apex, his chin resting on them as he watches me. And this is what he does, he watches me, or rather studies me because he is the one person I know who is not taken in by my act and who knows there's more. But I reveal nothing and to give him his due he doesn't pry.

He looks tired, pronounced crow's feet spread from the corners of his eyes and he's pale, too many hours at his computer is the usual cause. I know once he gets into his work he can pull an all-nighter and not realise he's missed a sleep until the next day though he says it takes its toll on him nowadays.

"I need to talk to you actually, about Kourtney," I say and I run over the discussion I'd had with her. I know Chris used to own and run a bookshop in a small town nearby but jacked it in a few years ago due to increased pressure from the mighty online competitors and the terrible imposition of having to be open and manning the place between certain hours. It inconvenienced his writing life so much that on some days he simply wouldn't bother.

I've been to his house. A small higgledy-piggledy thatched cottage at the smart end of the village and it was packed with books. Every nook, every cranny jammed with them. Each wall lined with bookshelves crammed two deep, wedged in above and filling every space. It was like he'd closed the shop and brought the entire contents home. He'd told me once I wasn't far wrong with that assumption.

But the point is that he has run a business and would know enough to get Kourtney started. He is also always willing to help, which is the most important bit.

The subject of our discussion appears bearing our order which she delivers to our table.

"Good evenin'," she says, with a smile, as she lowers the plates. She produces cutlery and napkins from her apron pocket and quickly sets the table, then hurries off before we have time to say anything beyond our muttered thanks. But she's back a moment later with mustard for him and ketchup for me, and places a dish of battered onion rings between us.

"We were just talking about you," Chris says, wanting to catch her before she rushes off again.

"Oh." She instantly looks uncomfortable and glances at me. I try to appear reassuring, however that is meant to look.

"I'm more than happy to give you some help in getting yourself set up, Kourtney. Are you free to come round for a chat Monday morning?"

"Yes, of course, thank you. What time?"

"Would ten suit? I might have a lie in," and he smiles at her, I know he hates an early start, he's happy to work until three in the morning but rarely sees a dawn.

"Yeah, awesome, thanks," she says with a beaming smile across her face now, "enjoy yer meal," and she's gone.

We turn our attention to our food; without discussion I move my mushrooms to Chris's plate and he reciprocates with his tomatoes then we eat. It's steak, it's always steak, rump, medium rare, juicy and tender, a slab of garlic butter on top of mine melting and running all over. Delicious, though there is none on Chris's, he won't touch the garlic. Chips, crisp shelled and filled with the softest potato are piled up, and we share the onion rings.

Midway through we finish our drinks and I pop to the bar and get some more, adding them to our tab. We chat as we eat, covering more of Kourtney's start up plans. Chris finishes first, places his knife and fork on the plate then pushes it a little away from him as he sits back and wipes his mouth with his napkin. Screwing that into a ball, he discards it onto his plate and reaches for his pint. Before he can say anything, I get in first.

"What have you been up to then?" Nothing much changes in our lives but we do like a catch up.

"I've been writing quite a bit actually, keeping myself busy." He's been living in the beautiful south for years but his northern brogue is undiminished.

"Still non-fiction?" I ask, and I catch a slightly sheepish look along with his smile.

"Yes," he pauses as if deciding whether to continue or not, then he does, "I'm trying a little something else though." I knew it! I raise my eyebrows at him in question as I pop my last forkful into my mouth. We've been socialising for probably three years now, firstly meeting at village gatherings, then chatting over a drink in The Birds until we eventually moved on to our current arrangement in which we meet up usually for dinner, sometimes just a drink, perhaps once a week, occasionally more often. We talk about many things, village life, current affairs, his writing. We listen, we support but we don't probe. However, I've always felt he was holding something back that he wasn't ready to share yet. But it now appears he is.

"Wonderful! Tell me more." I sit back; my stomach is full which always makes me content, and I drain the last of my drink. "Hold that thought, I'll get us another round in." The place is filling up and there's more competition for Josh's attention, so I place the glasses on the bar and he nods so I know he's seen them then I head for the ladies. The entrance to these is situated down a passageway that ends in a door which is a back route into the kitchen and as I enter this passage I see Kourtney. She has her back up against the wall, is holding her tray flat against her stomach with one hand while the other is pushing back against the chest of a guy standing directly in front of her and far too close for comfort. He's taller than she is, his hands pressed up against the wall to each side of her shoulders effectively pinning her in place. His attitude is threatening and she doesn't appear to be enjoying the attention. Neither has noticed me.

I don't like the way he looks at her.

Lecherous eyes that creep me out.

I feel a familiar shiver of fear from long ago slide down my spine and I shudder.

She lifts her chin defiantly and says, "Back off." I see him grin, but not make any effort to move, and as he leans in closer her jaw clenches.

"What's going on?" I say, as I approach. Kourtney turns her head towards me and there's a flicker of relief mixed with the anger on her face.

He pushes himself off the wall, takes a step backwards and says, "Nothing."

"Really? It didn't look like nothing to me. It looked like you were intimidating my friend here." I glance at Kourtney, "You alright?" She nods. "Do you know this guy?" She nods again.

"We were at school together." She sounds strong and I suspect given another few seconds he would have found himself on the floor clutching those parts he appears to do his thinking with in his hands.

"Yeah, we're friends," he interjects, making it sound like that means he can do what he likes.

"Sure you are, and do you want him in your face like that, Kourtney?"

"No." I look back at him.

"She says no, so move along and don't hassle her again." I sound tougher than I feel and do well to keep my voice steady. He holds my gaze and for a moment I think he's going to make some trouble but then I see it, the moment he backs down, his stance softening almost imperceptibly and he turns back to Kourtney as he says,

"I'll be seeing you around," and he walks away, his shoulder barging into mine as he passes me.

"Thanks," she says when he's gone, her voice quiet.

"It looked like you were dealing with it anyway. How long has he been hassling you?"

"A while, he's a coupla years older, an' it started at school. Usually he can't get 'ere but tonight a friend brought a car load over." I'd noticed the group of lads

42

at the end of the bar earlier. "I'd better get back to work," she says, and she walks off towards the door at the end of the corridor.

"Kourtney," I say as she turns back to me, "don't let any bloke put pressure on you, will you? Not for anything."

"I won't, I don't have time for it, or them, I've got a business to grow," and she grins at me. As I've said, in some ways she reminds me of me as I once was, but she is so much more than I ever hoped to be already. She has her priorities straight and already knows what she wants out of life; I didn't, and it took me so much longer to learn. I watch as she goes back to the kitchen.

I pop into the ladies and when I come out, go to retrieve the drinks. I see the lads standing together at the end of the bar and I get the evils from the aggressor but ignore him and instead reach for the glasses Josh has left for me.

"I thought you'd got lost," he jokes as he takes a break between customers.

"I got a bit distracted." I glance back over to the end of the bar. "Could you do me a favour?"

"Of course."

"Could you make sure someone walks Kourtney home tonight?" He follows my gaze to the group of young men and frowns.

"Absolutely. I'll do it myself. Is there a problem?"

"Hmm, one of those guys," and I indicate with a subtle tilt of my head, "is giving her a hard time."

"Don't worry, I'll make sure she gets home safely." He's solid, is Josh, just turned twenty and been working here for a couple of years already.

"Thanks," I say, and I return to Chris. "Sorry about the delay." I give him the highlights and then ask him to tell me more of his writing efforts.

"Oh, it's nothing much, I've just been trying my hand at a bit of fiction."

"Really?" I love reading, and although I grew up in a flat devoid of books, I'd devoured much of the school library, sneaking the books into my bedroom to avoid the scornful comments on what was considered to be a waste of time.

The film's always better, innit.

I'd heard this time and time again, but it hadn't put me off, not then and not now, I always had a book on the go. They had provided the education my school hadn't. This is something Chris and I discuss at length as he encourages me to try more literary works than the thrillers I romp through. Although actually he is just delighted I read at all, many youngsters don't anymore, he tells me. I can't imagine not doing so, not having that escapism in my life would be intolerable.

"Is it fantasy?" I tease, knowing his dislike for the genre, "are you aiming to be the next Martin or Tolkein?" He fixes me with his infinitely patient stare.

"It is *not* fantasy. It's contemporary fiction." I think for a moment that I've put him off from telling me more so I'm surprised when he continues. "You will relate to it actually because it's a story about a young woman."

"Oh yeah? I'm listening."

"Well, she has a mysterious background and moves to a village where everyone thinks she is one thing but in fact she is something very different." He watches me over the top of his glass as he takes a long draught and I can see the twinkle in his eyes.

"Oh, so what is she then?" I'm cool and am not about to satisfy him by rising to the bait I feel he is scattering before me by showing I may recognise the subject of his tale. How vain would that be? But I am

44

inquisitive and I want to hear the plot he's come up with. What he thinks he knows.

"I'm still working that out, but I can tell you what she's like." He's being mischievous which makes me want to know more.

"Go on then." I'm all ears.

"She's bright, pretty and independent."

"Well of course she is, she is your heroine after all and they are never thick, ugly and a bit clingy, are they?" I interject, teasing, a little, and he acknowledges the jibe with the merest tilt of his head, then he continues.

"She's popular, mixes well and is a good friend." I nod, as if this is nothing I wouldn't expect. He pauses for a moment in thought, before adding, "But, she's a loner and behind the façade she shows to the world she is lacking in confidence and has self-esteem issues caused, I wouldn't wonder, by her mysterious past." All at once I find it hard to swallow and he pauses and raises a finger as if he's only just thought of something: "and, she is nowhere near as strong as she'd have people believe." Clearly ridiculous. How can you have a heroine that's not strong?

"Wow, she sounds complex."

"She is." And there's a silence which is nowhere near as easy as those which usually come between us, and clearing my throat I need to move this on.

"So what's going to happen in the story?"

"I haven't got that far yet, I've still to come up with a likely scenario."

"Yeah?" I say, all nonchalant, "perhaps I can come up with some suggestions for you?" I take the slight nod of his head that accompanies his smile as encouragement and continue, counting off the ideas on my fingers as I rattle through them. "She could be an international spy, a drug smuggler, a jewel thief, or," and I'm warming to my subject now, "she could be in a witness protection programme or a mole planted by the government to keep tabs on a terrorist cell that's sprung up under the guise of the Village Hall Committee. The possibilities are endless." I grin at him.

"All a little far-fetched, don't you think?" His comment is delivered as dry as the dust in the Sahara, and we both laugh. "That's what comes of reading all those trashy thrillers, Madeleine, your imagination's running amok." He checks his watch. "Come on, let's settle up, I'm knackered and need an early night." The bar is busy now and as we look around we can see that most of the tables are filled and Kourtney is run off her feet. I check in with her as she rushes past when we're on our way out but she's too busy to be anything other than fine, and as we pay the bill Josh confirms he's still alright to get her home safely. Chris and I leave together a short while later but once outside we say our goodnights and head in opposite directions.

Chapter 6

The following morning, I have to go and get some shopping in as there are spaces in my cupboards that are making me anxious. So once I've had breakfast I reverse my car out from where I left it on the earth and grass approach to the old wooden garage that it rarely sees the inside of, and head towards the village. Diane is weeding in her front garden and flags me down.

"You okay?" I shout across to her as I wind down the passenger side window.

"Oh yes, fine, I wondered if you'd like to come for lunch. It'll only be soup."

"I'd love to, I'm just going shopping, do you need anything?"

"No, thanks. I'll see you later." I nod and pull away, raising the window as I do. As I arrive at the top of the road with the pub on one side and the church on the other, I see a few parishioners making their way up the pathway towards their weekly worship. I've never been to a regular service there, just one wedding and a few funerals, the population here being mostly what it is.

When I first moved in the village was consumed by grief. A little girl had died and her death and funeral overshadowed everything. I didn't go. I didn't know anyone then and I never got to know that family. Sadly, the tragedy destroyed them. The father left only a few months later and although I occasionally saw the mother out and about, first alone, then with a small dog and we did that automatic greeting thing, the one which separates out the townies from the villagers, when we crossed paths, I never got to know her. She moved away only a few months ago actually and I'd heard on the Crowbridge grapevine that she'd got a new job, miles away.

The village shop is closed on a Sunday so I drive to Oakton, which is the nearest place that has a supermarket, albeit a small one, and I find the carpark almost empty. It doesn't take me long to fill a basket with what I need to replenish my shelves and I buy a couple of cakes to take to Diane's.

I'm soon back home and much more at ease once the shopping is away and I know I have all I need, and more besides. I wonder if I'll ever get more relaxed about this aspect of my life. The village shop benefits greatly from my inability to barely let a day pass without buying something to add to my cupboards, fridge or freezer and although I know I could probably feed a family of four for a fortnight on my stocks it makes me feel better knowing I could withstand a siege, and never be hungry.

I walk up to Diane's later and rather than knock on the front door I wander round to the back, admiring her pretty garden as I do so. It's larger than mine and packed full of variety plus there's a vegetable garden and a huge number of herbs and other plants that are unknown to me but which Diane uses in the concoctions she makes up.

Locally, Diane is suspected of being a witch, gossip she is well aware of and I believe relishes as she loves nothing more than creating a bit of mystery. Her surname is Sampson and I've heard her discuss her ancestry as she's supposedly traced her family tree right back and found she was the direct descendant of one Agnes Sampson, a midwife and healer in the sixteenth century who was persecuted and tortured for being a witch. When I'd asked Diane if this was true she'd given me a wicked grin and suggested the coincidence was far too great for it not to be.

She makes up herbal remedies, whether asked to or not, for those who are ill, and ignores the disbelieving, and sometimes scornful, looks she gets when she delivers them because she knows that, more often than not, the recipient will be back for more. I find her fascinating and her home a place of peace and tranquillity. She's also very good at sensing people's auras and she tells me mine disturbs her because the calmness and strength I portray on the outside masks the fear and anxiety I'm filled with. She has a certain acceptance about this, so doesn't question me further and I don't reveal a thing but she loves nothing more than getting something soothing into me. From the tea she plies me with whenever I'm invited round, and that she sends me home with, to the food she gives me – I don't know what she puts in it, and I don't want to know, but it always has a calming effect on me.

"Hello," I call as I reach the half open back door.

"Come on in," I hear coming back at me and I push the door wider and enter a place that resembles The Burrow, home of the Weasleys. Admittedly there's no actual, obvious, magic going on but that doesn't matter, it's the atmosphere, the ambience. There's a large range with pots and pans piled up all over it and a huge black kettle coming to a boil. Bunches of plants hang drying from the ceiling and Diane is standing at the worn and well-scrubbed pine table using a pestle to mash stuff together in a huge grey stone mortar. The smell is divine. Woody, spicy scents mingle with citrus and flowers, all natural and raw, every element, fresh and dried, combining in a heady mix, and I take a deep breath as I put the cakes I bought onto the table.

"Can I do anything to help?" I ask, knowing what the answer is likely to be.

"No, no, no, just take a seat." And the minute I do Cat leaps onto my lap and I push him off. It is common belief that he is Diane's familiar, and I'm not a fan. He is stereotypically black and Diane is adamant that he is not hers hence the fact that he doesn't have a name, other than Cat. He simply arrived one day, she once told me, and as far as Diane is concerned he is a free spirit, able to come and go as he wishes. He disappears for long periods of time which doesn't worry Diane a jot as she believes that he is off helping people who need him. I'm not convinced and think he is merely tomcatting around but not wishing to ruin Diane's vision of him as a cat in shining armour I keep quiet on the subject.

Diane finishes mashing whatever it is she's working on and turns her attention to a vat of simmering liquid on the range. I peer into the mortar to see an uninspiring brown sludge at the base and briefly wonder what it might be used for. My thoughts are interrupted by a bowl of golden broth being placed in front of me, a hunk of homemade bread at its side. There is no ceremony here, no side plates needed and I break off a piece of the bread and dunk it into the soup. It is flavoursome, and hearty and I make soft noises of appreciation.

"What flavour is it?" I ask, my palate not sophisticated enough to dissect the ingredients that make up the deliciousness.

Diane shrugs, "Butternut, herbs, a bit of this and that." She's as dismissive as always and I realise I'd be disappointed if she were anything else. I know, from experience, she'd never be able to whip out a recipe for anything she produces. "Did you have a good time with Chris last night?"

"Yeah, he was in great form. Looked a bit tired though. He's been writing. Putting in long hours, I think."

"Oh? Usual stuff or something new?" And I hesitate, something holding me back from wanting to share the news of his latest project. I didn't want her discussing it with Chris, or more specifically, I didn't want him telling her the details about his main character, just in case she recognised anything about her. Again it's presumptuous of me as well as ridiculous because it is hardly likely to remain a secret, especially if he publishes it but whereas I know Chris sees the lie, if Diane does she just accepts it, and I prefer that. I briefly wonder if I should stop seeing him, if only to stop him *seeing* me but I swiftly realise I don't want to. I enjoy his company and I believe whatever he thinks he knows, he cares for me enough to be discreet about it.

"Just the usual, I think." I've finished my bread and start spooning the remaining soup into my mouth, my taste buds revelling in the creamy richness.

"Well that's enough to make anyone tired," and I nod in agreement. "You have steak?"

"Yes." She grins, like she knows it all. I finish my soup and as I push the bowl away Cat jumps back on to my lap. I push him off. "He only wants to help you," Diane explains.

"Help me with what?" She raises one arched eyebrow at me as if she knows better and I wonder if she is as unquestioning about me as I thought. Mine goes otherwise unanswered and I yawn, unexpectedly sleepy.

"Sorry," I apologise and not for the first time I look at the bowl I've just cleared and wonder if she's drugged me but as we ate the same thing I suspect not. I clear the table of our bowls and take them over to the sink that's piled high with the aftermath of her morning's work.

"Just leave them on the side, I'll deal with them later," Diane says, "You look like you could do with a nap."

"I could, do you mind if I eat and run?"

"Of course not! Though leave me one of those cakes, will you? I've got to get on as I've plenty to do yet but I'll have it later. You get off, you've got work tomorrow so need to be well rested." I loved the way she mothered me and thought it sad she hadn't had any children. Never the right time, she'd told me. I imagined she'd be the sort of mother who would have had mugs of hot chocolate and biscuits, straight from the oven, ready and waiting when school had finished.

I say my goodbyes, go home and head straight to bed.

I wake a couple of hours later and after a good stretch and yawn I get up. I have some work to do, and going to the cupboard I release the floorboard again and remove a folder from the space below, pushing the jewellery bag to one side in the process.

Once in the kitchen I place the folder on the table, and taking a tumbler from one cupboard and a bottle of Jack from another I pour a couple of fingers into the glass, taking a swig before sitting down to the task in hand. I take a sheaf of papers from the file and spread them out in front of me. I look through the notes I've made and update or add extra from the information I gathered from the coach trip on Friday. I run through the day. Everywhere I went, everything I saw. I'm methodical, my attention poring over every minute detail with nothing spared because I know the risks involved.

During this process I've refilled my glass twice and now finally satisfied I've captured everything, I drain the tumbler and place it in the sink. I put away all my papers and take the folder upstairs to hide it back in its safe place.

It's still only mid evening so I switch on the television and scroll through the channels. I see *Gone with the Wind* is showing; it's a good way through it but I click on it anyway to see where it's up to. Rhett is kissing Scarlett and telling her she should be kissed, and often, and by someone who knows how. I know this inside out and could recite it word for word, should I ever need to, so I change the channel.

Chapter 7

The next morning the start of the normal working week for most has arrived, and I set off fully made up and in my office wear, as I'm expected to do by anyone local who might see me. I leave the village and after a short while like many others I get on the dual-carriageway that leads in the direction of the city. Unlike many others though, I do not exit once the signs start directing traffic to the city centre but drive straight on, the traffic thinning and progress speeding up as I do. People, by which I mean the villagers, are constantly surprised when I tell them that I work in Hartleigh, a small market town some twenty-five miles from Crowbridge. They can't understand the concept of driving straight past a city where jobs in insurance must surely be easy to come by and travelling so much further to a market town no one ever goes to.

But that is exactly the point.

No one from where I live ever goes there because they get to the superior facilities in the city first and don't see the need to travel any further. This is how I like it and this is how I planned things because the life I live in Crowbridge is very different from the one I lead in Hartleigh. And it is there that I can be the real me.

As I do every work day morning, I stop outside the newsagents on the way into town and push the door open to a place time has forgotten. The fetid smell I walk into is a reminder of a life left behind but one immediately recreated in my mind. Mid-afternoon, and my arrival home from school greeted with no comforting hot chocolate or warm from the oven biscuits. The cheap curtains made of coarse fabric that hung in a haphazard fashion would be drawn against the bright sunlight but too thin to effectively block out the rays, the dirty burnt orange material would glow with the ferocity of summer happening in the outside world. Bright shards would pierce the room, finding their way through the smallest gap to show dust motes swirling in a fog of smoke. An old black and white would be on the telly and my entrance customarily ignored by the occupant of the settee as the clipped English of Celia Johnson would tell me *Brief Encounter* was the choice of the day. Word perfect on the script, I'd pass straight through feeling relieved if there was no one else there, less so if she had company. I'd go to my room where I'd stuff a towel under the door in an attempt to keep the smoke, and others, out, then I'd open the window to let the fresh air in.

I tell myself I only keep coming in here because it's convenient but I wonder if like picking a scab I didn't somehow like revisiting the pain.

It is a source of constant fascination to me that this shop continues to open every day as its owner, Sid, appears to care nothing for it, and even less for its customers, if there are any besides me, as I am yet to meet someone else in here. Dingy doesn't begin to describe the décor that I doubt has been refreshed since it first opened, which if the sign over the door is correct was 1947. My best guess is that the paintwork was probably originally green but it is difficult to tell as every surface is a mucky yellow, sticky with a noxious layer of nicotine. The smoking ban has been in place for several years but it has had little impact here and I make sure I touch nothing as I make my way to the shabby counter covered in piles of papers. To my right is the confectionery grandstand which I can't imagine anyone ever buying anything from, its contents well past their best before dates. Some possibly there are from before the time those dates even came into existence. Marathons, Opal Fruits and Spangles still appear in the line-up.

Trip-hazard lino makes an attempt to cover the floor. The gaps between the worn and broken patches show dirty concrete and you'd be hard pushed to describe the original colour of the inadequate flooring.

The shop signage, which looks to be the wooden original, cracked paint flaking and peeling in places reads, without further embellishment, 'Newsagents'. Sid doesn't go in for the twee names or corporate branding like others are starting to in the town and as a consequence I guess its days are numbered. I'd noticed the piles of papers getting smaller since the supermarket had opened its doors on the old cattle market site, not that Sid ever mentions it. He is a man of few words.

"Shop!" I'd yelled as I'd entered, the bell still jangling above my head and I'd left the door to close behind me, knowing from previous experience not to push it too as it was as unpleasant to touch as anything else in here, and unless you were able to wash your hands immediately afterwards, best avoided. I now look to the doorway in the corner behind the counter. Hanging from the doorframe is one of those curtains meant to keep flies out. I've seen more modern variations, beaded wood or metal links, even PVC strips. This one is of narrow strips of coloured plastic. Not all the strips are still present and of those that are, not all are whole. I hear a familiar hacking cough from the other side then what's left parts as Sid shuffles into view. He's got a fag on, which is standard, an untipped hard-core Senior Service if I'm not mistaken. In his wake strips of the curtain are left stuck together by the same noxious glue that coats the rest of the shop.

Shabby beige trousers made for a much larger man sag below a faded checked shirt and a baggy, worn cardigan that clings to meagre rounded shoulders. His scalp shows through the thinning strands of greasy, grey hair that reaches his collar.

"Good morning, Sidney, and how are you today?" My usual greeting that I know will only be replied to by a grunt, if that. He reaches the till and I push forward the two national papers I want and hand him a crisp fiver. "Just these two please." I am as determined as ever not to go through the whole exchange without some social interaction and it is just as well that I'm persistent and endowed with unending quantities of patience because to date I have been unsuccessful. This is our daily routine though and I am convinced that one day I will get him to join in. He looks at me, the whites of his rheumy eyes yellow, bloodshot and watery, as if having to get me change is an imposition. The till isn't in use as an actual till anymore but works as more of a drawer arrangement. I suspect this is because it has never been decimalised but he opens it and gnarled fingers, yellowed from a lifetime of tobacco use and tipped with blackened overgrown nails, scratch around for the coins I need.

I watch as the lengthening ash tip of his cigarette grows perilous. I'm mesmerised as to how long it will stay attached to the whole and Sid remains unconcerned as it eventually parts company and falls onto the papers I'm buying. I tip them up so it rolls off as I hold out my hand for the change.

"Have a very good day, Sidney." But as I pocket the shrapnel, he's already turned and is shambling back to beyond the sticky curtain and whatever newsagenty delights await him there. I'm not sure why I continue coming in here every day other than for the convenience, but I know I'd miss the banter, that life enhancing touch of human interaction, if I didn't.

Back in the car I flick though the papers quickly, but finding nothing of specific interest to me I leave them on the passenger seat, start the engine and head for the leisure centre.

This morning I'm leaving the weights, the cardio and the sweating and it's all about the swimming. There are only three others in the water and taking to the fast lane I plough up and down. It's a decent size pool, three breaths a length, freestyle, tumble turns, the lot and I go on length after length. I have plenty to think about and this is my time to do it. I vary the stroke, twenty freestyle, twenty breast stroke, twenty backstroke but I leave the butterfly well alone. Never have been able to get the hang of that. In between each twenty I take a breather for a couple of minutes. Three walls of the gym are glass and I can see straight into it from here and in my breaks I watch those on a different sort of work out. Most I recognise and know by name, regulars working the same daily pattern, one I've seen before but haven't yet spoken to, a new guy currently on the rowing machine. Well, he's newish, he's been coming here every day for a week or more, and although he might be new in town judging by his physique he's not new to working out. I watch him for a moment, his dark blond hair flopping over a sweaty forehead.

Today there are only men in the gym and this is the usual situation. I am one of the few women that like working out on the machines, or at least I am at the times I come here. In the evenings this place may be a frenetic hive of female activity for all I know. The centre has other studios available as well though and they put on a range of classes to suit all tastes. Yoga,

Pilates, aerobics, step, body pump and the increasingly popular Zumba groups fill these rooms and the pool caters to those who love the aqua aerobics sessions. I find it is to these areas that other women are attracted and they come in their droves, flitting by in lurid Lycra outfits as they bend, flex and tone their bodies into submission. After which they'll meet for coffee, cake and conversation in the on-site café.

It's Monday, it's a working day and I realise my current activity doesn't come across as very work-like, and we'll come on to that, but every week day morning I start off here. It's where I fit in, it's where I'm comfortable, it's where I can be me and, it's where I find my type. Which is why I like the male to female ratio being in my favour during my morning workout. My needs are simple. Young, fit and with a good recovery rate. It's not much to ask.

I finish with a final twenty of freestyle and leave the pool. Looking back into the gym I see Mike on the closest running machine to me; he holds up his hand, fingers splayed, and I nod.

I shower thoroughly, soaping myself with a potent flowery gel, shampooing my hair, conditioning it, ridding myself of the chlorine that clings to every pore and follicle. Then I blow dry my hair. It's dark, long and has plenty of body so I keep it layered and it ends in a point somewhere between my shoulders. I replace the silver earrings I took out before my swim and redo my makeup. Packing up my stuff, I leave the changing room. Mike is waiting in the reception area checking his phone but he looks up as I get to him.

"Hello." He's smiling, his mouth filled with perfect white teeth. "Do you want anything to eat?" He always asks, but I never do.

"No I'm fine, you ready to go?" In response to his nod we leave. After dumping my bag in my car we cross the road to a bank of new builds designed in a range of different styles so as to provide the town with its visual diversity for the future. We reach a tidy end of terrace and Mike opens the door standing aside to let me enter. I brush past him, deliberately, then linger in the hall as he closes the door.

He reaches for me immediately and doesn't waste a moment, pulling me towards him, his lips on mine.

There's barely a word spoken because there's no need, I know what he's like after the gym, he's horny as hell and feverish in his desire for me.

A while later I'm lying in his bed with much to appreciate. There is nothing like a bit of afternoon delight to get the week off to a good start. Mike is a man of organisation, of duty, of order. He does his day job Tuesday to Saturday and works out at the gym every evening. Sunday, he tells me, is for getting his chores done, and there's not a thing out of place here, not a speck of dust to be found in his pristine pad. Clean sheets, scented with wild flowers fresh and lovely are softly wrapped around us. Monday morning, he does the gym. Monday afternoon, he does me. And it takes all afternoon, every time. It's like he's been saving it up all week but I'm not complaining. Like everything else in his life he's methodical in his attention to detail and he gets me off, every time, another reason to be thankful. The sex is satisfying and fun, though there are few words and he puts me through it because I know he won't be satiated until late in the afternoon. When we eventually get to that point he lies back and stretches. Then, he glances at the bedside clock.

And that's my cue.

Because *we* have an arrangement, and it works. He asks if I'm okay as I dress and I say I am, and I mean it.

Because we don't do feelings.

60

He tells me Monday evening is his time; he showers and I suspect he changes the sheets, again, he eats and watches the telly for the evening.

I travel home, shower, eat and watch the television. We're not so very different but we never consider sharing these things.

Tuesday starts off much the same, like most households that have a weekday routine, the only change being that Kourtney is on my doorstep as I'm about to leave and is eager to make a start on her first official cleaning job. I make sure she is alright after the issue with the bloke the other night and she is totally fine, much as I expected, and I hand over a key for future use and leave her to it. On my way into Hartleigh I pop in to see Sidney who is his usual ebullient self. I have a quick glance through the papers once I'm in the car but nothing in them delays me long and I'm soon at the gym.

Today I'm on the machines, getting the cardio in, the toning, the weights and I work my way round the room to include each piece of equipment during my workout. My headphones are in and I'm uninterrupted but I do look to see who else is going through their paces and a couple raise their hands, or nod in greeting.

Towards the end of my session Ricky comes over. I've not seen him here in a while and he asks how I am. I pull the earbuds out as I carry on with my cool down.

"Fine, and you? Haven't seen you in here recently." He looks like he's had a hard night, like he's dealing with a hangover, which wouldn't surprise me; we've known each other a couple of years at least and it's not uncommon for him to be in this state. I can smell the alcohol sweating out of him, but it doesn't put me off, not one little bit.

"Yeah, I'm okay. You busy?"

I shake my head, then back it up with a simple, "No."

"We on then?" He tilts his head as he leaves the question hanging there and I feel the faintest tingle of anticipation.

I nod, then as he starts to turn away, I say, "Don't shower." He grins in that way that's guaranteed to get the juices flowing and wanders off to the changing room.

Now this may come as a surprise to some people, it might even be a bit of a shock, but putting aside the whole stealing the necklace bit for a moment, if up until this point anyone had any positive thoughts towards me at all I'm afraid they *might* be about to be dashed.

Because I fear that what is about to happen is going to change people's opinion about me, and although I hate the thought that I'm going to become a disappointment, there is sadly little I can do about it.

How people do feel, of course, does rather depend on their own moral compass. What they consider to be right or wrong, or decent.

I'll be honest; I am not a one-guy kind of woman. I'd been given a hard lesson early in life when the only man that had mattered had left. Amid desperately whispered promises of his return he'd hugged me goodbye and wept as he did so. From the distance of time that I now view these scraps of memory, I guess he couldn't cope any longer but I won't ever forgive him for leaving me to pick up the pieces.

I was eight, and I never saw him again.

His departure simultaneously robbed me of my childhood and abandoned me to poverty and a mother who from that moment on gave up on even the vaguest pretence of looking after me.

Since then, and with only one or two exceptions, I'd never found any reason why I should put my trust in, or involve myself further with a man other than, as I got older, to use him purely to satisfy my own sexual needs.

Ricky and I walk out minutes later. Passing the front glass wall of the gym we make our way to the car park and I see the new boy is on the running machine, his headphones in as he's pounding away the miles and I briefly meet his eyes then look away. Ricky and I leave in separate cars. I follow him out of the car park, and out of town. We turn off the main road and up a concrete track which has tufts of weeds growing through where it's starting to break up. It ends where a wood begins but we carry on over a rougher track following the edge of a field until we are on the other side of the woods. We both get out and look around, checking we're alone. We've been here before and never seen anyone else yet, though Ricky would probably prefer it if we did.

He grabs hold of my hand and leads me into the woods for a little alfresco. He is as opposite to Mike as it is possible to be although I find they are equally satisfying. However, when I want sex hard and fast Ricky works for me, he likes to be rough and he loves it that I give him what he wants. He prefers me dirty and this works fine for me too. We are well matched and I can sense his agitation, heightened like my own, when he decides we've gone far enough and he turns back towards me.

And there's that grin again, that wicked glint in his eye that sends a hot lick of excitement running through me.

I like some ink on a man and as Ricky regains his breath a while later I run my hands over that which decorates his skin. We know each other like this inside and out but neither of us wants to know anything more. This is what we do, this is all we do, all that we have in common. I know he comes to me because I give him what others won't and that suits us both just fine.

Because I know that's what girls like me are for. To take up the slack, to fill in the gaps of what, men tell me, would otherwise be the totally fulfilling relationships they have elsewhere.

It's not like every afternoon is spent like this. Clearly that would be exhausting. Sometimes I wander off to have a mosey around the library or take a gentle walk in the park. Sometimes I even have to go into the office. But it's hard for someone like me to say no when the possibility, no, opportunity, for a little affection comes knocking.

I am well aware that if people who think they know me knew this side of me I'd feel their judgement; I'd hear them tutting at what they'd consider to be my loose morals. Perhaps, if they were feeling sympathetic, they'd blame all those bad men for leading me down this path. But they shouldn't. They shouldn't go thinking I'm a victim in all this at all. I can assure them I am not. I have things exactly as I want them. No ties and everything on my own terms, what's not to like about that?

I have rules and I'm careful. And I don't just have sex with any old random, there are no unplanned hook-ups or one-night stands for me, thank you very much. I like to get to know a man before ever doing the deed so there's always some level of friendship between us, and I can generally tell by then that they're not crazy or into some sort of weird shit. I ensure other people, admittedly mostly only those at the gym, know who I'm with and on a personal level I take appropriate precautions. No one is coming near me bareback, of that I can assure you.

My chosen lifestyle comes down to the fact that I like having the lack of commitment a relationship would require and enjoy the variety of having more than one man in my life. And it's not always them that does the asking either.

Chapter 8

You watch her. Not like just now when she passed by the sheet of glass that separates you. But, like, whenever she is nearby, her very essence telling you when that is the case. You do it surreptitiously, of course, and you know you probably shouldn't do it at all but you can't help yourself, she fascinates you, you find the way she behaves both intriguing and off-putting in equal measure.

Forgetting for the time being about the things that make you uncomfortable about her, the welcome result of the level of curiosity you are showing in the glorious Madeleine is that it has pushed aside those leftover thoughts for another that have been harbouring deep inside for far too long. It's been cathartic to rid yourself of the festering mess of emotion you'd been left with when all that ended.

You note that you've totally blanked the fact that she is on her way to what is no doubt going to be an afternoon of pleasure at the hands of that creep, Ricky. That, you don't want to think about. Not one little bit.

Despite your reservations you're not immune to the attraction you feel for her, the inevitable reaction she arouses, but while you're only too familiar with the physical response she engenders in you, you and many of the other blokes in here you'd be willing to bet, even that isn't straightforward. Because, in the cauldron of mixed emotions you have for her that in itself doesn't appear to be enough to whet your appetite sufficiently for you to do anything about it as the minute you think about her behaviour the negative feeling you get is almost palpable.

And this is confusing you.

In the circumstances you've kept a low profile, made sure you've not made eye contact. Until just now. Unavoidable really, you on the treadmill minding your own business and her passing by, glancing over, and just like that, contact was made. It was fleeting and she looked away again as though it hadn't registered at all, and you can't help wondering if it did.

You're not a prude, you think as you stand in the shower washing away the sweat of the morning's efforts when you've finished. At least you don't believe you are. You imagine she'd probably consider your views old fashioned, and you try and rationalise them as you simply being more traditional in your way of thinking, although not entirely successfully.

Of course all this preoccupation coming on top of your general state of mind isn't helping.

You know your day to day base level of discomfort has nothing to do with her and everything to do with the fact you're still coming to terms with having been sent here by your family. The inescapable truth that your nearest and dearest had come to the end of their tether with your inability to stick at anything so that when this opportunity had come along they'd jumped at it quicker than a terrier after a rat, has been a tough one to adjust to. You know it's early days but you remain to be convinced that this new start is the answer to their prayers and that it will settle you down. It is, after all, hardly the thrill a minute career you were seeking and you're already feeling restless.

You put the key in the lock of the door to your flat and once inside take a look around, letting out a deep sigh as you do. It's a decent enough place. Modern, attractively furnished, masculine. But you've wondered, more than once, if you've made a mistake in moving here instead of into the city. This is handy for work of course but there's nothing going on. There's *precious little nightlife to entertain anyone in Hartleigh and few opportunities to create your own, as far as you can see.*

She, who causes you all this distraction, could be a huge improvement to your social life and a massive boost to your amusement levels. You know that. But you are equally certain of one other thing. You know you cannot become one of the masses, that is just not in your make up. And you doubt whether changing is in hers.

Then of course there's the other complication, and when she finds out about that, well, you can't see her being too happy with you at all.

Chapter 9

The following morning starts the same though Sidney takes so long coming out to serve me I start flicking through the papers while I wait and try to ignore the sound of him coughing up God knows what from what remains of his lungs. It's publication day for the local rag and I'm delighted there's nothing in there about the necklace, the weight of which I can feel in the pocket of my leather jacket.

I'm distracted, reading another story, when Sidney finally makes it out to the shop. I ask if he's alright as I hand my money over, receiving an incoherent mumble by way of response, and as I collect my change his eyes focus on mine, the creases around them deepening as he frowns. *I'll take that*, I think as I leave to return to my car, that tiny acknowledgement of my existence, it's more than I usually get.

Julie is behind the leisure centre reception desk as I hand over my gym pass for scanning and I try not to stare, but fail miserably. We exchange greetings because I'm a regular but she's not a gym bunny, preferring to run the classes instead, and she is one magnificent woman. Toned to perfection. I've never seen her in anything other than Lycra and she fills every inch with voluptuous glory. I'm not even that way inclined and I would totally go there. I can only imagine the effect she has on the more testosterone-fuelled among us.

I put in a decent showing at the gym, the usual Wednesday crowd are in and there's a good atmosphere here, because we're mostly all friends. Okay, sometimes more than friends.

I'm topping up my water bottle later on and Steve, one of the personal trainers, comes over. The black tee-shirt he wears fits tightly over his body-builder physique and there's not an ounce of spare fat on him. He takes his role very seriously and is something for all here to aspire to. I get in first.

"I'm going to work, Steve; I have an appointment."

"Oh okay, no problem I was just coming over to check on how you were getting on."

"Sure you were," I reply, sounding unconvinced as I smile at him and he laughs slightly self-consciously.

"I wouldn't delay you for long."

"You're not exactly selling it to me, Steve." But I know he tells the truth. Our relationship took place strictly within the leisure centre and could best be described as frantic. However today I am not in the mood for a quick thrill heightened by the potential risk of discovery.

"Alright, point taken. I'll catch you another time," and he wanders off and out to the staff room.

As I said earlier, I am the one in control here. I am the one calling the shots.

Which is exactly as I like it.

I check my watch and decide I've got time to put in a few lengths before I finish.

I manage to squeeze into a parking space on the street right in front of the offices of Watson & Grove and as I get out of my car I hear the clock on the nearby town hall tower start to strike two. After the swim I'd got ready for the afternoon and treated myself to lunch in the café at the gym so, fully sustained and feeling virtuous with a light salad inside me, I stride briskly into reception and smile at Helen behind the desk.

"He's expecting me at two, can I go straight in?" I've barely slowed my pace when, as I anticipate, she nods and tells me to go ahead. Bypassing her desk, I go straight down the passageway to the side. There are a couple of doors that lead off along the way but I have no idea what goes on in those rooms. At the end the corridor opens up into a larger area with a couple of chairs and a few not-at-all interesting looking magazines on the exciting world of insurance placed on a small table between them. Ignoring all that, I open the door right in front of me and walk into Cubby's office.

But he is not alone.

Seated in a chair in front of his desk is the new guy from the gym. His messy rough blond hair is smoothly combed and he has his back to me but I've seen him enough times from that angle over the last couple of weeks to know exactly who he is.

"I'm sorry," I mutter, embarrassed to have walked in on a meeting, "Helen told me you were free." I don't like the unexpected and this has thrown me. As I back out of the room the new guy turns to look at me and appears to be nowhere near as surprised to see me as I am him.

Cubby leaps to his feet as I'm making my exit. "Hey wait up, Madeleine, it's fine, come on in." I stop and he beckons me forward. Meanwhile the new guy stands and I don't like the way he is studying me. Encouraged by Cubby though I approach the desk.

"Madeleine, let me introduce you. This is my nephew, Daniel Travers." I raise my chin at Daniel in greeting but he has his hand out so I shake that and wonder what he is doing here.

"Call me Dan," he says, "everyone other than family does." I see Cubby smile at this.

Dan says, "Take a seat," like this is his office, and his meeting, which it isn't, and the sense of unease this generates prickles the hairs on the back of my neck. He fixes me with a slate grey gaze and indicates the chair next to the one he was previously occupying, showing no sign of leaving and in fact every likelihood of sitting back down again. This concerns me.

I look at Cubby and raise one eyebrow in question. "Our meetings are always private, Cubby."

"I know, Madeleine, but I need Daniel to meet you, to understand, about you."

He needs Dan to meet me? Why?

"Well now we have, I'll come back another time, when you're alone."

"What's the problem?" Dan interjects, "Is there something else you're meant to be *doing* this afternoon?" The intent in that question might have been lost on Cubby but I know exactly what Dan is getting at and I don't appreciate the implication, not one little bit. It annoys me that he has known all along who I was and never said anything until now. It's like I've been spied on, and that makes me uncomfortable.

"Not at all," I say, and I sit in the other chair next to Dan's. "Why is he here?" I speak to Cubby, who is looking at us like he senses something is going on but can't quite put his finger on what that something is.

"I need him to understand, that's all, about you, and about our arrangement."

"Why?" I don't like hints or guessing games and prefer people to be direct with me so I wish Cubby would cut to the chase and spit out what this is all about.

He sighs and places his hands on the desktop. He spreads his fingers wide then straightening his arms he braces against them and take in a deep breath. With this build up I don't feel like anything good is about to come in my direction but Cubby and I have always been straight with each other and I trust him. He fixes me with one of his I-mean-business looks and says, "I had intended on telling you this a while ago, but the time never seemed to be right. The fact is, Madeleine, I shall be retiring soon. Daniel will be taking over my role." There's a long silence as I digest this.

"Your role here?" I need to clarify what this means and indicate with my hand to the offices in general.

"Yes."

"And your role, with me?" My voice is quieter, my hand on my chest where it can feel the rise and fall of my breaths, the increased drumming of my heart.

"Yes." His eyes, which had remained fixed on mine until that moment now fall away and I sense his discomfort.

He might as well have pulled the carpet right out from under my feet. I hate change, loathe it in fact and this one potentially spells disaster for me and I'm immediately unsettled.

I glance at Dan who doesn't say a word although he does meet my gaze, his eyes dark-lashed and steady, but when I speak it is to Cubby, "When did you decide this?" I realise I have no rights over his personal life. But still I ask.

"It's been coming for a while, Maddy, look at me. I'm not getting any younger." I hate the fact that he's shortened my name because he only does that when he wants to placate me, when he wants me to do something I don't want to do, when he wants to cajole me in some way. But then I do look at him and I see what I always see. Steel blue eyes that crinkle up at the corners when he laughs, weathered skin that's tanned after a summer spent as much out of the office as he can manage, a head of still thick, more salt than pepper hair. Arms that make me feel safe when they wrap around me and I realise that I've never even thought about the age of this man who I love. I'm surprised to feel tears pricking at the backs of my eyes and I look down and blink the moment away.

"Okay," I say, I'm not but for the moment I have to be and my voice is soft. "Business?"

Cubby smiles at me and nods, "Business."

I reach into the inside pocket of my leather jacket and take out the drawstring bag then lean forward and put it on the desk. Cubby picks it up and shakes the necklace out onto his hand. He makes a soft whistling sound as he examines it then shows it to Dan. Like me, he's freshly showered and as he leans forward to take the necklace from Cubby for a closer look I get a hit of body wash from him. It's cool, fragrant, and not entirely unappealing.

"There was nothing in the paper," I clarify and Cubby nods in agreement, I know he will have checked too.

"The owner hasn't reported the loss to us yet either." His face breaks into a mischievous grin and his eyes widen as he says, "Let's give him a call, shall we?" My interaction has been purely with Cubby, as always, although I'm acutely aware of Dan's presence and I allow myself to briefly wonder what he is thinking. Cubby reaches to the end of his desk and pulls a file off a pile there. He brings it closer and, reaching for his glasses, checks the name on the top, grunting in satisfaction that it's the right one. Flipping the cover open he runs a finger down the contact details on the sheet stapled to the inside and lifts the phone from its cradle at the same time. Dan and I sit in silence as Cubby dials the number and puts it on speaker-phone so we can hear when the ringing tone starts. It's picked up after only three rings, the greeting abrupt.

"Mehew." Public school formality barked out in those two simple syllables.

74

"Ah, Mr Mehew, good afternoon, it's Mr Wilton here from Watson & Grove."

"Good afternoon, Mr Wilton, what can I do for you?" I can hear in the question he's surprised to be receiving this call.

"I need to talk to you about your current insurance arrangements as I feel that you are not perhaps taking the necessary precautions for the cover provided."

"Really! Everything seems to be working perfectly adequately to me." His response is guarded.

"Well if it was I wouldn't be sitting here with your wife's diamond and sapphire necklace in my hand, now would I?"

"What! How did you get that? You must be mistaken; it can't be hers." He's in denial, disbelief etched into every word.

"What makes you think that, Mr Mehew? Is it because our agreement is that this necklace is either adorning the neck of the lovely Mrs Mehew or, that it's locked up in your safe?"

"Well of course that's where it is, hold on a minute." Mr Mehew is sounding more than a little agitated now and we can hear him calling to his wife. *Uh oh.*

Cubby raises his eyebrows to me and I smile. We can hear a muttered conversation and it seems as if the hunt is underway for the cherished necklace. Mr Mehew is on the move and I try to picture where he is in the house. I think he goes to the safe first which, although I haven't been in there, I know is in his office, then I can hear his breathing becoming heavier as he mounts the stairs. I hear the murmurings between him and his wife and I imagine them now in their bedroom and he's asking her how she could have been so bloody stupid as not to have put it away and she's saying she's sorry and I do feel for her, though not because of her

75

carelessness but in light of the fact that I know what a shit he is.

And yes, I'm entirely aware of my hypocrisy in happily bonking the most-definitely-married Ricky one day while being so entirely judgemental of the Mehew situation on the next. But I'm not the one breaking my vows now, am I.

He comes back on the line, and goes on the attack. "It's not here, Wilton, and I'm bloody furious that someone has broken into the house." Cubby is cool and calm in his response.

"We would have a problem of a whole other level if the house had been broken into, Mr Mehew, because of course if that had been the case the alarm would have gone off, wouldn't it? Because the alarm is, as you have assured us, always set when you leave the house. That again being part of our agreement, the one that we have in place to allow you to benefit from vastly reduced premiums." There's silence on the other end of the phone so Cubby continues. "And yet, Mr Mehew, the fact remains that my agent walked into your house in broad daylight, and took the necklace, while you were there."

"That's preposterous!"

"Indeed, it does sound so, doesn't it, and yet it's completely true."

"I don't believe it! I don't see how he could have got in here without me knowing about it."

"She, actually." He doesn't respond to the correction.

"You're damn well going to have to prove it."

"Alright, Mr Mehew, she's right here with me now. I'll have her tell you what happened, shall I?" There's a grunt and nothing more so I take that as my cue to proceed.

"Good afternoon, Mr Mehew. I'm a security consultant and I work with Watson & Grove. Last Saturday afternoon I entered your house via the woods at the back."

"But my children, my wife, you could have frightened them."

"I could have done, Mr Mehew, but I didn't. I waited until they went out on the dog walk. You came out into the garden, and I walked out of the woods and entered the house." There's a snort of disbelief as to how I could have possibly got past him but as no question or other utterance is forthcoming, I carry on. "I went to your bedroom, found the necklace on the dressing table and left."

"I don't believe you could have done all that without me being aware of your presence." He sounds angry that what he considers to be his foolproof vigilance could have been outwitted.

"Well you were a little distracted," I add, delighted to get the opportunity to increase the pressure, purely for my own satisfaction. Though that will not have been on Cubby's agenda and he is now looking at me with his eyebrows raised in question. I smile a smile tinged with wickedness at him as I listen to what Mr Mehew has to say next.

"By what?"

"By a phone call you took. I heard you, I was on the stairs."

"Oh." There's a lengthy thought-laden pause that stretches out after that response and I'm hoping, desperately hoping I get the chance to elaborate so I jog things along a bit.

"Would you like me to give you the details of the call, to refresh your memory?"

"No. No that won't be necessary." He's dismissive and wants to move off this subject but his wife has overheard at least part of what I've just said. "Who was on the phone, darling?" I hear her say and he tells her, just someone from the office, a work thing. "On a Saturday?" is her incredulous response, and by its tone she's clearly flabbergasted that anything as crass as work could possibly interrupt a weekend in the country. "Yes, dear, even on a Saturday," is his tired and patronising reply to her before he pauses and comes back to me. "I think we have said all we need to say to each other on this subject." This is a somewhat disappointing conclusion to the conversation for me but it seems his questions have ended and although I say I'm happy to clarify anything further if he wishes, he apparently doesn't, which is no great surprise, and trying not to show my disappointment I hand back to Cubby.

"So, Mr Mehew, this is the situation. The necklace is valued at fifty thousand pounds and is only one part of your wife's collection. As you know, we offer bespoke insurance arrangements to our select clients and you negotiated a substantially reduced premium with us on the understanding that certain procedures would be followed."

"That still doesn't mean you can break into my property." A last ditch attempt at outrage on Mr Mehew's part.

"I think we have established that we did not break in, Mr Mehew, and your policy clearly states that we have the right to test out your security arrangements, a right we have taken up."

"I think we should have been warned that such a test was going to take place."

Oh for goodness sake! What a dimwit!

"Now what would be the point in that?" There's no answer forthcoming and I'm amazed, as I always am, at how good Cubby is at staying calm. "I need to return

78

the necklace to you," he continues, "and I think it would be a good opportunity for us to have a further discussion about your ongoing security arrangements and perhaps a renegotiation of your premium, Mr Mehew, *if* you do not wish to put in place further security measures. Would you prefer to come here or shall I come to you?" Mr Mehew is sounding considerably more conciliatory now, no doubt still intent on getting a good deal out of Watson & Grove but I hope this time Cubby will have the upper hand. A short while later and with the arrangements made, Cubby ends the call and gives me a broad smile.

"Well done, Madeleine." This is greeted with a snort of derision from Dan.

"Well done! I can't believe you condone her stealing another person's property." Cubby and I turn to look at him and my impression is that to Cubby this reaction doesn't come as a surprise. I feel a twist of nausea, anger flaring like a flash of electricity through my veins and I'm aware my salad is not sitting as comfortably as it once was.

"Clearly you have no idea what I do as I've saved the company thousands," I blurt out through gritted teeth in an attempt to protect my position. Dan looks ready to launch back a retaliation to this statement but Cubby verbally steps between us as with a raised hand he tells Dan not to say another word.

Although I'd been surprised by the news of Cubby's retirement and wary of Dan's inclusion in this meeting, I hadn't realised until this moment that somebody in the room wasn't on board with the methods Cubby uses, even though I do appreciate they are not the most orthodox. The fact that this somebody is the one who's going to be taking over could prove problematic. Out of the blue my future here is as shaky as my burst of anger has made me feel, and I have no idea how to go about proving my worth with words or whether I should be fighting my corner at all, so I'm relieved when Cubby turns on him and I decide to hold back and watch how things develop.

"I told you, Daniel, Madeleine is a key part of the set up here. She has been for four years and it works well, so you are going to have to deal with it." I wonder how I'm ever going to manage to work with Dan if he doesn't believe in what I do. Then it occurs to me that I may never even get the chance because if, and I change that to when, he takes over he could simply sack me. Dan stays silent but looks mutinous and very much as if he has no intention of dealing with it at all. I can feel the hostility building like a wall between us and I try to think of something I can say to improve the situation, but as nothing comes to mind I appreciate I probably look as sulky as Dan does right now. I look over at Cubby who is sitting back and watching the two of us, probably wishing he could bang our heads together.

In the end he holds up his hands as if to calm the simmering anger he can no doubt feel before either of us says something we might later regret, and I'm thankful for the intervention because I can't help thinking that anything that comes out of my mouth now is unlikely to be helpful.

"We need to move this on," Cubby says, "clearly, Daniel, you are finding the rather unusual working arrangement Madeleine and I have to be something of a challenge. And I appreciate that the news of Daniel coming on board has come as a surprise to you, Maddy. You both need to be given some time to process how it's going to work." Dan goes to speak but Cubby holds up a hand and the accompanying glare causes him to remain silent. "So this is how we're going to proceed. You two," and we each receive his sternest of looks, "are going to spend some time in each other's company so that you learn how to play nicely." I want to object and say that I can't see how that is ever going to work but I don't as when Dan tries to interject for a second time, presumably with a similar objection, he is silenced again by Cubby's raised hand. Dan sits back in his chair and I get the distinct impression he is not used to being told off.

Cubby then reaches again to the end of the desk and takes the next two files off the pile there. He pushes them across to me and I pick them up and place them on my lap. He has moved back into business mode, for which I am grateful and I check the name on the top one then raise my astonished eyes to Cubby.

"Mrs Fortescue? Again?"

"I know, unbelievable, isn't it. Her bag went missing from the front seat. Another warning please, somehow we have to get her to change her habits," and he sighs in frustration. I have a quick check through the top pages of the inch-thick file that I've seen several times before, update myself on the latest details, then slide it back onto the desk. The second file is thinner and as I open it up Cubby says,

"I know you've been working on Danewright House for a while," as he nods towards the file, "but as this is your most complicated job to date, here is a copy of all the intelligence we have gathered so you can take it away with you."

"Ah, that's great, thanks." I close the file knowing I can peruse the details in my own time later.

"Are you planning on visiting the House any time soon?" he then asks me.

"Yes, Saturday."

"Excellent, then you can take Daniel with you." *What?* My reaction shows on my face as Cubby adds, "He might as well find out more about what you do." I suppose he's right but the idea isn't any more appealing to me than it appears to be to Dan when I glance across at him. He looks back at me and grudgingly suggests we swop contact details.

That done, I get up to leave. I say goodbye to Cubby then in an attempt to be more gracious I say to Dan, "Maybe I'll see you at the gym, tomorrow?"

"More than likely you will," is his underwhelming response and I catch Cubby's broad grin.

"There, you see, I knew you two would have something in common."

Chapter 10

Officially I'm not an employee at Watson & Grove. I'm on a retainer. It's not a huge sum but I live modestly and it covers my needs. When I moved to this area I had few job opportunities open to me, due to a complete lack of provable working history to put forward to give any credibility to me being a suitable candidate for a normal vacancy. So I created my own, unique role in this business based on my specialised, but rather dubious, skillset. I was and always will be eternally grateful to Cubby for seeing the potential, and for asking no questions. He has been my handler, for want of a better description, and I could kick myself for never thinking of the possibility that this situation might one day change.

I arrived in this area four years ago. But I did so having planned my escape and new existence with great precision. Once I was set up I knew I would need an income and while a fake CV with much on it to excite any potential employer was no problem, there would be more of an issue should they want to speak to any previous companies to get references. So I'd planned on taking a different approach. I thought long and hard about it, did my research then I went out one night and stole a ring.

It wasn't difficult. People are basically lazy and instead of bothering to lock their valuables away they leave them scattered all over the place, turning to their insurance companies for recompense when they go missing. I know my actions were wrong but we all pay for such carelessness in our increased premiums so with the service I was planning to provide you could say that in the greater scheme of things I was doing everyone a favour.

I knew that although Watson & Grove had a quiet and unassuming profile and their offices were based in an unremarkable town, all of that was done to keep it low key and protect the identities of what I was interested in, its elite clientele. My living where I did wasn't a fluke. I'd come across the company in my past life, and its location and where I ended up living was all in the planning. I watched the offices, followed a few possible marks until one ticked all the boxes and then I took her ring. I won't bore you with how, as it was not dissimilar to the trick I'd just pulled on the Mehews.

The following morning I'd presented myself in the offices of Watson & Grove. There was a lot riding on that meeting and I could well remember the sleepless night I'd had and feeling sick with nerves as I'd waited in the reception area but, getting used to playing the part in my new life in Crowbridge, I'd put on a confident front as I'd waited to meet Mr Wilton for the first time.

I didn't have an appointment so I'd said I'd wait until he was free. I could sense the tension in the office. An irate client had already been on the phone demanding action. I was sitting in reception when she'd called back. I could hear her high-pitched indignation from across the room and I knew it was the owner of the ring that was currently nestled in my jacket pocket. Mr Wilton was, she was told, engaged with another client so a message was left with promises to the caller that as soon as he was free he would ring her back.

It was important to me that I met with Mr Wilton before he spoke to the client so once the phone was quiet again I told the receptionist I might be able to help with the situation and I remember her look of disbelief as she'd called through to Mr Wilton's office. I was told to go through a moment later. I realised that rather than being engaged he was merely delaying the encounter for as long as possible, probably having to gird his loins in order to make the call back and meeting me was, for him, just a welcome distraction before having to face the inevitable.

Therefore, as soon as I walked in I was aware Mr Wilton was only humouring me as being one more thing to deal with before he tackled the situation at hand, and I knew I had to make an impression. I introduced myself and, getting straight down to business, placed the ring box on the green leather top of the oak desk in front of him. Then I sat down and waited.

He'd looked at the box, at me, and then at the box again. I'd indicated with the briefest nod that he should open it, and when he did his eyes widened and he'd breathed out an expletive, one I don't need to repeat.

"Where did you get this?"

"Her kitchen table."

"She told Helen it was in the safe."

"She lied." He'd gazed at me for a moment then called through to the receptionist, Helen, told her to hold his calls and ordered coffee. He'd looked up at me and mouthed the word 'coffee' as a question as he did that, and I'd nodded.

"Why have you done this?" He was intrigued and having gained his attention I hoped I'd get him round to my way of thinking before he thought to call the police.

"To show you I could, because I have a proposal for you." He'd acknowledged this with the merest tilt of his head, indicating for me to go on. "You have clients who are, to put it politely, slack with their security arrangements and careless with their possessions. This results in your company having to pay out large sums in claims made. I can provide you with an advisory service, of sorts, to get them to, how should I put it, take their responsibilities a little more seriously.

"As a consequence their possessions will be protected better, fewer claims will be made and premiums will go down – it's a win-win." His eyes had narrowed as he contemplated my words and thought through the implications, and I'd seen the moment when he'd decided that it might actually be something worth considering. Before he could say anything further though the door had opened and the coffee brought in, a tray placed on his desk.

"Help yourself," he'd murmured, after thanking Helen for delivering it. I take mine black so had simply leaned forward to lift a cup from the tray and I'd watched him carefully as he remained thoughtful throughout the process of adding milk and sugar to his. It wasn't until he'd taken his first tentative sip, wary of scalding himself, that he spoken again.

"How do you suggest I deal with this current situation? Our client is furious and the police have already been notified." I'd feared that might have happened.

"I suggest you call her and explain that you have her ring safely in your possession. You can tell her that as part of your company policy on testing security measures she was chosen at random and the ring was taken to show how easy it was, and that in order to abide by the terms and conditions that she signed up to, she should have had it locked away. She may say again that it was locked in the safe at which point you can tell her it was taken from the kitchen table and I daresay that will take the wind out of her sails."

"We don't have such a policy."

"She's not to know that and is unlikely to question it as she has the ring back and is probably going to be flustered at having been caught out in a lie. I would think she would want to put the whole thing behind her. *If* we come to an arrangement, we can add in the appropriate wording to the terms and conditions for the future."

"Okay, but what about the police?" Now this *was* going to be trickier to deal with. I'd pretended to be giving it a great deal of thought for a few moments, before saying,

"Find out who has been to the property and put a call into them immediately. We need to stop SOCO looking for fingerprints, and any other possible forensic evidence." I was sure they'd find nothing but it was best to be on the safe side and I didn't want there to be anything linking back to me. "Explain your change in security testing and apologise for not informing them first. They'll probably appreciate you doing all you can to heighten your clients' awareness. But most of all you need to convince them not to take this any further. Again, should we consider working together we can inform the police appropriately in future." He'd given me a smile, one that lit up his eyes that crinkled at the corners, and it was at that moment that I knew I really wanted us to work together.

"You've thought of everything."

"It's what I do." I'd spoken confidently, wanting to reassure him because I needed him to believe in me.

"And what if they want to speak to you?"

"I was never here." With my sleeve I'd wiped my mug free of fingerprints before I'd put it on the tray. "You will have to gloss over my part in all this, *if* we are to do further business." I'd hesitated for a moment, then finished, "Are you in?" I could see him falter, his face etched with concern at the trouble he had swiftly realised I might be bringing his way, and I'd waited. I'd known better than to force the situation and was well aware he had to come to me, and although I'd appeared cool, not a trace of emotion showing on my face, my body belied my appearance. My heart hammered as with every cell, every molecule of my being I was willing him to say yes.

Say yes, say yes.

The seconds ticked past, each one weighing like an hour.

Say yes, say yes.

And then he had. He had said yes and a wave of relief had swept through me.

He'd made the calls. He'd smoothed the turbulent waters with his client, put things right with the police and he'd finally hung up the phone with a huge grin and a sigh of satisfaction.

"I think we can do some business," he'd said, we'd shaken hands and he'd told me to call him Cubby. Since then we've carved out our own special way of working together. I sometimes have quick, easy jobs and others are longer and more complex. Some are local while others are further afield which I might have to stay away for and I don't mind that. The only person likely to notice if I don't come home is Diane, and I tell her I'm off seeing old friends or family which she never questions. This is why I like not having the responsibility of anything relying on me, it gives me the flexibility to come and go as I please.

I care for Cubby, probably more than I should, and I like to think he cares for me in return. In our early days together we'd spent a lot of time getting to know each other and working out how and where I could be used in the business. I'd come to the office and we'd talk through cases and client histories and we'd try out various possibilities. He'd called me his security tester, and I'd often be used on larger jobs where a security system had been installed and I'd be sent in to see if there were weaknesses in it. Most of all though he was genuinely interested in me, and while I was guarded about what I told him of my past life I knew he took in anything I let slip and no doubt joined the dots in the sketchy history I shared.

However, I'd never experienced a relationship like this before, and having only ever been used to men wanting one thing from me I'd initially read things wrong, and one day I'd made a clumsy attempt at a pass at him.

My foolishness could have been the end for us but to his credit he'd managed to rebuff my advances with kindness and a joke about his age. At the same time, he'd smothered my embarrassment by wrapping his arms around me, telling me that one day someone was going to hug me so tight that all of my broken pieces would stick back together. I'd doubted that was possible, he thought he knew me but love him as I might, Cubby had no idea how utterly damaged I was.

Chapter 11

The following morning, I set off for Hartleigh, calling in on Sidney for our usual bout of sparkly repartee and then going straight on to the gym. I'd slept badly, exhausted by vicious dreams of running, of pelting along darkened streets slick with rain, of gasping for air as blackened bony fingers reached out Dementor-like to thwart my escape. But I knew what was likely to be hunting me and it was no work of fiction that had startled me awake in the early hours.

I'd lain with my heart pounding and pulse racing, it taking ages to calm myself enough to get back to sleep. When I'd finally woken again, the alarm causing me just that, I'd been so tensely coiled I'd had to do some stretches to ease my aching muscles before I'd left the cottage. My head hurt from the lack of a decent amount of sleep, my eyes were scratchy and I could have done with going back to bed but I have to keep up the pretence of having a 'normal' job so I'd headed off as always. Fortunately, with modern times being what they are, gone are the days when office wear meant suits and I can dress quite casually in trousers and a top and it not be remarked on.

I can only put my disturbed night down to my unease at what I consider to be Dan's intrusion in what had, until the previous day, been my ordered life. The shadows of my past were taking advantage of my unsettled mind to make an appearance. I'd been seething since leaving Cubby's office, building up a detailed depiction of Dan's privileged life in my mind. I imagined him at some exclusive private school, followed by university, of course, summers vacationing in the south of France, winters spent skiing. How else did he get his hair like that? And resentment gnaws at me because it must be nice not to not have any worries because nepotism has secured your future for you.

I wish Cubby had tipped me off earlier about his impending retirement and the changes that would bring, though I guess whenever he had done it I would have felt like this at some point and he probably thought similarly. Telling me at the same time as me meeting Dan at least dealt with the shock all in one go and I wondered when he was actually leaving. He hadn't mentioned that, and I hadn't asked, which was thoughtless of me but I'd been selfishly focused on the uncertainty that clouded my future and I would have to put that right with him.

As I change into my gym gear I decide I can't be bothered to do any weight training today, my body is too tired, so I plan to put in a few miles on the treadmill and then swim, as I figure that will be best for stretching out my aching muscles.

There's no sign of Dan when I enter the gym and I nod a hello to Steve who is chatting to one of the other guys about increasing their training programme. I flick on my iPod and choose a much needed motivational playlist before starting on the treadmill. As I run I pick up the rhythm which helps, and I let my mind wander. I'm still not sure how real the risk to my future is from Dan. At the moment I'm under the impression he doesn't think much of me and sees what I do as a waste of time, and no doubt money. I'm not sure why he's taken against me on our first proper meeting and I don't know what I can do to improve things between us. But as far as I'm concerned our personal relationship is of lesser consideration and the far more important issue, and the one that is making me anxious, is that I need him to appreciate my input to the business, and I don't know how to go about proving that to him. Let's face it, if Cubby hasn't managed to then he's hardly like to believe me now, is he?

I'm aware when one of the younger guys, Pete, starts running on the machine next to mine but I remain focused on getting my stint over with as today every step feels like hard work and I'm not enjoying myself at all. Pete is in his late teens and has been coming here for a few months in the run up to joining the army. He initially started working out to get through the medical but now he's been accepted he's hoping to get a head start on the basic training weeks he'll be facing shortly.

Finally, I reach the end of my target run and I slow the pace bringing it down to a jog and then a walk as I calm my breathing. I take my earbuds out and hear Pete say, "Are you finished now?"

"No, I'm off for a swim next."

"Fancy hooking up later?" Direct, that's what I like.

"Sure, I'll see you when you're done." Pete and I have been enjoying each other regularly since he's been coming here. He's a little too hair-triggered for my liking but at his age his recovery rate is admirable and he's always a fun way to while away an afternoon, albeit one that due to the lack of any better facility would most likely be in the back of his car, although that does add a certain frisson to the proceedings.

As I swim my lengths, my mind keeps going back to the situation with Dan and I'm surprised he hasn't shown up this morning. Maybe Cubby has him actually doing some work in the office as he presumably won't be able to spend every morning at the gym instead of at his desk once he gets going properly in his new role. That will be a good thing. It will be far easier to only have to deal with him in the office. However, I've still got our outing to get through on Saturday and I hope his presence isn't going to make things too difficult.

There's no sign of Pete when I come out of the changing room and I take a seat in the reception area to wait for him. I've only been there a couple of minutes when Dan enters through the main doors.

"You're late," I say, the words out before I realise they could come across as antagonistic when I only meant them in jest. Fortunately, he appears to take them in the manner in which they were intended.

"That all depends on what time I was meant to be here, doesn't it," and he smiles before clarifying, "I got caught up in some stuff in the office and have only just managed to get away."

"I was thinking you were probably unlikely to be able to take every morning off when you got going."

"Indeed, I know Cubby escapes as often as he can but even he doesn't manage that." He grins again and seems so much more relaxed than he had been in the office the previous day. "So why are you still hanging around?"

At that moment Pete walks out of the changing room and as I start to say, "I'm waiting for..." I see Dan's face darken as he catches sight of Pete and then looks back at me.

He cuts me short with, "Oh, I see," and before I get the chance to say anything further he walks off, straight past Pete, who he doesn't acknowledge at all, and into the changing room. I watch him go and frown, bewildered at the change in him.

When Pete reaches me he says, "Are you ready?" and I nod as we turn and walk out together.

There's a chill in the air on Friday morning and as if Sidney doesn't already do everything he can to make me feel like a cared for and appreciated customer I notice he has a dewdrop clinging precariously to the end of his nose, which is delightful. I hand over the correct money then try not to shudder as the droplet detaches and splashes down onto the paper I'm about to take away and seamlessly I slide out the next one down from the top of the pile instead. He really is a special man and I wonder if there is a Mrs Sidney. If there is, she must count her blessings every day.

I go through my usual routine at the gym and am keen to get done early so I can stop off to get some shopping on the way home. I have built a short day on Friday into my fictional working week so there will be no surprises if I'm home early. I want to go over my notes in readiness for the trip to Danewright House tomorrow. I'm keen to make sure I'm on top of my game to show Dan I know what I'm doing.

There's no sign of him again in the gym, which suits me fine, but just as I'm about to get into my car he drives into the car park and takes the free space next to me. I feel it's a little churlish to just drive off so I wait until he gets out and, trying to keep it light and chatty, I say, "Hello, I nearly missed you completely today."

"I know, all this working is going to become very inconvenient." He looks at me and frowns, then has a quick check round the car park. "Blimey, are you taking an afternoon off?"

For a split second I don't know what he's talking about then just as quick it's as clear as crystal and the insinuation hits me so hard he might as well have given me a backhander. I feel colour rise in my cheeks but try to cover any tell that he's shaken me and say, in a voice edged with steel, "I shall see you in the morning," giving him no chance to respond as I get in my car and drive away.

I think about his comment on the way home. His words were a dig, a slight against me, the sentence laden with sarcasm which with each repetition lay heavy and festering in my mind. There was a time when such a comment would never have gone unchallenged, and the violence of the verbal backlash I'd hand out then would, I suspect, be of a level Dan had never encountered. But that had been in another lifetime, in the days when I pleased wherever I could in order to be popular, in the hope of being liked and of finding myself on the receiving end of some affection. I am well aware of the things that have been said about me, of the names I have been called both to my face and behind my back, and whereas now I brush them off back then I'd tackle head on what I took as jealousy from the girls and ignorance or bitterness from the boys. With absolute certainty I would never have allowed a quip like Dan's today to pass without defending myself and I wonder if I've become weak. Perhaps living among the gentle people of Crowbridge has pacified me and maybe that is what I want; after all there had been a time when I'd left my promiscuous life behind before in an attempt to have a more settled existence with one man, but then that had brought me nothing but trouble.

I ponder on the possibility that I'd been mistaken. Maybe he was genuinely referring to an afternoon off from work but try as I might I can't make that explanation sit comfortably.

Chapter 12

I drive straight past the turning down to my cottage when I get back to the village, and on reaching the top of the High Street I turn round on the junction and come to a standstill outside the shop. We are lucky to still have this facility and I try to support it whenever I can. Unfortunately, I'm not keen on the latest people to have taken it over. She's alright, Pat, a bit colourless but she's friendly enough, hardworking and nothing is ever too much trouble. The word that springs to mind when I think of her is efficient, both in manner and body. She's in her fifties but keeps herself lean and fit with all her racing about. No, it's him. To be fair, most of the time he's not around as he has a job somewhere else but that's only part-time so sometimes he's here, like today, when he's supposedly helping her. Usually if I see he's in I walk back out but I know I have to get past this problem I have with him and today I force myself to stay.

While Pat bustles around serving the customers, busily managing and organising whichever part-time staff she has in, stocking shelves, sorting the deli counter, the cheese, slicing the meat, putting in orders as well as making up fresh, tasty rolls and cooking the hot items for takeaways, pasties, sausage rolls and the like, he sits behind the counter like a loathsome toad. That's what I call him: The Toad. Only in the privacy of my own head though, naturally. Everything about him is bloated. His thick, meaty arms are crossed and rest on rolls of fat as he overflows the stool he squats upon. His mouth is wide, thin, wet lips drawn down at the corners by life's disappointments. He watches me now as I browse the shelves, his dull little piggy eyes pink-rimmed and watery and I avoid making eye contact because he does nothing to hide his lascivious thoughts, his tongue salaciously flicking out to moisten cracked lips.

I feel flushed, my skin crawling with discomfort as his eyes walk all over me.

And that's all that's needed.

That's all that's ever needed.

A lecher, giving me the once over.

The simple trigger for the split-second memory of waking in the night with a darkness looming in my room, a shadow right in my face and the stench of hot beery breath and fags from a mouth too close to mine. Bile rises in me now as fear had done back then as I'd struggled against the weight that had pressed me into the mattress, a rough hand tight over my mouth to stifle the cries that had gone unheeded, even though I could hear the telly on and knew *she* was only in the lounge.

I shake myself away from this train of thought and find I'm gripping the edge of one of the display tables, my fingertips pinched white with the pressure they are under. I force myself to swallow and take a deep breath.

She never went out. Ever. She couldn't. That's what she'd told me. That's why I had to do the shopping, she'd said, although that was hardly an arduous task consisting as it did of buying little more than cheap white bread, own brand beans and riffling through the out-of-date shelf for anything we could afford. I was young so it had taken me a while to wonder where the booze and fags had come from. Initially I'd resented the fact she'd obviously managed to go out and buy those, and to find the money for them, when she couldn't make the effort for anything else. It was only later when I saw the men arrive with cans, bottles and cartons, like gifts, that the penny dropped.

I'd hated the way they'd looked at me, at the way they were over friendly, like they knew me, like we were pals, and I'd recoil when they touched me. Though not openly, that never went down well and I'd be made to regret it. There was an unending supply of alcohol and cigarettes for her though and as I grew up I came to realise what else she'd traded for those, beside herself.

Shaking my head to dispel the dizziness as a wave of nausea rolls through me, I force myself to concentrate on the here and now. I shudder, and turn my face to the window, the late afternoon sun golden and low in the pink blushed sky as I push the dark thoughts back into the hidden recesses of my mind where I know they'll crouch like menacing demons ready to return soon enough to haunt my nights.

It is because of the thoughts that surface in his presence that makes me steer clear of this place if he's around and I have no idea what Pat sees in him. Though as I watch her plate up and then hand him a huge sausage roll which he munches into like a pig at a trough, flecks of pastry and spittle flying, I wonder if she isn't merely playing the long game of feeding him into an early death.

Nice.

It has often surprised me that with such a fabulous source of delicious delicacies on the doorstep there isn't an obesity crisis hitting the village. Though perhaps others here have more willpower than I. Fortunately I do enough exercise to burn off the calorific intake of having such temptations within far too easy reach.

Letitia is currently being served and is keeping Pat busy by ordering all sorts from the deli counter because, as she says loudly, they have people coming over, not that anyone has asked, Ben's work people, business people, very important, she gushes. She's fully made up and wearing a white top under a navy jacket, gold jewellery, and plenty of it, jangling, white jeans and a pair of heels so high I would have been tottering. High heels to go to the village shop? I wander around the shelving and try to keep out of her eye line, but it's not that big a place and as she's looking round for something else to buy she spots me.

"Maddy darling, how lovely to see you. Day off?"

"Oh, hi, Letitia," I mutter, then I carry on with no idea why I feel the need to explain, "I've been into work but often have a short day on Friday."

"Oh wow, lucky you! I often say to Ben how fantastic it must be to have a job so that you can get holiday and have days off because of course there's no time off for me at all, not with everything I have to do." I should clarify at this point that she has never had a job, other than her brief stint as Ben's secretary, which from what I can gather mostly involved lying on her back, so she has no idea what it is like to run a home as well as manage to hold down a job that's needed to pay the bills. I am fully aware I have it easy compared to most as there's just me, but Letitia's lack of any empathy for anyone else's situation is honestly astonishing. She also fails to take into consideration that having tennis lessons, playing golf, going shopping, getting her hair done, her nails done, being spray tanned or waxed, meeting the girls for coffee, brunch, afternoon tea or the regular days out she has at the spa does not amount to a job. She frequently says things that are totally baffling in their insensitivity, however even I'm not prepared for her next offering.

"Though of course with you being single you don't know how hard it is to do what I do." If I didn't feel so much like slapping her across the face to wipe off that look of pity she is now giving me I might just feel sorry for her, and not just for her stupidity, she is with Ben after all. I mean, imagine having to keep having sex with that? She continues, "It's a shame, isn't it, that you don't seem to be able to find a suitable man, we'll have to see if we can set you up with someone."

No sooner has this horrific thought unexpectedly popped into her vacant mind than clearly a suitable victim follows as she squeaks, "Oooh, I know! Ben has a new guy working in the sales team, he's single too, we'll have to get you two together." She claps her hands, rapidly and more than once, totally thrilled she's solved my problem and I imagine she is already seeing herself buying a hat for the wedding and being godmother to all our future offspring, so undyingly grateful are we going to be for her matchmaking skills.

"Don't," I say, as firmly as I can, because from experience I find people like Letitia take little notice of the word no and plough on in their own thick-skinned way totally disregarding anyone else's wants or desires. "I'm perfectly happy as I am."

"Awww." She tilts her head in that most pitying of ways, drawing the corners of her mouth down in feigned sadness then reaches out to hug me and it's all I can do not to punch her. "You can thank me later."

See what I mean?

She relinquishes her hold on me and returns to the counter to pay Pat. As she picks up her bags she turns back to me. "I'll be in touch once I've organised something. Ciao!"

Ciao? What the...

I go to speak then shut my mouth, I know there is little point and I let her pass without further comment.

Pat grins at me, raising her eyebrows ever so slightly, but ever the diplomat she says nothing and starts to ring my purchases through the till. The Toad is watching me again, but I refuse to acknowledge him or even glance in his direction, needing to keep my memories well and truly buried and not be witness to him scoffing down the remains of the sausage roll. He belches and Pat flinches, briefly closing her eyes. I can't help but feel his presence does nothing to promote business. Once I have finished paying I pile my goods up in my arms and return home.

Joe is in my garden; it's a dark evergreen tie today, with a nice weave pattern to it and after dumping the shopping on the kitchen counter I walk out the rear door to see what he's been doing. Mostly tidying up, he tells me, getting the garden ready for winter. I look up and the horses are close by my garden wall so I walk over to talk to them. The larger of the two is brown, the smaller grey. Joe told me that. I thought it was white but he told me horses are never white, only grey. Diane suggested early on when I was renting the cottage that he come and help me manage the garden, and one day he'd encouraged me to touch the horses when they came to see me. I wasn't sure at first, a little afraid I suppose but he told me they were friendly and showed me how to stroke them. I loved the velvety softness of the skin around their mouths and nostrils and it made me laugh when they blew out of their noses, their nostrils vibrating with the action. Joe had sat and talked to me that first time, told me how as a lad he had worked with horses, racehorses mostly. It was hard work with long hours but he'd taken them out on exercise and even ridden in a few races. A young man's game, he'd said. He'd had to pack that in when his parents became ill. He'd come home and cared for them then brought up his younger brothers and sisters when they'd died within a few weeks of each other. He'd grown food to eke out what they could afford to buy and that was his start in gardening.

I'd asked him once if he'd regretted not staying in racing but he'd said there was no point thinking about what might have been you can only go with the flow of what is. He is probably the most laid-back person I know and quite content with where life has taken him. I wonder if I shall ever be that relaxed with how things work out for me.

I lean on the wall now and watch the horses as they graze. They are not interested in coming over to be petted today but are close enough for me to hear the sound of the grass being torn as their teeth clamp down on it and of them grinding it between flat molars before reaching out for another bite. They are so peaceful I can happily watch them for hours.

Joe joins me at the wall. He's drawing on his pipe as he holds the flame of his lighter to the tobacco. I watch it catch and flare with orange heat as he inhales and moments later exhales, the smoke coming out on his soft breath. "You should look into learning to ride," he says. The scent of the pipe tobacco wafts in my direction and I wonder why it is that I like the smell of it so much when the stench of cigarette smoke makes my stomach turn.

"Oh I wouldn't know where to start."

"Have a word with that Letitia, she goes riding." That is definitely not going to happen but I don't want to pour cold water on his suggestion.

"Hmm, maybe. I'll think about it," I say, having no intention of doing any such thing.

"Okay, well I'd best be getting off," he says as he ambles over to retrieve his jacket from the bench seat I have under the kitchen window. We say our goodbyes and I watch the horses for a few more minutes until they move further away before going back indoors and settling down to work.

I run through all my notes on Danewright House then pack them away in their hidden space. I'm just starting to think about what to have for dinner when I'm saved by the bell as a text arrives from Chris – *Hungry?* is all it says, and I reply, *Yes*.

He's already in our booth when I get there and tells me he's ordered. The fire has not long been lit. The kindling cracking as flames lick up from the balled up newspaper and there's a smell of coal dust on the air.

"That's presumptuous," I tease, sitting opposite and reaching for the cider he's chosen for me.

"I didn't want to waste any time, I'm starving. I've been writing all day and completely lost track of when I last ate." He downs half his pint before placing the glass back on the table.

"Oh yeah? Dusty old stuff or juicy new fiction?" He raises a quizzical eyebrow at me.

"I'll have you know, madam, my *stuff* is not old or dusty. Anyway it wasn't that, I was concentrating on the new work today. It's starting to take shape."

"Oh, exciting, tell me more." At that point Kourtney arrives with our steaks and we are side-tracked as we organise ourselves with condiments and cutlery.

"How are you getting on with that flyer?" Chris asks Kourtney.

"I've done it; can I pop in on Monday to print it off? I've got some time in the afternoon to deliver it round the village."

"Absolutely. I'll be in, so any time after about..." He pauses as if to think for a minute.

"Ten?" she asks, smiling.

"That would be perfect, no use rushing at these things, is there?" Kourtney shakes her head and thanks him before she heads off to another table to deliver menus and on to a third to take the order.

103

Chris is clearly famished and has already made a start on his steak so after swopping the usual accompaniments we eat in silence. A short while later he takes a breath and sits back, putting his cutlery down for a moment.

"Better?" I say.

"Better," he replies, with some relief. I pause with him and take a draught of my cider as he lifts his glass to his lips.

"So, go on then, tell me a bit more about your story." I pick up my cutlery again, using the fork to reach for an onion ring from the pot we share.

"What have I told you already?"

"Only about the heroine, how she's bright, pretty and blah, blah, blah."

"And that she has a mysterious past?"

"Oh yes, and that." How could I forget? "Are you any further along?"

"I've developed her character a bit and I'm pretty sure she might be running away, or hiding, from something, or someone, in her past." I want to make a spooky *oooh* noise, but I don't.

"So how's that going to affect her? Do you have some crazy psycho of an ex about to spring out of the shadows and do her a mischief?" He grins, at my lack of subtlety, no doubt.

"You and your thrillers, Madeleine. I'm not sure the past features at all actually, the story is more about the impact it's had on the way she lives now." I'm lost and shrug as I say,

"Which is…?"

"By living in solitude, by spurning the advances of those who might want to get closer to her. It's just a commentary on her life and how she lives it based on her experiences."

104

"Oh." I have a slight sinking sensation as I wonder if I will like reading what Chris has written. To be honest it sounds a little boring but he's my friend and although I want to support him I'm filled with concern that I might hate it. I carry on eating and think I shall have to worry about that another day, it will be ages before he is ready to publish anything anyway. That's if he even gets a publisher, he's forever telling me dire stories of the state of the publishing industry so it may well never see the light of day.

"Don't worry, Madeleine, I shall be injecting some drama into it." I breathe out a visible sigh of relief.

"Thank goodness, I thought for one moment then that it was going to be dreadfully dull." He laughs out loud at that.

"God forbid there should be a story without sex and violence in it."

"I hadn't even mentioned sex." I ponder on that for a moment but then can't help but be inquisitive. "Is there going to be any of that?" He's finishing his final mouthful as I continue clearing my plate.

"Probably not. I'm not sure I'm the right man to be writing sex scenes," and he chuckles, "anyway like I said she's keeping herself to herself so although there's the promise of a romance in the air I think her past will influence how she deals with that. We shall see," he ends mysteriously as if he doesn't really know where his story is going when I bet he knows exactly how it all pans out.

"Do you fancy a pudding?" he asks, surprising me.

"Go on then." I take no persuading at all and when Kourtney comes to clear our plates we order two chocolate fudge cakes.

"Warm?" she asks, knowing she really doesn't need to.

"Of course," is our joint response.

105

When she's gone again I say, "You haven't told me her name."

"Who?"

"Your heroine. She has got a name, I assume."

"Absolutely," and he beams, "it's Gabriella."

"Oooh, classy!"

"Isn't it just," and he smiles knowingly at me.

Chapter 13

As arranged Dan picks me up late Saturday morning for our trip to Danewright House. I'm not keen on this as I prefer the independence of having my own transport but he had insisted, saying it made sense as he was coming from the city and would be driving straight past the village so not wanting to rile him further, I agreed.

After receiving the file from Cubby I had read through all it contained and incorporated any new information into my own notes. It was not long until this project was due to come to fruition and this could well be my last visit to the House.

Dan doesn't refer to my abrupt departure the previous day and seems to be in a relaxed frame of mind, which comes as something of a relief. We've only been travelling for a few minutes when he says, "Cubby has kept me in the dark about why we're going to Danewright House, I guess so we'd have something to talk about," and he smiles, "so can you fill me in on what you're doing there?" Before agreeing to this outing I had checked with Cubby that Dan hadn't already met anyone involved with the House. Cubby has been liaising with one of the trustees, Arthur Ramsey, and the last thing I wanted was to get there, for someone to recognise Dan and for there to be a link to me.

"Of course," and I take a deep breath and hope he's going to be receptive to my role rather than instantly dismissing it as a waste of time. "In the next couple of weeks Danewright House is hosting the Duchess de Havilland's Jewellery Collection. It's loaned out by the trustees who run the charity that was set up when the

Duchess died. They offer the collection to various houses and museums to support them in increasing visitor numbers and funds by way of entrance fees.

"Watson & Grove insure the collection and it is my job to test the security of the House and see if it can be breached. The owners of Danewright House are satisfied they have the appropriate security in place but if I do get in, extra measures might have to be taken."

"That sounds like a useful exercise." I'm amazed. He actually seems quite amenable to the idea, which surprises me although I suppose to him it appeals as it's a more palatable option than walking into people's homes and taking their stuff.

"This is the first time Danewright House has hosted such a collection so it's important to them that everything goes smoothly."

He's quiet for a moment then says, "I hope you don't mind me asking but how did you get qualified to test such security arrangements?"

"I'm sure Cubby has a file on me, have you not looked at that?"

"I have, but it can best be described as sketchy and gives no information about you at all other than where you live now." Good old Cubby, I love his discretion, but I do think that if Dan and I are ever going to work successfully together I'm going to have to tell him more, or at least as much as I think he needs to know.

"Cubby is being discreet but basically the skills I have are the product of a misspent youth."

"Really! And there's me thinking you must have taken some burglary course at college or been on an apprenticeship scheme." His humour is arid in its dryness.

"I did, just not in the way you'd understand what with your private education polished off by a stint at university." I have a dig back and hope I haven't overstepped the mark.

"That's what you think, is it? I hate to put a dent in your prejudiced opinion of me but there was no private education," he replies and shakes his head.

"Really? You surprise me."

"I went to a comprehensive, probably just like you, though I admit I did go to university."

"What did you study?"

"History of Art." I have no idea what that covers and precious little about art at all so I say nothing further and he continues, moving away from that subject anyway. "So is this a fact finding mission today?"

"Yes, although I've already done most of my planning. But I want to have a final look around and make sure nothing has changed. I was only here a week or so ago so I'm not expecting there to be anything new. But as they are starting to get set up for the exhibition there might have been some alterations."

"Okay. Well I haven't ever been here so I shall be interested to see the place anyway."

"Don't you come from round here then?" I thought it unlikely that if he was local he wouldn't have been to the House at some point. It was a favourite school trip destination.

"No, I was brought up a few hours away."

"So it's only the opportunity to take over the family firm that has made you move here then?"

"Pretty much, and I really appreciate the nepotism dig by the way."

"You're welcome." I smile, enjoying the banter, "Has it always been your dream to work in insurance?" Is that anyone's dream? I can't help prodding, just a touch more.

"Unsurprisingly, no it hasn't. The truth is that I've taken a little time to settle down. I didn't at school, and university was meant to fix that but I left there with still no idea of what I wanted to do."

"So you're here reluctantly?" He nods.

"My mum is Cubby's sister and he and I have always got on so I guess she thought he might be a good influence and with his retirement on the horizon he's given me a chance."

"But you don't approve of his methods?" He looks askance at me, before saying, with some care,

"I don't see the point of doing things unnecessarily."

"Uh huh," and I tell him to get off at the next exit. We take to the country roads for a few miles and then turn into the gates of Danewright House. It will be some time before we get to see the 16th Century mansion, home originally to generations of the Beauchance family and now that of the Duke and Duchess of Cranborough. I'd brought the leaflet I'd picked up on my visit here a week ago, thinking Dan might be interested, and I can feel the thickness of it, the weight of it, as it lies between my fingers. The rough textured parchment-like quality speaks volumes for the place that will come into view around the next corner.

I watch Dan, his eyes widening as he sees our destination for the first time.

"Blimey, that is one big house." An understatement, if ever there was one.

Danewright House is impressive in both size and splendour. Soft cream stone rises two storeys, topped with a parapet behind which a further layer lined with skylight type windows shows the extent of the living quarters. There are drives and gravel laid paths, arches and colonnades, and symmetrical rows of identical windows face the ample parkland, woods and formal gardens.

"You should find plenty to entertain you here, Dan. It has one of the country's most superb collections of fine art adorning the State Rooms apparently." I wave the leaflet, and add, "it says so, right here." He makes some sort of noncommittal noise, then says,

"Hmm, perhaps I should say at this point that I didn't actually get my degree."

"Oh! Why not?"

"I found other entertainment more appealing, didn't do any work and left after the second year." Then he elaborates, "I jumped actually, rather than wait to be pushed."

"So you're not about to give me an informed guide of the work around us as we peruse the art while surrounded by fine examples of furniture, tapestries, carpets and porcelain?" I say, reading the last part directly from the leaflet. Even if he didn't get his degree at least there will be something of interest for him to look at today, I think, which will add some authenticity to the trip.

"Sorry to disappoint," he says, and shrugs, but it doesn't bother me at all, in fact it's quite a relief to find out he's not the over-achieving, highly qualified, family successor I'd been imagining he was. It makes him less intimidating. I'm also surprised he's been so open but it's made me feel closer to him. Maybe that's part of his plan; if he shares then he might be hoping I will too. I shall have to watch out for that.

We pull into the car park, and with it being the end of season there are only a few other cars here which suits me, and as Dan turns off the engine I get out.

"So what's the plan?" he asks.

"We'll follow the tourist route through the house first then check out the gardens and the approach."

A short while later we're wandering along the plush carpeting of the State Rooms paying appropriate attention to the displays. Dan seems uninterested as I read out some of the descriptions below the paintings and keeping my voice low, I say,

"Considering you did history of art, you don't seem at all interested in what's hanging on the walls."

"I'm not," he whispers, as if letting me in on some big secret, then speaking normally he elaborates. "The truth is I wanted to do history, but I didn't get the grades so I went through clearing and got History of Art offered to me. I thought once I got to uni I'd be able to swop courses but they were having none of it and then the course started and I simply couldn't summon up the interest."

"Hence the eventual leaving," I finish for him.

"Exactly."

We push on and I note the discreet cameras that are positioned through the main rooms. This building is listed, obviously, and is the actual home of the Duke and Duchess of Cranborough in the closed season and because of that there have been as few changes as possible to accommodate the opening of the house to the public, so that in the winter months it can easily revert to becoming a family home again.

At the end of the main gallery there are double doors that lead to the library and it is in here that the jewellery is to be displayed. To all intents and purposes, and as far as the public is concerned, there is only one door into this room.

But I know better.

At least I think I do.

The library is magnificent. Oak panelled and lined floor to ceiling with bookshelves it has upper galleries reached by spiral staircases straight from Beauty and the Beast. It's flooded with light from an atrium roof and I love the feel of it, the smell of it, of books: camphorous, oily, the musty woody smell from leather-bound volumes to vintage paperbacks, that's oh so comforting. It's warm and golden in here; and if this were my home I doubt I'd ever be far away from it. There are tables to work at and comfortable sofas scattered around for cosying up in to read away an afternoon. Utter bliss.

I'm a stickler for research, for planning my work down to the last detail and with this being my biggest job to date I had read everything I could find about the House. In doing so I'd stumbled upon something useful, hopefully. Once upon a time way back in the days when libraries were put together and maintained as a status symbol (think Darcy and Pemberley) there was a full time librarian who lived and worked here, an enviable role indeed. As a sign of his status he lived in a cottage on the estate, rather than in the servants' quarters; and so that he did not disturb the family with his comings and goings there was a separate entrance into the library. This was hidden, covered by a section of bookshelves that swung free of the rest but unless you knew what you were looking for you were unlikely to spot it. This secret entrance is not something referred to on the tourist trail, which I found surprising but I'd discovered its brief mention in an old tome about the hidden gems found on estates in which Danewright barely got a mention so perhaps it's not widely known. The information on its whereabouts was also sketchy so potentially it could be a complete fabrication or no longer accessible. I sincerely hope neither of these possibilities turn out to be true.

On my visits here I had narrowed down the options for where the entrance could be situated to three places. Visitors aren't given free rein to wander the library at will so I'd only been able to look at the alternatives from a distance and make an educated guess as to where it was likely to be. As I was going to be approaching it from the other side I didn't actually have to find it but what I needed to know was that it wasn't either blocked by furniture or hampered by the rolling ladder being in the way. Two of the most likely entrance points could be compromised by the ladder while the third was completely clear of that possible obstruction but being in the furthest corner had every chance of being blocked by furniture. Particularly as what was in here already was probably going to be moved around to accommodate the display.

There is a sign up announcing the impending visit of the Duchess de Havilland's Jewellery Collection and I can see that part of the library has already been cleared in readiness but as I look around I note that at the moment all three of my potential entrance points are still clear, which is a relief.

If I was a betting woman I would put my money on the option in the furthest corner as being the two to one favourite and I was keen to see if, in a week or two, that would have been a safe place for my money.

Dan is looking round the library in awe, saying "This is amazing," and I'm delighted my favourite room gets this reaction from him.

"Do you read?" I ask.

"Of course." He sounds slightly indignant that I would think he didn't but I'm surprised he says this as it's not my usual experience of men. Again, he pleases me.

"What sort of book do you like?"

"Oh, you know, the usual, a bit of horror though more often crime, thrillers, psychological stuff." I nod, our tastes are much the same and his eyes meet mine as he says, "Have you seen all you need to?"

"Yes, shall we go and visit the gardens?"

"Absolutely, though let's get something to eat first shall we?" We are at the end of the open section of the house anyway so we walk out of the library and head for the tearoom nearby. I haven't sampled the delights it has to offer whenever I've been before and imagine in the height of summer the place must be heaving, but today all is quiet. Inside, the blue gingham tablecloths brighten tables that are only being used by a few punters. We gaze at the menu written neatly in chalk on the blackboards behind the counter and choose sandwiches and drinks.

"We're going to sit outside," I tell the young waitress and she nods as she finishes writing our order up and tears it off her pad. There's no need to give a table number, she says, they'll find us.

Outside, tables spill across a paved area dotted with planters and we walk though these to one farthest from the buildings. From here we can see right across the unstructured lawns in front of the House to where they drop away down to the informal lake and the parkland beyond where I can see sheep grazing. I prefer this area to the formal gardens behind the House that the vast majority of the public come to see. I sit down making sure I face the building and Dan takes the chair opposite.

"Tell me about this jewellery collection then."

"There's quite an interesting history to it actually. A lady from a well-to-do family became the Duchess de Havilland when she married the much older Duke in the late 1960's. He had been something of a playboy in his time and had failed to settle down and have a family. She was brought in to right that omission but before he managed to impregnate her he died, leaving her his fortune. To everyone's horror she upped and sold off the family estate and then with plenty of money in the bank set out to lead a rather hedonistic lifestyle.

"As part of that she started buying racehorses and in doing so caught the eye of the princes of Saudi Arabia. She became quite the darling of that set, and in their bids to outdo each other for her attention, jewels rained down upon her and the collection came into being. It wasn't until her death, however, that the jewellery was collated. She was patron of several charities serving the countryside and on her death the De Havilland Trust was formed to preserve the collection and loan it out where it could be useful in supporting estates that are constantly struggling for money."

"She sounds like quite a live wire."

"She was, and do you know what?" It was a rhetorical question so I carry on, though lower my voice; "it was said she took more than a thousand lovers."

"Imagine that." I note the sarcastic twist in his response and that he doesn't seem particularly interested in what I thought was a fascinating fact but I'm distracted from pursuing it any further as he changes the subject asking, "Have you got what you wanted from today, so far at least?" Until this moment Dan has been relaxed, and conversation has been easy between us, but I feel a subtle change come over him with even the briefest touch back on business, which is the reason why we are here after all.

"Yes. There have been no changes that concern me, which is the main thing. But we'll have a wander through the gardens after this." He nods and I see the waitress bringing a tray towards us and decide to leave anything further until she has gone.

She unloads a proper teapot, together with cups and saucers, as well as our sandwiches. Like everything else here, this is quality. Delicate porcelain cups in a pretty blue and white floral design match the rest of the crockery.

Dan says, "Shall I?" indicating the teapot and I give him the briefest of nods as a response. Then as he's pouring milk into the cups I decide I should tackle the elephant in the parkland, so to speak.

"I know you don't agree with what I do, Dan, but I don't understand what the problem is so I think we should discuss it, don't you?" He looks a little surprised, I'm assuming because I've been so direct, but he murmurs his agreement. "Go on then," I prompt, "what are your issues?" He takes the lid off the teapot and stirs the leaves before replacing it, and presumably satisfied he pours the tea as he says,

"Are we talking business?" That confuses me, because what else would we be talking about?

"Yes, of course, that's why we're here." He fixes me with his steely gaze for a moment as if coming to a decision about how to start.

"Okay, well I think it's risky, and I don't understand why Cubby goes about things in such an unorthodox manner."

"Well probably because I initially talked him into it."

"So I gather, but," —he looks exasperated— "well, take the last job you did, the necklace?" He says this as if to remind me and I say, yes, wondering what's coming. "What would have happened if you'd set off the alarm? Mr Mehew could have caught you in his house and you would have been at serious risk of being attacked by him because he would think you were a burglar."

So he's worried about me? This is an interesting development, and not what I was expecting.

"True, but then he'd have to catch me first, and I'm pretty sure I could outrun him," I grin at Dan but apparently we are not in a joking mood, so I drop the smile from my face and clear my throat before continuing, in a matter of fact manner, "no one puts their alarm on when they're at home, Dan, that's the thing to remember. That's why I carried out the job when I did. Also, I do put a lot of planning into what I do, you know. I don't just rock up on the off chance hoping it'll turn out okay." I sip my tea and turn my attention to the sandwich in front of me. This is not just any old ham sandwich, of course, it's chunky for a start. Thick slices of posh white bread enclose plenty of crumbly smoked ham carved straight off the bone, dry and flaking. Red onion chutney makes the perfect accompaniment as I sink my teeth into the deliciousness.

"How did you know the necklace was going to be there?" I've made a slight miscalculation in the size of mouthful I took and it takes a moment or two to clear my mouth enough to speak. I watch Dan tuck into his brie and bacon round as he waits for me.

"Because, like I said, I do my homework. The previous night it had been the ball at the school. I knew the Mehews were going, and at a do like that the jewels are going to come out, aren't they? Good sandwich?" He nods, now in the same position I was in only moments before.

"I guess so, but what if the necklace hadn't been there? Would you have gone and broken into the safe?"

"Of course not, because that's where the necklace should have been. Besides I'm no safe-cracker, Dan, and I'm not out to steal stuff just because I can. Cubby's clients have made various agreements over covering their expensive belongings and my job is to make sure they are holding up their end of the bargain.

Why should insurance companies have to keep paying out purely because their clients are reckless with their possessions?" I risk another decent sized mouthful.

"Good point," he concedes, I feel somewhat reluctantly, "so if it had been where it should have been, would you have just walked away?"

"Of course." Dan has finished his food so I crack on with mine and wash it down with the rest of my tea then lean forward to refill our cups, draining the teapot in the process.

Dan is watching me. I don't think he's convinced at all but I have no idea what else I can do to prove my worth. Then he surprises me by asking, "Would you like an ice-cream?"

"Yes please, anything chocolaty." He smiles, his face relaxing again as he does so, and rises from the table to go and see what he can find in the end of season supplies of the tearoom. While he's gone I study the House, or at least the parts of it I can see. There are floodlights fitted that I know are used to illuminate various areas of the outside when particular events are on but are not in everyday use. There are also some security spotlights that react to movement and a couple of cameras as well but nothing that I wasn't expecting to see.

Dan is soon back and we wander off down to the lake, eating on the way. He has chosen well, at least he's chosen mine well. A crisp chocolate outer shell contains rich chocolate ice cream and there's even a hint of a dark chocolate sauce in there as well. His looks to be of a more dubious variety. A pink raspberry filling is covered in white chocolate. I shake my head; chocolate and fruit, never a good combination in my humble opinion.

Beside the lake there are a few picnic tables and we sit again and look back up to the House. We've lapsed into silence, but it's comfortable and I feel as though I could sit here forever, it's that relaxing. I shade my eyes against the soft sunshine that brightens late September days. It's still warm but I can sense the imminent onset of autumn in the light breeze. There's the faintest hint of a bonfire burning somewhere, and when I look at the trees dotted around I see the leaves are turning, shades of yellow and gold mellowing the branches.

I finish my ice cream but having eaten don't feel like moving at all and could just as easily nod off. When I look across to Dan he appears to be in the same frame of mind and is sitting gazing across the lake. I watch his eyes close as he turns his head towards the sun. Long lashes that many a girl would envy outline the curve above high cheekbones.

"Come on," I say, stirring into motion, "the gardens await." We climb back up to the tearoom, the slope feeling far greater than the one we came down. We dispose of our rubbish and follow the signs towards the formal gardens. Behind the tearoom I see the Portacabin that has been brought in as a base for the additional security that will be on site while the jewellery is here. I saw it being set up when I came on the coach trip. Whoever is in there will be monitoring the cameras and I'm expecting them to be patrolling the grounds as well.

Dan is quiet, somewhere far away in his thoughts and I wonder if he is brooding on my role in what is soon to be his business. Perhaps he is thinking about how to fire me. Whatever is going on in his mind, there is little I can do about that so I try to lighten the mood again.

"Do you know much about horticulture, Dan?" I ask. He glances across at me, having been pulled out of his reverie.

"Not really, certainly not as much as you."

"What makes you think I know anything?" I frown, genuinely perplexed.

"I've been to your place, remember, and seen the garden. It looks great, so you must know something."

"Ahh, yeah, no, that's not me, that's Joe, my gardener."

"You have a gardener! How terribly grown up." His response makes me laugh.

"I guess it is, I've never really thought about it, as Joe kind of came with the garden." I explain how I'd originally rented then bought the cottage. "I don't know much although Joe does try to educate me on plants and stuff."

"Stuff?"

"Country lore, you know, things like you know it's going to rain because all the cows are lying down."

"That's useful," he says in that way where you know he doesn't think it's useful at all but then comes back with more; "so you're not a country girl born and bred then?"

"No, city, London actually."

"Really? Very trendy."

"Not at all, as least not where I lived," I say and I go on to tell him about the borough, the streets, the buildings I grew up among and all the while I'm telling myself to shut up. I've never told anyone this much but once I've started I can't seem to stop, for fear it then looks suspicious, so I finish by changing the subject. "Nice roses," I comment feebly, as we pause and take a look around for a minute. We're in a walled garden and there are beds of various bushy type roses which are pretty but, for me, nowhere near as nice as those which are climbing up and clambering over the surrounding walls. "I wonder why they became the flower of love? Above all others, I mean."

"Well they don't all mean love, there's far more to it than that," Dan responds and I glance at him in surprise.

"Really? What do they mean then?"

"Well red is for your passionate love situation of course, but white is for purity, pink admiration and yellow for friendship." He speaks as though he knows what he is talking about, but I narrow my eyes as I meet the grey of his because I don't know if he's winding me up. He grins and I can see he's enjoying himself. We wander on as I say,

"Are you kidding me?"

"Not at all," he says, and he's all sincerity, "it's well known that flowers have meanings. You know that the poppy depicts consolation and we use it for remembrance." I do indeed know that and I nod. He continues, "So, lily of the valley, for example, means happiness, the glorious daffodil stands for chivalry, then we have the tulip which tells its recipient, I'll be back, and if you're ever handed a chrysanthemum you'd better watch out because you have a secret admirer."

"You're making those up," and as he laughs I realise I've forgotten what I'm meant to be doing here. I turn on my heel and glance back at the house, making sure that I have my bearings, but I'm enjoying myself and when I turn back he's watching me and there's something in the way he is doing so that makes me unexpectedly self-conscious.

"Not all of them, Maddy." He pauses for a moment then decides to show off more of what I believe to be his suspect knowledge; "they can also be used to describe people."

"Oh yeah, what flower would I be then?" *This should be interesting*, I think.

"Oh definitely a freesia." I have no idea what one of those is but I'm interested in why he thinks that's me. "It means you're spirited, or a free spirit." Okay, I can live with that.

"That's how you see me."

"Yes, I think so." He nods in agreement as much with himself as with me and he looks down at the path we're walking along.

"And you?"

"Oh I'm ivy."

"Not a flower, but go on," I push for the explanation.

"Fidelity, Maddy. I hang on in there like grim death, right to the bitter end," and he laughs but there's a sadness to it and I know immediately his heart's been broken and if he truly is ivy then that's going to be hard to let go of. Unlike me who can simply walk away.

We've been wandering through the maze of flower beds and borders while talking, which has been enjoyable but I've not been paying attention to my surroundings in the way that I should have been. However, he's grown on me, and interested in finding out more I abandon my plans, realising I've learnt a lesson here and in future there are some things I clearly have to do alone.

"You sound like that trait has caused you problems." I tread carefully.

"It was all a while ago now. We fell in love, were together a few years and while I thought it was for keeps she didn't feel the same way. That's when I found out I was ivy."

"And what was she?"

"Fickle, that's what she was and to be honest breaking up was the right thing to do, it just took me a while to realise it. Sorry. You don't need to hear all that." His foot scuffs through the dust and gravel of the path we're on, showing his frustration. I sympathise, hopefully appropriately and try to make all the right noises, then as we're nearly back at the car park I lead him over to a perfectly shaped horse chestnut tree that I adore. I scour the ground searching for conkers in the grass. I'm in luck and pick up one of the spiky protective casings that has fallen. Breaking it open, I free the burnished brown conkers within, marvelling over the rich glossy skin patterned with lines like the contours of a map, which I show to Dan. I know I'm grinning like a goofy kid when I hand one to him and then there's a moment.

The briefest moment.

When our hands meet.

His, warm and dry.

Mine, the skin tingling at his touch.

And it surprises us both.

We're close, too close, and I look up at him and want to feel his arms around me, to feel his lips on mine and I know it's not wise and that this will be complicated but right now, right in this moment nothing else matters. His eyes search mine as he says,

"I'm not about to become one of your disposable pleasures, Maddy."

And I'm brought right back down to earth with the harshest of landings. I take a step back, exhale and look away. He raises one hand from his side as though to reach out to me, but then it falls back, as if he thinks better of it.

"I'm sorry," he says, his brow furrowed in a frown, "that came out wrong."

"Don't worry yourself." I'm brisk as I brush it off and say we should leave, and I walk away towards his car to cover the fact I'm flustered, anger burning my cheeks.

I am well aware of what I am and I make no excuses for it, because I live my life the way I want to and yet in one sentence he manages to make me feel cheap when none of the others do.

You gonna lay on your back, girl, yer might as well get paid for it.

Echoes from the past, and I shiver at the ghost of an unwelcome reminder not yet laid to rest.

Chapter 14

We're heading back towards Crowbridge and there's an uncomfortable tension between us now which I don't feel inclined to do anything about. It's a shame because we'd been having a good time together until he said what he did and ruined it. Perhaps it's best that his feelings have been aired but I doubt we're going to be able to work together, not with him thinking of me like that. I feel a pang of concern over the future as I'm not sure what I'm going to do for work. There are not many companies like Watson & Grove, certainly not around here and I don't really want to move house. I ponder whether I could talk Cubby into writing me a decent reference. I might have to get a proper job, but immediately the thought of having to clock in and out at certain times makes me shudder. Dan notices.

"You okay?"

"I'm fine," is my cool response, as I remain focused on staring out of the windscreen.

There's a left turn coming up and as we're approaching it a white convertible, roof down, flashes across the road ahead of us. In the driver's seat is a woman, pale with red lipstick, her blonde hair held immaculately in place by a headscarf, the ends of which are flying out behind her; she's impossible glamorous but an Isadora Duncan style accident waiting to happen.

"Turn left, Dan." I say immediately, readjusting myself in my seat so as to lean slightly forward.

"What?"

"Now! Follow that car," I order. There's only a moment to react before we'll be past the junction but he does what I say. The brakes go on and we turn, but

126

we're going far too fast and Dan is tight-lipped as he struggles to make the corner; we've left rubber on the road as the tyres squeal in protest, but then we're round and still in one piece. I'm amazed he even reacted to my demand in the first place and can hardly blame him when once we're travelling along steadily again he rounds on me.

"What the hell is going on?" I give it to him straight, because this is business.

"That car, the woman, it's Mrs Fortescue. Cubby gave me the file the other day?"

"I remember." He frowns. "Why are we following her?"

"Don't get too close," I warn him, ignoring his question for a moment. We're on a country road with little traffic and are heading towards a large village with the kind of facilities that I have an idea will tempt Mrs Fortescue into displaying her slapdash ways. "There are no turnings off this road until the next village so as long as we can see the car now and then on the road ahead we'll be fine."

"So why are we following her?" comes his impatient repeat.

"I've been set the challenge and this is an opportunity not to be missed." I turn to look at him for a moment, before adding, "plus it has the added bonus of you getting to see what I do and being able to give me a hand."

"I don't want anything to do with your work, thanks." He sounds grumpy.

"Really? Well let's see how you feel when you see how one of your clients treats their 'insured by your company' possessions, shall we?" We lapse back into a stony silence.

I keep a close eye on the road ahead, catching occasional glimpses of white through the hedges that line each side. As we come round the next corner I can see the signs indicating the entrance to the village. Mrs Fortescue barely brakes to get through the traffic calming measures and certainly doesn't reduce her speed enough to make the village limit. I tell Dan to slow down.

"But won't we lose her?" I detect a slight interest, a little competitive edge creeping into his voice.

"Not if she's about to do what I think she's going to," I say, and I hope I'm building up the intrigue enough to get him into my way of thinking. "Plus I don't want to draw attention by exceeding the speed limit."

"No, God forbid you should break the law," he mutters under his breath and I throw him a look icy enough for him to feel the chill of the response I'm not going to dignify that with.

We're travelling around a sweeping bend and as the road straightens again I can see the crossroads ahead. The heart of the village. At the moment though there is not one person in sight. There's a village shop on one corner and sure enough there is the convertible, parked on the double yellows outside.

Mrs Fortescue is a delightful woman but her failing is that she is all about the convenience of doing exactly what suits her. I tell Dan to slow down and park up well behind her. As he stops I say, "Call Cubby now, tell him what I'm doing." And I get out. We're twenty metres behind the target car and I run the distance. As I suspect, when I approach the vehicle I can hear the engine running so without missing a stride I leap in, slam it into gear and pull away from the curb. My heart is racing and I can feel the blood pumping in my veins with the adrenalin spike. In a matter of only a couple of minutes, and even with sticking to the speed limit, I'm out the other side of the village. Once I get to a gateway I stop and reverse the car into it before turning the engine off.

I don't have to wait long before my phone's buzzing. It's Dan.

"Cubby is talking to her, and he says you're to come back now."

"Okay, I'm on my way. How does she seem?"

"Amazingly unperturbed." He sounds incredulous but it doesn't surprise me. Not at all. I've seen that reaction too many times before, and not only from Mrs Fortescue.

I drive slowly back and cruise past the shop before turning the car around and pulling it in in front of Dan's car. But I keep it off the double yellows, being the rule follower that I am.

Mrs Fortescue is on the pavement, standing with Dan, and is as calm and collected as if she were merely waiting for a bus (not that I imagine she even understands the concept of public transport). I turn off the engine and getting out I walk towards her.

"Hello, Madeleine dear," she says in greeting, and for one awful moment I think she is going to do that kissing thing but apparently we don't know each other well enough, yet. "Cubby is terribly cross with me and I'm so sorry to put you out again, I simply forget." She waves her hand in the air as if it really is all too much for her to think about. That's the thing with rich people, they can afford to be airheaded and careless. They know there will always be someone to pick up the pieces and replace that which they have lost.

"Just doing my job, Mrs Fortescue." I don't say anything further to her as I know Cubby will have said all he needed to so I hand her back her keys and wish her a good day, managing not to add that no doubt I'd be seeing her again. Because I will be, I know that. She is a frequent flyer for Watson & Grove. Though it suddenly occurs to me that of course I might not, not once Dan takes over.

We walk back to his car and get in. He doesn't go to move off right away but sits staring out of the windscreen and I look over.

"You okay?" I say.

"Yeah," and he hesitates for a moment, "do you want to go for a drink?" This invitation appears to come as much as a surprise to him as it does to me but this bout of collaboration seems to have overcome the tension between us so I reply,

"Alright." I only have the prospect of a quiet evening in ahead of me otherwise so sure, why not. "Where do you want to go?"

"I don't know this area that well but there's a pub in Crowbridge, isn't there? Shall we head back there?" I'd far rather keep him away from the curious glances of the neighbours, so suggest one instead in the next village. In less than ten minutes we're pulling into the car park of The White Hart. It's not a pub I've been to before but I've heard it's been recently refurbished and sure enough when we go in it's all sleek wooden floors, subtle lighting and those faux aged roughened leather sofas, that you sink into so deeply you wonder how you're ever going to climb back out of their comfortable embrace. They do food here; the specials are up on a blackboard. I doubt many dishes will come on plates, with the preference being for wooden boards or slates around here, and when I glance through to the dining area there isn't one table that has matching chairs around it. How very modern.

I join Dan in ordering cider but make mine a half. I'm not sure how this evening is going to go, or why he has a sudden desire to prolong his time with me. But with him taking over from Cubby and his rather negative feelings about my role, as well as the way I run my private life, so I've found out today, I want to make sure I'm in full control of my faculties and don't let myself down.

I take a seat at one of the tables in the bar area, not wanting to relax into the intimacies of the friendlier sofa section. Dan follows me over and on sitting immediately holds up his glass, and I clink mine against his.

"To," —and he hesitates for a moment as if thinking of a toast, then smiles— "to misbehaving clients, may they continue to bring us the opportunity to work together." Amazed at how positive that sounds, I find myself smiling back at him, then he downs a decent draught of his glass, and I can see he enjoys it. I'm surprised by the toast, perhaps he really has mellowed in his view of my input to the business. Despite my need to be on my guard, my spirits lift along with my confidence that my work may yet continue. He's only having the one, he'd told me at the bar, and however well things now seem to be going I'm relieved that he's not planning on staying that long.

"I've ordered us a sharing platter of tapas," he says as he puts down his pint. "I'm famished."

"Okay, thanks," I say and although I've heard of it I wonder what tapas is, it not having been part of my menu choices to date.

"So how did you get into working with Cubby?" Along with the toast I see this interest as a step towards him coming round to my way of doing business. I wonder if he has been told anything and suspect not, so decide to give him the highlights.

"I had recently moved here and needed work. I'd researched Watson & Grove and found they had the client base I was looking for so I set up a robbery to show Cubby what I could do."

"Now *that* is an unusual way to approach job hunting," he says, and he seems genuine. "It must have taken some guts to do it."

"It was tricky and pretty tight on the timing. I needed to get Cubby on my side ideally before the client found out and called the police. Unfortunately, both of those things had already happened and it was a bit touch and go."

"So how did you get away with it?"

"Well I had planned for the possibility, and fortunately Cubby was quick to see the potential so we managed to wiggle our way out of the situation."

"I see. So the example you've just shown me, is that typical of the jobs you do?" We're interrupted by the tapas arriving as a waiter lowers a large slate onto the table and we move our glasses out of the way to accommodate it. It turns out tapas is a selection of spicy sliced meats and tiny sausages, cubes of cheese in oil and herbs along with dishes of olives and dips with bread on the side for the actual dipping. As soon as we're alone again I reply,

"Fairly." I reach for some bread and try one of the dips which turns out to be tasty, and strong on the garlic. "With the likes of Mrs Fortescue I have to wait for the opportunity, just like a real thief would do if they're stealing to order. She doesn't realise that there are people out there who will target her car for a specific client, and will do exactly what we have just done and follow her until she is careless. Which with her is rather more often than you would like. The last time I also found her handbag on the passenger seat because she was 'just popping in to see a friend'," and I do a passable impression of Mrs Fortescue which makes him laugh. I decide to see where his thoughts are at and as he's helping himself to the olives, which he is welcome to as I've tried those before, I question,

"Can I ask? Are you feeling any more sympathetic towards what I do yet?" He shrugs.

"Possibly, in places I guess."

"What do you mean by that?"

"I still don't like the thought of you breaking into someone's home, stealing personal stuff and potentially traumatising them but I can see the value of your work at Danewright House."

"I don't break in, Dan; I don't cause damage; I never have done. I try to be subtler than that, the idea being that no one even knows I've been in their place, and I've never traumatised anyone."

"No, but you could do. I just don't like it, that's all." I don't want to get into an argument about the rights and wrongs of my work so I leave it and concentrate on the food instead. It's delicious and I enjoy trying the different things, although I don't want to show my ignorance to Dan by asking what anything is.

Unexpectedly he then adds, "I will say one thing though." He pauses after popping an olive in his mouth and I wait expectantly. "I do think that with a few changes to how you do things you could add a certain level of excitement to what I was foreseeing as an unutterably dull existence in this job." I grin, his words, the most positive thing he's said so far, warming me instantly.

I sit back a while later having eaten plenty and study Dan as he clears the rest of the slate then wipes his fingers on his napkin, and I wonder if he's planning on ordering anything else. Apparently not, as noticing I've finished my drink he downs the rest of his and says, "Shall we go?"

As we leave the pub the night is already drawing in, the air cooler than when we entered. I shiver in just my shirt sleeves and am keen to get into the car. Dan flicks on the heating then reaches into the back and passes me a jumper that's lying there. I thank him and pull it on, inhaling the comfortable musky smell of him as I do. It's only a few miles to Crowbridge but we cover those in silence and as I'm left to my own thoughts I realise that even though it's not one, this evening, in fact the whole day, is the closest I have ever been to having gone on a date, which seems a trifle sad. I've enjoyed it, on the whole. Despite his reservations about me I like Dan, he's attractive, good company and a decent person if possibly a little too morally upright for my tastes.

By the time we're bumping along the track to my cottage the clear sky has a sprinkling of stars across it, making themselves obvious against the deepening indigo blue. I'd said he could drop me at the top of the road but he wouldn't hear of it. What sort of gentleman would that make him? he'd said, which had made me smile. He turns the car around and once he's stopped I say,

"Thanks for a lovely day, it's been mostly unexpectedly enjoyable." His eyebrows raise at this rather backhanded compliment.

"You're welcome, it's been an enlightening one for me, that's for sure." He hesitates and I think he's going to say something else but then the moment passes and I get out, taking off and passing back his jumper before I walk away.

He still hasn't driven off as I'm putting my key in the lock and I wonder if he is that old fashioned that he's making sure I get in safely before he leaves. Other than in the films I've watched, I've never been exposed to this kind of behaviour. However, as I turn the key and push the door open I realise he's out of the car as he calls out,

"Wait!" I turn to see him coming up the path towards me.

"What's the matter?"

"Nothing, that is, everything." He stops right in front of me and exhales, clearly gathering himself for something. "I'm sorry, I wanted to say I'm sorry for what I said earlier. It was unkind." I don't understand; is he apologising because he's changed his stance on my behaviour? I doubt it.

"It's fine, Dan, you're entitled to have whatever opinion of me you like." I'm not sure what he wants of me but I do know there's a connection between us and I wonder if he's wanting to take that further. "Do you want to come in?" I say as I gesture over my shoulder. I'm not sure why I do that because no one gets invited back here, ever, and certainly not just for sex. It's my space and I treasure it. But I wonder, for a brief moment, if perhaps this could be something worth bringing back into my home.

"Oh no, sorry." His hands are up and I know I've misjudged the situation again as he continues, "I can't become…" He pauses and shakes his head as if trying to refocus on what he was trying to say, and then he continues, "I have no intention of becoming one of your fuck buddies from the gym, Maddy," and again I feel the low blow of his judgement. I'm reeling but before I even have a chance to process, and react to, what he's just said he changes direction again and it's so fast it's surprising I'm not suffering from whiplash when he leans closer, his lips brushing my cheek as I feel the warmth of his breath and he says, "I want much more from you than that."

And then he kisses me.

It's chaste.

It's on the cheek.

And its touch burns like a brand on my skin.

Chapter 15

I wake in my usual ball of tension but in addition feel tired and irritable after a bad night of broken sleep. Vivid images of soft grey eyes turning graphite with disapproval had haunted my dreams and my feelings had swung confusingly between desire for this man, which I knew was reciprocated, and anger because of the way he'd spoken, and what he thought of me.

I'd been left on my doorstep rather stunned, my hand to my face like some love-struck fan after their idol has kissed them and they've vowed never to wash again. Except he wasn't my idol, he was only a man, and one that didn't think too much of me judging by what he'd said. He'd driven off leaving me with much to think about.

I've never questioned my behaviour because I'd never known any other way. I was *that* girl growing up, the one that went with whoever, at school and elsewhere, losing my virginity and I guess my reputation, if I'd ever had one to begin with, at a ridiculously young age. Things did change for a while though. When I was fifteen someone came along who took me away from all that, who wanted to make me all his. Only I hadn't realised at the time that he'd wanted much more from me than just being his girlfriend so eventually I'd run away from that life and on arriving here had returned quite happily to my previous pattern of behaviour. It had never been called into question before as it's always seemed perfectly natural to me to have sex with the men I'm attracted to. I mean, doesn't everyone do that? Although having said that I do realise I'm conflicted in my thoughts on this, because much as I have no shame about how I choose to act I have kept that side of my life well away from the village, so on some level I am concerned my lifestyle choice would probably be frowned on here.

But now there's this man, Dan. I know there's an attraction there, and his kiss? Well, let's just say its effect was unexpected and leave it at that. However, it all feels too complicated and judging by his response last night I suspect he's not willing to take things further until he's the only one I'm seeing, and I need to consider that carefully. One part of me feels why should I be the one to change who I am, particularly for something so new and untested. The other can still feel the heat of that kiss, the pathway it ignited, and it's difficult to ignore that reaction.

The cold breath of autumn hits me as I walk out the door and I turn back to reach for my leather jacket. I'm so lost in my thoughts as I drive off to get some shopping I nearly miss Diane who's waving at me to stop, so that when I do I have to reverse up before winding down the window.

"You look tired," she says, bending down and peering in the window.

"I didn't sleep well. Can I get you anything at the shops, eye of newt, tongue of frog, perhaps?" I manage a weak smile.

"Of course you can, if they've got any, though they've been out of stock all summer," she grins back. "I'm just making some soup if you fancy some for lunch, we haven't had a chat for a while."

"That would be lovely, I'll see you in a bit."

I don't do shopping lists, usually managing to remember the things I need but today my mind is preoccupied and other than getting some Danish pastries and a large chocolate cake I wander round the store with my basket and no idea as to what I wanted. I end up filling it with a random selection of things I like and when I get back find I've now got duplicates of most of them.

I'd made a quick detour on my way home and had turned off into the old estate pulling up in front of the house where Kourtney lives. I'd picked up the chocolate cake from the passenger seat and made my way to the front door. Whenever I'd been here before the grass had always been long enough to take a decent hay crop off it but today it's short, the edges trimmed and it made a huge difference to the place. I'd knocked on the door and Kourtney had answered, she had a barefoot child on her hip and shifted him a little, easing the weight, as she smiled at me.

"Happy birthday, Kourtney." I'd held out the cake to her and her little brother had reached out stretching two chubby hands towards it, his face lighting up. She'd laughed at his reaction looking at him fondly.

"Thanks for rememberin', an' for this, it looks delicious."

"You're welcome." I'd reached into my back pocket and pulled out a bundle of notes. "This is for the driving lessons. Have you got any booked yet?" She was briefly distracted by another small person, a sister, who'd appeared and gazed at me shyly from where she remained half hidden by Kourtney's leg.

"Thanks. I've got the first one tomorra'." Her face was bright with excitement and I was thrilled. Things were really looking up for her. I looked back at the lawn.

"This is tidy."

"That's my brother," —then glancing at the one in her arms, she'd clarified— "the oldest one. I'm putting 'im to work on gardens, so we've got to make this look alright haven't we?" I'd nodded as she'd carried on, "it's all about the image, ain't it. I told 'im, we can't

138

expect people to take us on if our own garden looks a mess, now can we?"

"No, that's true." I had been amazed at her ambition, and the fact she had expansion plans already.

"Joe is showin' 'im the ropes though he's mostly just cuttin' grass at the moment."

"Oh that's good of Joe. That reminds me, I'd best be getting off actually." I'd checked my watch. "I'm due at Diane's. Have a good birthday, and what time's your lesson tomorrow? I'll make sure I'm not on the road when you're having it." I'd grinned at her and she'd laughed again.

"Lol. It's at eleven, I'll keep an eye out for yer." The few minutes' respite from my thoughts had only managed to distract me until I got home.

I'm still mulling over the previous day's events with Dan when I walk up to Diane's and as always enter round the back. Cat is perched on the windowsill right next to the open door and as I walk past and into the kitchen he silently drops to the ground and follows me in. There's no sign of Diane but as I put the Danish pastries onto the table she enters from the other room.

"Hello," she says, "thanks for those," indicating towards my gift.

"You're welcome, how are you?" I say as I sit down heavily onto the kitchen chair. Cat immediately lands in my lap and is pushed off.

"I'm fine thanks, and you? You look exhausted," she says, frowning at me. "I'll fix you a pick me up," and she turns to her dresser and starts searching through the myriad of small drawers it contains, pulling out what look to me to be odd bits of twig and leaf. As I watch her I'm pleased to see how well she's looking. Her bright blue eyes are vibrant and alert, her hair short and an attractive steel grey. Frankly she looks in a much better state than I currently feel. I don't fight against whatever concoction it is she is putting together for me, I know there's no point as she will wear me down into taking it anyway. And who knows, if it stops me thinking, or dreaming, about a pair of slate grey eyes and a disturbing kiss I'll take it.

She pushes the kettle onto the hot plate to boil and wraps the stuff she's gathered in a square of muslin before tying it up with a piece of string, then turns back to me. While she has been doing all this no words have passed between us but she doesn't miss much and her first words are straight to the point.

"What's going on with you, Maddy?" I hadn't planned on talking to her about my issues and now I wonder what, if anything, I should say, but then, too weary to think of any clever way of skirting around the issue, I decide to come right out with it.

"What do you think of promiscuity?" She doesn't bat an eyelid.

"Oh I'm all in favour of it," she says, which makes me smile but then she looks at me and frowns, "but then I think you know that. Why on earth do you ask? It's not as if you're overindulging, is it." This is said as a statement, not a question, it's a throwaway line that she ends with a confident smile as she reaches for the kettle and pours the now boiling water onto the muslin bag. I remain silent and it's that silence that tells her everything. She has her back to me and as if something clicks into place she pauses in her movements and breathes out a quiet, "Ahh." She brings the mug she's brewing for me over to the table, sits down opposite looking at me as if for the first time and acts like she's totally cool with everything.

"Do you want to talk?" she says.

"I haven't been entirely honest with you."

"No reason why you should have been. It's your life. But you seem troubled. Is there something I can help with?" I shrug because I honestly don't know and I have no idea where I'm going with this.

"I have a more active social life than I've led you to believe."

"Okay, and presumably that's away from here?"

"Yes, I've wanted to keep it separate from my village life. Everyone here thinks I'm such a good person."

"Just because you're sexually adventurous doesn't make you any less of a good person, Maddy," she says, gently.

"I think that depends on your views, Diane, there are people here who would be judgemental."

"You're not wrong there," she nods in agreement, "we all are to some degree or other, aren't we? So go on, what's the problem?"

"I've met a man and there's something between us but I don't think he wants to get any closer because he disapproves of my behaviour."

"Well, he would, wouldn't he? Men don't like to share, Maddy."

"The others don't have a problem."

"But that's different, it's casual sex for them. You probably like these other men and they like you but that's as far as it goes. It sounds like this new one maybe wants something more serious with you, and that's not a bad thing, is it?"

"Perhaps not, but part of me objects to having to change for him when I have no idea if it's going to go anywhere, especially…" and I tail off.

"Especially what?" Diane probes.

"Well it's made more complicated by the fact that he's soon going to be my boss."

"Ahh." She cocks her head as she thinks. "I don't see that that is necessarily a problem. You would need to work out a way to keep your business and personal lives separate, or, alternatively you could just get a job elsewhere. There are other insurance companies, you know." She smiles but she's not to know it's not that straightforward, and as I can't go into all that with her I just agree that yes I could get another job. She carries on, "Presumably if it's causing you all this angst you think you might also have stronger than normal feelings for him?"

"Hmm, maybe, but I'm not sure because one minute we're getting along fine and then he says something that really hurts and I don't understand how can I have feelings for someone who makes me feel bad about myself."

"Sometimes it is a little baffling," she smiles a little ruefully, "but we can't control who we're attracted to."

"I guess not, although we can ignore those feelings."

"We can try." She sounds wistful, as if she knows from experience, but then focuses back on me. "You've been in love before, haven't you?"

"Yes."

"Then you'll know anything worth having is not without its faults. Think back to last time, it wasn't perfect, was it?" No it certainly wasn't, and I do think back for a moment to the man I'd loved and left behind. Our relationship was the casualty in my need to forge a new life and I realised that getting together with him had not been totally dissimilar to the situation I was in now. He had also wanted me all to himself but he had wanted me for far more than that as well. "As for changing for him," she continues, "I can understand your reticence but make sure you're not just being stubborn, Maddy, and think about where this relationship could go, if you give it a chance. You could think of it as a compromise rather than a change. Isn't that what we do all the time in the relationships that are important to us? That is what love is after all, it's putting someone else's needs before your own, however much it might pain you to do it. Anyway," and she gives me a wicked smile, a sparkle coming to those eyes of hers, "if it doesn't work out, you can always go back to your bad old ways." She laughs and makes me laugh too. How true that was.

She pushes the mug towards me having extracted the muslin bag of twigs, and urges me to drink it. I tentatively sip at the contents and am not surprised to find it tastes disgusting.

"What the hell is that?" I say, grimacing and peering at the murky brown contents of the mug.

"That, my friend, is magic, get it down you." I know there is no escaping this but still I have a quick check round to see if there is anywhere I can surreptitiously tip it. However, she has her beady eye on me so I take a deep breath, raise the mug, and down the contents in one go. I take a couple of deep breaths after, pleased to find the contents of my stomach do not appear to be about to come straight back up again, and I put the mug back down on the table.

"There you go, you see, that wasn't so bad," Diane says with deep satisfaction, "shall I get the soup?"

I leave an hour or so later having eaten a bowl of something that tasted remarkably like straightforward tomato soup and then I'd stayed for a while chatting as I'd watched Diane start making up some other potion.

Cat had made repeated attempts to conquer the summit of landing on my lap, assaults I'd continued to brush away despite Diane telling me it would do me a lot of good to give him a cuddle and when I eventually head for home I'm in remarkably good spirits.

I walk back towards my cottage full of good cheer and much lighter of heart than I had been before my visit, and I wonder how much that has to do with opening up to Diane and how much is down to the supposedly magic concoction she'd made me swallow.

Dan continues to occupy my thoughts through the evening, though as the situation remains unresolved in my mind I decide to catch him at the gym in the morning and have a chat with him then.

Chapter 16

It's Monday and the start of another abnormal working week for me. I set off as usual, though I meet Joe in my front garden as I leave the house and he tells me he's starting at mine this week as I'm apparently getting out of hand. I look around, assuming he's talking about the garden and not actually me, and it all looks pretty perfect in my eyes but then what do I know, so I leave him to it.

Sidney is in poor form. I can hear the rattle of his chest as he makes his way to the till and moments later with a great heave his hacking cough wracks his frail body. He doesn't cover his mouth and I'm exposed to a wave of possibly the worst breath I've ever experienced as a blast of ashtray odours and rotting teeth assails me and I wish I'd been quicker to start breathing through my mouth.

Having made the decision last night to try to talk to Dan today, I'm then disappointed to discover he's not at the gym when I get there, because I'm all geared up to tackle whatever it is that's going on between us.

I say hi to the others already there and see that Steve is spotting for Mike on the weights across the other side. I get on with my routine but as I work through the machines I find myself having imaginary arguments with Dan. I know I'm being unreasonable but I'm irked that he hasn't turned up, not that he said he would of course but I was prepared, and had my lines ready and everything, and now all that preparation has been wasted and completely irrationally I'm blaming him. Then it occurs to me that perhaps he's avoiding me and, amid my internal ranting, I decide he probably finds I'm too much at odds with his own moral code to have anything more to do with. I had thought I'd speak to him, sort a few things out in my head and know what it was I wanted this morning but by the time I'm on my cool down I'm frustrated by his non-appearance and as I go to shower I pass Mike and say, "you on?"

He nods and answers, "I'll be done in five."

After showering I pack up my stuff and leave the changing room. Mike is already waiting in the reception area checking his phone, but he looks up as I get to him.

"Hello," he's smiling, his mouth filled with perfect white teeth, "do you want anything to eat?" He always asks, but I never do.

"No, I'm fine, you ready to go?" In response to his nod we leave. Passing the front glass wall of the gym we make our way to the car park. After dumping my bag in my car we cross the road and Mike opens the door of his house, standing aside to let me enter. I brush past him, deliberately, then linger in the hall as he closes the door.

He turns and reaches for me, pulling me towards him, his lips on mine.

There's barely a word spoken because there's no need, I know what he's like after the gym…

It's late afternoon, I'm in Mike's bed and he finally lies back and stretches. Then, he glances at the bedside clock.

And that's my cue to leave.

But something's changed.

No.

Everything has.

Because I don't know if Dan is going to feature in my future but I do know I don't want this anymore. What I do want is a bit extra, a hug, a little cuddle, the possibility of being asked to stay the night, but rules are rules and *we* have an arrangement, and it works, it really does. He asks if I'm okay and I'm cool, because of course we have this arrangement, and we know where we stand and I say I am, and I sound as though I mean it. I don't want to outstay my welcome so I get dressed and as I do I look back at the bed and see that he has already dozed off so I finish getting ready to go in silence, and I leave, with no goodbyes and no one to even see me to the door, doing what I know I have to do.

Because we don't do feelings. We don't do caring or emotions…or love.

He tells me Monday evening is his time, he showers, eats and watches the telly. I could join him; I've thought this before. Thought it but never voiced that thought. I have the time, and I wouldn't mind that, a bit of a snuggle in front of the box, but I'm not invited and I console myself with the thought that he'd be horrible to sleep with anyway, I mean to actually sleep with. He's hard, all slabs of muscle with not a millimetre of give, and it would be uncomfortable to snuggle up against that now. Wouldn't it?

I'm overwhelmed by a sense of loneliness as I travel home and I try to pick myself up from the sadness enveloping me by pathetically looking forward to the ready meal I will soon be warming up, knowing that it will fill the unexpected emptiness I feel inside. If only temporarily.

I stand under the shower, the hot water trying to wash away my day, but it's not enough, not anymore and I run a bath. A deep one into which I pour gels and oils, their pungency released by the heat that I have as high as I can bear. I submerge my body under the surface, I exfoliate, scrubbing every inch of skin, I wash my hair and I emerge as cleansed as I can be, at least physically.

It's Tuesday, and I'm on auto-pilot. Kourtney arrives at the cottage before I've left and is talking at me as she sets about her work. She's had her first driving lesson, tells me she has three new clients and while I love the enthusiasm that's pouring out of her I'm even more pleased she doesn't notice my lack of response. I'm relieved when I eventually reach the sanctuary of my car where I appreciate the return of silence. Tired and subdued, I'm pondering on my time with Mike as I drive to work and at how differently I'd felt being with him yesterday. I hadn't slept well and much of that was due to the irritation I felt at being knocked out of my comfort zone. The gym and everything that went with that was where I had, until the last few days, felt at home. It was where I could be myself, at least that was what I had thought. But now all that was mixed up and as I drive to Hartleigh I'm annoyed that the person who has messed everything up for me didn't even show the previous day. Not only that but he has made no contact at all, just left me hanging with those final words on Saturday – *I want much more from you than that.*

What does that even mean?

It keeps going over in my mind but there's been no follow up and I have no idea what he wants, or what I want. I have little work on via Cubby this week, which is another irritation as I could do with being busy, but this is the nature of our business and I know he's leaving me alone to prepare for the big one.

Sidney looks terrible and is his usual less than monosyllabic self and I arrive at the gym not really in the mood for exercise but knowing I will feel better if I get on with it.

There's no sign of Dan, again, and I start off on the treadmill as a warm up, putting in a couple of miles before my general feeling of despondency makes me pull out my earbuds and step off the machine.

Steve joins me as I cross the gym to fill my water bottle.

"You okay?" he asks, to which I shrug, not really knowing the answer. He then follows me over to one of the machines so I can work on my abdominals and as he gets me set up on it and keeping his voice low he says, "Fancy a bit of light relief? That'll perk you right up!" He's grinning but I barely manage to smile back. Only a few days ago I would have totally taken him up on his offer believing that to be the salve to cure most problems, but my experience with Mike the day before has shaken me. I really don't want to feel like that again.

"No thanks, I appreciate the offer though," I say, as casual as you like.

"Seriously?" His brow is creased in something between surprise and annoyance. "You're turning me down again?"

"Yeah, sorry, Steve. Things have changed for me recently. I'm just not into it at the moment."

"Okay," and he sighs, putting on a jokey voice as he continues, "well don't you go forgetting about yer good friend Stevie when you are back in the mood, alright?"

"I won't." I smile at him and he reciprocates so I know we're cool, then he leaves me to go and help out a guy who's just walked in and I set about giving my abs a seriously hard time.

Once I'm done I shower, then since I have nothing on for the rest of the day I decide to treat myself to lunch in the café before leaving to go home.

Later, as I approach my car, I'm hunting in the bottom of my bag for my elusive keys and when I eventually close my hand around them and look up I see Dan coming across the car park towards me.

"Hi," he says, as he stops in front of me. He's smiling, his eyes creasing at the corners. "I couldn't get here yesterday so I'm pleased I've caught you."

"Really? I'm not sure why when you're so disapproving of me." These words are out of my mouth before I can stop them and clearly show my frustration.

The smile is gone as he says, "Can you blame me? Don't you care what people say about you?" I wonder then what he's heard as I've been unaware of anyone saying anything.

However, I retaliate with, "What does it matter what anyone says?" while at the same time realising that I'm the one with the thick skin, the one who is used to this. Sure, words have been spoken in the past, names called out of jealousy and spite but I have always been more than capable of dealing with my detractors, it is they that have the problem after all.

"It matters to me what is said about you, Maddy, and some of the guys you go with are married, did you know that?" and he brandishes his arm in the direction of the leisure centre.

"So, go and have a pop at them then. I'm not the one who's made vows, Dan."

"I know, I know," he exhales in frustration, "I'm not judging you."

"Oh I think you are." The sarcasm drips heavily over my response like thick icing on warm cake. I turn to go and he puts out a hand, placing it on my forearm to stop me.

"Maddy," his voice is softer now, "I just want you all to myself, that's all."

I don't know how to respond to this. My head is filled with the anger of this exchange, my body, well, that's having a totally different reaction to him and I wish it wouldn't.

"I'm going now," I mutter, and pull my arm away from him.

"Don't," he says, and I see him falter, a flicker of uncertainty in his eyes, his jaw clenching like he's biting back whatever's coming next, and while I know he's unsure how to proceed, I give him nothing.

"See you around," are my parting words as I get in my car and, without looking at him again, I drive off knowing he's watching me leave.

I go home slowly, annoyed that after all my preparation to have a proper conversation with him we ended up in what feels like an argument, one that repeats over and over, festering and building in my mind as I come up with all the things I should have said, and didn't. Even though I stop off for some shopping on the way I'm still home much earlier than normal but I don't care. I've always been particular about keeping realistic hours so no suspicions are raised but today I couldn't give a damn, deciding to plead illness should anyone ask. Which they don't, so then I question why I've bothered with such an elaborate ruse to date.

At least entering my cottage brings me a little lift of the spirits. I'd forgotten about Kourtney's visit earlier and now, like a show home, it is immaculate. Everything is in its place and each surface gleams, which is a delight. I get changed into cosy tracksuit bottoms, thick socks and a well-worn oversized sweatshirt. I flick the kettle on to make a large mug of hot chocolate and while I wait for it to come to the boil I wonder if it's too early to add a little livener to it. Deciding it is, I stick to my original plan and curl up on the sofa wrapped in a thick fleecy blanket, the latest thriller in my hand and a packet of my favourite biscuits at my elbow. I'm soon buried in the storyline and it's only when I realise I'm squinting to read that I notice it's getting dark and get up to draw the curtains. I turn on a couple of lamps, the room instantly becoming warm and comforting, and I return to the sofa, and my book. I finish the read, and the biscuits, late into the night and, not bothering to make myself a proper meal, I go to bed.

It matters to me what is said about you, Maddy.

Is that because he cares about me, or worries about what people think? This is what comes to mind as I'm trying to get off to sleep and it makes that eventuality a long time coming.

Wednesday. It's colder this morning, a real nip in the air, made more so by a stiffening wind adding a chill factor. Now we've flipped over into October, autumn has well and truly set in. I stand with coffee in hand and look out of my kitchen window. The trees are sheathed more in yellowy golds and browns than green and I know in only a few weeks those same branches will be bare. There's a crisp crunch of leaves underfoot as I make my way to my car and head off to Hartleigh. I had considered staying in bed for the day, the thought of blissfully making my way through another book while remaining under the covers a most tempting one, but I knew I needed to keep up some semblance of normality.

Hit by the drop in temperature as I'd left the house I'd turned back to get a more substantial coat, and once I'm in the car I put the heating on. I hate to be cold and take steps to ensure I never am these days. However, I remember a time at primary school when I was found in the playground so frozen my lips were turning blue, my teeth chattering as I shivered and I was taken inside, warmed in blue scratchy blankets that smelt vaguely antiseptic then later chastised for turning up without a suitable coat. I took the verbal ear-bashing, too proud to admit I didn't own one. My form teacher, Mrs Snow, had been looking on and later brought me an unclaimed coat from Lost Property. She never said a word by way of explanation, just handed it to me and told me to put it on at break time. I soon cottoned on to the treasure trove of unnamed stuff that was lying in the Lost Property bins and from then on got most of my uniform that way. Mrs Snow remained complicit though, occasionally handing me a sweatshirt or pair of trousers, no comment, no discussion. She was a diamond like that.

She was also the one who spotted my hunger.

While on the one hand my mother refused to allow me to have free school dinners— *We ain't acceptin' no charity!*—on the other she failed to provide me with anything as a replacement. Mrs Snow saw me wandering around the playground one day when everyone else was eating and called me in, telling me to hurry up and join the queue to get my lunch. She was so matter of fact about it no one even checked me for a dinner pass, and this became the norm throughout my school life. A familiar face is never questioned, so be brazen, look like you belong and it's amazing what you'll get away with. A lesson learnt indeed.

I have my usual one-sided chit-chat with Sidney, who looks no better and sounds worse, and on my way to the gym I consider the reputation I have made for myself there. This is not something I've ever given much thought to, yet after Dan's stinging words yesterday it is now making me unexpectedly anxious and I wonder if I should change gyms, start again somewhere else. But that would probably mean having to travel to one in the city instead and I really don't like the thought of that. However, I've come to realise that something needs to change, and if that's my behaviour and I'm not willing to go to another gym I'm going to have to tough it out here, until all get the message. Then see where things go from there.

Most of the machines are already in use when I enter and I return a couple of greetings before making my way to a free treadmill. I put in a few miles hoping to keep myself to myself but a short while later Pete appears at my side and asks what I'm doing later. I say I'm busy, and start to slow down my run.

"That's a shame, I was hoping to keep you company." He grins a grin that would usually warm the cockles of my heart but is incapable of even thawing mine today. However, I do smile back at him, not wanting to cause any hurt. Then I stop and turn to him.

"I'm always going to be busy from now on, Pete."

"Really? Why? Have I done something to offend you?" He's speaking quietly but looks genuinely upset.

"No," I reassure him, "It's not you. I'm making a few changes in my life, that's all."

"Oh, okay," he shrugs and starts jogging on the treadmill next to mine, "I'm off to basic training soon anyway. Are you still going to be coming here?"

"Yes, that's the plan."

"Cool, I'll see you around then," and he gets into his stride.

I pick up my water bottle and as I go to leave, say, "Yeah, I'll see you around too, Pete," but he's already plugged in his earbuds and, concentrating on the task in hand, there's no response.

Following on from Dan's comment yesterday I wonder if the men here do talk about me, if I'm discussed as a sure thing, if they compare notes, and the more I think about it the more I wish I hadn't let my mind wander in this direction. I see Steve chatting to a bloke by the weights, sharing a joke, having a laugh and I feel the paranoia creeping in like the tendrils of a vigorous plant, wrapping themselves around and choking the life out of any confidence I had. There is nothing I can do about it now, but feeling uncomfortable I decide to go to the relative isolation of the pool instead.

As I push the gym door open I meet Dan entering.

"Hello," he says. His tone is upbeat which surprises me, given our last exchange, and he hesitates as if he wants to stop and talk, or something.

"Morning, Dan," I respond, and having nothing else to say I walk on past and go to change into my swimming costume.

I'm home early again but this time I'm spotted by Diane who waves me down.

"You okay?" she says as I wind down the window to speak to her, the gust of cold air that enters making me shiver.

"I'm not feeling too good actually, so decided to take a bit of time off this week to try and get over whatever it is."

"You do look peaky," she says, a frown line deepening between her eyes, "I'll make you up a little something and drop it over later."

"That would be lovely, thanks," and I smile at her hoping it's not the same revolting brew she made me before.

I get home and go through a similar routine as the previous day, though I cut out the biscuits and make a simple supper instead. Diane knocks on the door early evening and holds out a steaming glass to me. I take it, surprised it hasn't shattered under the heat, and she instructs me to down it as soon as it's cool enough.

"What is it?" I ask, staring suspiciously at the contents.

"Oh, a bit of this and a bit of that, you know," she says briskly. I invite her in but she refuses, telling me to take my medicine and get an early night. I return to my book and when the liquid is cool enough I do indeed down it. It tastes surprisingly like a straightforward hot toddy. Whisky tempered with honey and lemon. Spices too, I can taste cinnamon and clove, and something else which I can't quite put my finger on but I suspect it is this added extra that makes me so drowsy, and within half an hour I stagger to my bed for the earliest night I've had since I was a child and I sleep the sleep of the dead.

The usual crowd for a Thursday are in, plus Ricky for whom there is no discernible pattern of attendance. It wouldn't surprise me if he only actually came along when he wanted sex. He needs me because I give him what others won't, and there's this thing between us, a chemistry that pulls us closer, and for the time that we're together I can make myself believe that he likes me but I shake off all those thoughts because he is about to find out I am a changed woman. Albeit one with a lot on her mind. I notice that today he hasn't even bothered to take off his ring, and this strengthens my resolve. At least when he'd removed it before it was like he'd cared enough to keep up the pretence.

I'm subdued but acknowledge those I pass then enter my personal zone by putting my earbuds in and my iPod on shuffle as I start my workout. I feel better as soon as I begin the familiar routine and my confidence grows as I concentrate purely on working hard.

So deep am I in my thoughts that as I change from the cross trainer to the running machine Ricky has to step in front of me to get my attention. I look up and he grins at me. I wish he wouldn't as the Pavlovian response of my body immediately distracts me; however, determined to change my ways I pull my earbuds out and wait for whatever it is he wants.

"Are you free later?" he murmurs, keeping his voice low.

"You'll be lucky, mate," chips in Pete who walks past at that precise moment slapping Ricky on the back in the process. "She's ditching us all." He gives me a wink that I find both supportive and conspiratorial, over Ricky's shoulder, and walks on.

I smile at Ricky and say I'm not available as if to back up Pete's comment.

"That can't be true, Maddy," Ricky beseeches, and to be honest spending the next couple of hours with him is certainly appealing. He'd always had the ability to bang the stresses right out of me but I smile at him again and reply.

"It's like Pete said, Ricky." He holds up his hands.

"Yeah but you don't mean me though do you, babe? I'm married yet I still make myself available for you." And I have to laugh at that.

"That's very generous of you, Ricky, but perhaps you should try giving the monogamy thing a go, you know, for your wife's sake. It's just a thought." He looks perplexed, as if this is a concept that has never occurred to him.

As far as I'm concerned our conversation is at an end and I'm about to go and get on when I hear a mumbled, "Excuse me," from behind, I turn, surprised to find Dan standing there and I move out of the way to let him come past. Without making eye contact he says a quiet hello which I reciprocate but I'm flustered and, annoyed to find I'm blushing, I look away. He's taken me by surprise and I have no idea how much he heard of that exchange. Replacing my earbuds, I start running, determined to take no further notice of him.

I finish my routine, pick up my stuff and as I pass Ricky on the way out he says, "It's not too late to change your mind!" his face brightening with his cheeky grin.

"No, Ricky, go home to your wife," I say, but I smile at him, pleased to see his ego hasn't taken that big a knock.

It's Friday and when I wake I find I've overslept. At least I would have done, had I had a proper job to go to. At some point I must have turned off the alarm, and I lie gazing at the clock that sits on my bedside table and I don't want to move. In fact, I'm not convinced I can move, my limbs feel like lead, the duvet being all that's needed to keep me pinned to the bed. This is the problem with working as I do, self-motivation. Generally, I don't have an issue with it. I've worked so long and hard on keeping up the persona I wear here that I've always stuck to my routine and never let my mask drop. Until now, when I find I couldn't give a damn anymore. I decide I'm ill, or at least sickening for something, and being out of sorts I drift back off to sleep.

I'm startled awake a couple of hours later by my ringtone, and the spell holding my body in its state of inertia is broken the moment I move my arm to pick up my phone.

"Yeah?" I mumble.

"Oh! You're not dead!" It's Diane. I can hear relief in her voice and as I focus on the clock again I see it's nearly midday. The car's in the drive and the curtains are still drawn, so it's not unreasonable of her to have thought I'd come to some sort of harm. This is one of the joys of living in a village and it's good to know that someone out there cares.

"Very much alive, Diane, although I am still in bed. I'm coming down with something, I think." I know the minute the words are out of my mouth that I should not have said this.

"I'll drop round a little something later." There's no arguing with the tone that is in her voice so I thank her and end the call.

I get up, shower and dress before thinking about what I'm going to do with the rest of the day. I decide I need to get some food in, not that I really do, so I put on a jacket and wander up to the village.

As I'm nearing the shop I see a car approach; it's Paul's, and he's not alone. In the passenger seat is a woman, fresh faced and pretty. She's grinning across at him and he's laughing and they look great together, relaxed and enjoying each other's company in the way I guess a normal relationship is meant to be. I feel a little tug of envy, because it looks so easy but I'm pleased for him, for them both actually and I enter the shop.

There's a melancholy that descends over my day. I read, I watch a film, finding myself reaching for an old black and white, wrapping myself in a past I thought I'd left long behind. Diane visits for a while, her concern for me obvious and she gives me a potion that she calls a tonic. It's rich in vitamins, minerals and anti-oxidants, apparently, and it's to revitalise those under the weather, she tells me. I'll take whatever she's handing out and hope it has a similar effect on my spirits.

She asks me what's wrong and I tell her I don't know. I can hardly tell her that it seems that having stopped being sexually adventurous the life appears to have gone right out of me. I feel fragile, as though the slightest setback now could break me, and lost, like I don't even know who I am anymore. I'm saddened to

159

discover that I'm so shallow; the only reason I ever felt good before was because men found me desirable and I responded to that.

I caught sight of myself in the mirror earlier. My makeup-free skin was pale and smooth. Thickly lashed green eyes peered out solemnly from a face framed by dark hair that fell onto pallid shoulders and I wonder who people see when they look at me. I'm having a crisis of identity, the first since I became Madeleine, and I wonder if the pressure of living this lie day after day has finally caught up with me.

Diane asks if I've seen the man I'd told her about. I tell her his name is Dan and no, other than a greeting in passing I haven't seen or heard anything from him, and I doubt I will. I think he has been exposed to all he needs to know about me and has moved on. I'm not worth his trouble, and as I say this out loud I realise how disappointed I am at this outcome. She tells me to call him, to make the first move but I say no. It's not that I'm afraid of doing that, of being forward, of making the running. I've done that many times, I've been the one to call the shots, the one in control of the situation, but it's not my place now. Not this time. If Dan wants me he has to make the move, and I'm convinced that if it wasn't for the fact I knew that at some point I'd be seeing him at the offices of Watson & Grove, and even then most likely only to be fired, I doubted I'd ever see him again.

Despite this I'm pleased I've moved on. It feels like I've made a cathartic change in my life and one I was ready for.

Chapter 17

It's the weekend, and I have nothing planned. I try not to feel too bad about that, or like I'm wasting time. The jewellery collection arrives at Danewright House next weekend so I shall be building up to that over the course of the following week and I tell myself that I deserve a weekend off, doing nothing.

I see that Joe is working in Diane's garden on Saturday morning and wander up to have a chat on the pretence of thanking him for helping Kourtney out with her expansion plans.

"Well I shan't be here forever," he says, "I might as well pass on what I know." Not exactly the uplifting words I want to hear from him right now but he's down to earth and I appreciate that. He's wiry and strong and I can't imagine he'll be going anywhere anytime soon. I have a coffee with him and Diane, and silently question my need to seek them out this morning. Perhaps I'm not quite as able to live without human interaction as I thought.

In the evening I'm relieved when Chris calls with his one-word pub question. Damn right I'll join him and I don't know why I didn't think to ring him earlier. That would have brought much needed focus to my day. We're eating our steaks, our meeting strangely without its usual conversation, when I realise he's paused, put down his knife and fork, and is watching me.

"What's the matter?" he asks. I look up from my plate and shrug.

"Nothing. Why do you ask?"

"You're not your usual self," and he peers at me. "You're not wearing makeup and you have no perfume on, it's unlike you." Like I've said before, he sees me. I imagine he'd be the most unreliable of boyfriends because he's forgetful of the minutiae of life. However, he would remember how you smelled, what you wore, every story you'd ever told him, the important stuff. We don't often touch upon his love life and he seems ambivalent about it so while I appreciate every moment I get to spend with him I hope he eventually finds someone who deserves him.

"I've been a bit under the weather, probably coming down with something," I say, "so I'm resting and relaxing this weekend." He makes a murmuring sound as if he doesn't quite believe me, so to distract I ask him how his writing is going as I resume eating.

"Slowly, I've had a load of work on this week that actually pays me some money so I've been doing that. But I have worked out the story line, at least as far as the climatic point, so that feels like a step forward. I just need to write it now though I should be able to crack on with getting a few words down over the next week."

"I shall look forward to getting to read it, have you contacted a publisher yet?"

"Nah, I'm a way off that, anyway it's tough getting published, Madeleine."

"You've told me that before, but you must have contacts already." I know he's had plenty of his work published before.

"Different ball game. That was academic, non-fiction. Everyone's writing a book nowadays, the market is awash with them so unless you have a celebrity name to guarantee more than a few copies going out the door, publishers don't want to know. I'll probably self-publish, when I get that far."

I have no idea what that is but as long as I get a copy, for him to sign and for me to read, I don't much care how it gets to me.

I have pudding, chocolate fudge cake, warm and gooey comfort food. I need the sugar, I kid myself. Chris doesn't partake, choosing to watch me over the rim of the coffee he's having instead. He's keeping an eye on his waistline he tells me, though I know he's having a laugh. Kourtney asks if I'm okay when she delivers my dessert and I decide I must be looking rough for people to keep checking on me like this.

"I'm fine, how are things going with you?" I ask her.

"Brilliant, thanks." Her eyes are bright, shining with enthusiasm. "I've got four new cleanin' clients and one more lawn to mow. Keep goin' at this rate, I'll be takin' me own staff on." She grins at the idea. "I'm meeting with Chris next week, aren't I, Chris?" She looks to him for confirmation and I see him nod. "'E's gonna make sure I set it up all legal 'n' proper."

"I certainly am," he says, and looks rightly proud of her. I was wrong to have ever had my concerns about this girl, she's got her head screwed on and knows exactly what she wants. I was envious of her, but she would never believe that if I told her.

It's Sunday evening and I'm in the lengthening shadows of another day that's stretched out behind me with little to show for it. I slept solidly enough though I've taken to clamping my jaw tight shut and woke with that aching, along with everything else. I did some stretches and seriously considered taking up yoga to enable me to do this more effectively.

I don't obsess or reflect on things that have happened, at least not in the daylight hours when I can control what comes to mind. Since leaving my old life behind I've kept so busy it's been easy not to give my past much of a second thought. But one of the problems of having all this time is that it has allowed thoughts and feelings from that time to resurface, which I've found disturbing.

Unwelcome glimpses of my childhood keep popping into my head, rising unbidden from those places where I've been happy to suppress them. I don't know how to deal with the emotions associated with them and too often tears come, in gentle sadness or body-wracking fury.

I find myself dwelling on the confused thoughts I have of the life and man I left behind too. I smile when I recall his startling blue eyes, the feel of my fingers slipping through his mass of black hair or of his lips on mine. But then the smile is gone when I acknowledge the things I did, the reason for my inability to relax at night, for the grinding of my teeth, for waking protectively foetal. I wonder if he is still looking for me, if, in fact, he ever looked. It's the not knowing that's eating away at my nerves, and I ponder on how much time will need to pass for him not to have such an influence over my dreams.

I occupied a couple of hours of the morning on housework chores although with Kourtney's thoroughness there wasn't much to do. I went out and chatted to the horses until they tired of me and wandered off to graze then I sat for ages on the bench watching them instead. I've eaten, read, watched the television and now with a glass in my hand I'm going over the notes for Danewright House again while I play some music. It's not loud but it's loud enough for me to question whether I heard a knock at the door, or not.

I'm on my feet anyway, caught between refreshing my glass and returning to the sofa, when I hear it again. I expect it to be Diane delivering another potion so I'm surprised to find Dan standing there, his hands buried deep in the pockets of his jeans.

"Oh! Hello." My surprise is evident and my welcome guarded.

"Hi," he says, then he turns a little awkwardly and looks back over to his car adding, "I was just passing."

"Course you were, it's how most people end up at my door." I feel exposed and totally unprepared for him. Today had been another day without makeup, though I've also gone further and removed my nail varnish, my toes feeling bare and virginal without it. My hair is as it was when I got up this morning and I've removed my earrings, in fact all my jewellery. I'm wearing a comfortable pair of lounge trousers and until recently a sweatshirt but I've been dancing so I discarded that a while ago and now I greet Dan in a vest top, and no bra. A blast of cold from the open door is not helping my lack of attire and I glance at my chest then reach for my sweatshirt which I clutch to my body self-consciously. I raise my tumbler; it has two fingers of bourbon in it, my drink of choice. This is me stripped down and he might as well see it all.

"Fancy a drink?" He nods, steps into the room and I close the door behind him. He follows me through to the kitchen and I'm acutely aware of him, my cosy rooms unusually feeling too small. As I put my sweatshirt back on I ask him if he wants the same as me to drink.

"Yeah, though with rocks, if you have them." I fish around in my jam-packed freezer, having to remove many things to uncover the tray of ice cubes I know I have somewhere, and I see the look of astonishment on his face at the amount of food I have in there, then my hand emerges triumphant and I crack a few into his glass. Replacing the contents so they'll all fit in, but with the ice cubes closer to the surface this time, is like a challenge on the Krypton Factor but I succeed and once I've poured his drink I lead the way back to the sitting room.

The music's still going, it's on shuffle playing a calming playlist, so I leave it running though turn it down a notch or two. Up until this point I've had things to keep me occupied, and he's quietly watched me, his eyes on me at every moment but now I feel nerves take flight in my stomach and I don't know what to say. I take a slug of my drink and put the glass down, it's not been my first.

"How have you been?" he says, breaking the silence at last.

"Fine," I lie, "and you?"

"I've had better weeks." I glance at him. There are shadows under his eyes, and I can sense the tension in him.

I whisper, "Yeah," and look away.

"I didn't see you Friday…at the gym?"

"No, I haven't been feeling that great, so I stayed home."

"I see. Are you okay now?"

"Yes." Another fib. The conversation is horribly stilted and as he reaches for his glass, so do I and I sip at it for something to do as much as wanting it. He tilts his head to the file on the table.

"Next week's job?" I nod, relieved he's seized on something we can discuss.

"Would you like to see what I have planned?" I ask.

"Absolutely." He seems as relieved as I am, and sounding keen sits on the edge of the sofa then he leans forward as I pull the coffee table towards us. He's wearing a blue and white checked shirt, open at the neck. His sleeves are turned back a couple of times and as he moves I can smell the subtle scent of body wash emanating from him and wish I'd been in the shower as recently.

Cubby has done a terrific job for me in pulling together the information I need to tackle a job like Danewright House. One film I can still bear to watch is *The Great Escape* and if he were to be cast in that Cubby would play the part of Hendley, The Scrounger. Anything I want he will get for me, discreetly, of course. It wouldn't do for our intentions to be signalled in advance. On this occasion he has provided me with a priceless piece in the shape of the floor plans of the House. There are a couple of them and I roll them out now so they cover the low table. I show Dan the rooms we visited on our outing, the route we followed, and the library where the collection will be displayed so that he can get his bearings.

He's absorbed in the details, his hair flopping over his forehead in which small creases form as he concentrates. His fingers run over the plans as I show him what I'm intending. He edges further forward moving nearer to me and I'm acutely conscious of him. I can feel his heat radiating across the gap we've carefully preserved between us. His arm is in close proximity, his thigh running parallel to mine, and I can feel the pull, the subtle forces drawing us together, and I feel warm and think I should maybe lay off the Jack.

I've memorised these plans. I know the exact route I'm going to take but as most of the House has been physically out of bounds to me a lot of my planning has relied on the fact that these drawings are still accurate and that there haven't been any changes, such as building works, which could mean I unexpectedly come across closed off accesses on the night. I've therefore checked out alternatives, and a variety of exit routes.

I take pride in what I do, my sole goal being to outwit the security in place. However, I'm more than willing to put my hands up, and admit defeat, if I find the measures are too difficult for me to get past. That hasn't happened to date, but there's always a first time.

The challenge for all those involved with the smooth running of the House is that the collection is only there for two weeks, therefore there is only a limited amount of security it's worth forking out for, so in a situation like this it's not going to involve pressure pads under the carpet and lasers beams trained across the room. That's *Mission Impossible* territory, that is, and well out of my league. I know I'm beaten if we start getting into all that.

Dan asks me about timings, and routes in and out, what the exit plan is and what my alternatives are and he seems genuinely interested, even putting forward a few suggestions. He appears oblivious to the underlying tension between us as we discuss the merits or otherwise of his input. I reach across to show him where I believe the three possible entrances connect with the library and our fingers brush. It's momentary, the lightest of touches but it only strengthens the attraction I feel for him and I pull my hand away though try not to make it obvious; however I can feel his gaze on me and although I try not to, I glance across at him and our eyes meet. There's a hint of blue accentuated in the grey, I notice, his shirt setting them off a treat and their intensity as he watches me makes me uncomfortable.

I turn my attention back to the paperwork, needing something to do, and knowing I can't leave it out I slide off the sofa landing on my knees by the coffee table and mutter something about putting this all away now. I fold everything up and put it back in the folder and all the time I can feel him watching what I do but I have no idea what he's thinking. I sit back down and reach for my drink. I see he's finished his so I down what's left of mine. If he's planning on driving I doubt he'll stay for another so as he's made the first move by coming here it feels like the right time to see where his head's at.

I'm nervous and I don't know why. It's not like I'm a novice at seducing men after all and usually have no problem in asking for and getting exactly what I want. But with him I'm not that sure of myself and I think there are two things making me jittery. Firstly, I've never had a man come to my home before. This is my space, my territory, and him being here is breaking new ground for me and that makes all the difference. Secondly, I realise that I actually care what happens. All of a sudden it matters how this goes. He's already knocked me back twice and I'm not sure how keen I am to have that happen again. But then he wouldn't have come here tonight if he wasn't interested, would he? I wish I still had a full glass to get through, something to give me more courage, but I don't and I'm simply going to have to go for it.

"So you have a choice before you," I say as I stand, trying to keep my voice light but it betrays me by breaking slightly, and as I bend to pick up the folder I clear my throat.

"I do?" His eyebrows raise slightly. I'm committed so come right out with it and I watch him, wanting to see his reaction as I say.

"Are you going to stay, or say goodnight?" His eyes widen, and I think I see a flash of relief before his slow smile as he stands. I hold out my hand and will him to take it. As he does he holds it for a moment, his skin dry and warm against mine, and he gazes at me. Even now I believe this could still be a no, that he's thinking about it, that maybe he's going to try to let me down gently. As my stomach clenches in readiness for another rejection coming my way, there's pressure in my chest as though my heart is shrinking, tightening and hardening, like it knows I'm not worthy of him and prepares to protect itself.

He moves closer, his other hand wrapping around my waist, and into the small of my back pulling me towards him. He brings my hand to his lips and kisses the palm before letting it go.

He can't say no now, I know he can't, he's too close. I can see the desire in his eyes, feel it in the heat of his body pressed against mine and that thought alone frees my heart which I feel beating rapidly like a bird that's trying to escape its cage. My breath catches and for a moment I'm light-headed. He lifts my chin, his fingers light against my jaw, and we kiss.

It's brief, the barest brush of his lips against mine and it ends as quickly as it began but the touch is like lighting a fuse, a path set burning down to my core. I'm still holding the folder, and wish I wasn't, but I bring my free hand up to his face. There's a slight bristle, a day's growth but no more and as I touch his cheek we kiss again, his lips initially soft but this time he doesn't stop, he can't pull away and they harden as he holds me tight up against him. His tongue gently flicks against mine, it's intimate and exploring and I feel his breath catch as I moan softly at the touch.

I put my hand on his chest to halt him and he pulls back a little although his arm stays around me.

"So I guess you're staying then?" and I grin at him.

"If I'm still invited." Without saying another word, I take his hand in my free one and lead him up the stairs as he asks, "You're bringing the folder with you?"

"Absolutely, it never leaves my side. I can't have it fall into the wrong hands." I'm only half joking as I know there are people out there who would give a lot to have this file and I would not be being diligent if I didn't keep it where I knew it would be safe. With Dan here I am not about to reveal my hidey-hole under the cupboard, so when I reach the bedroom I tuck it under the mattress.

"Nowhere safer," he says. I agree, but for the moment I'm more interested in the fact I now have two hands free and as we kiss again I undo his shirt. I pull it open and out of his trousers, my hands running over his body beneath it then I move them up his chest, pushing the shirt over his shoulders so that he has to let go of me for a moment to allow it to drop to the floor.

His body is well muscled but not in that narcissistic way that requires selfishly long hours in order to achieve the perfect six pack. His chest has a light covering of hair though a darker line trails down his stomach before disappearing into his jeans.

I reach for his belt but he interrupts me by grabbing the bottom hem of both sweatshirt and vest top lifting them up and off my arms and over my head. He pauses and gazes at me, then reaches for me once more, and moving closer I inhale his scent, delight in feeling my breasts pressing up against his chest. I shiver as he cups one in his hand, running his thumb across my nipple, which stiffens at his touch.

I return to his belt, undo it and his jeans, but again he is quicker and he pushes the elasticated top of my trousers down over my hips and bottom after which they are in freefall to the ground. He kneels before me running his fingers under the edges of my pants then peels them down my legs and I step out of them. They're black, cotton, bikini cut and supremely comfortable everyday pants. I wish I'd made more of an effort but this is the problem with spontaneity, you simply can't plan for it, and anyway, he doesn't seem disappointed.

"Sit down," he says, more command than request, and as I do he reaches for one foot, then the other, removing my socks. What then comes as a surprise is that this is where he starts, my feet. No one ever touches them yet he lifts them in turn, kissing the toes, the instep; his touch is firm as he smooths his hands over the skin with an attention bordering on reverence and throughout he keeps checking in with me, making eye contact, and when he does it is smouldering. He works his way higher, trailing his hands up my legs, my skin tingling beneath his fingers. He's leading the way, doing exactly what he wants, and I am happy to let him.

His voice is thick as he tells me to lie down and as I push myself back on the bed he stands, removing the rest of his clothes as he does so. He leans over me, continuing his travels up my body, kissing, tasting, exploring and it's becoming too much. I reach out, I want to touch him, I need to pull him towards me, to feel his hardness and his weight on me. My fingers are in his hair and I'm drawing him up my body, he's kissing my breast, his tongue teasing my nipple and while I'm never wanting it to end my body cries out for more. I ache to have him inside me and I tear open a condom and roll it onto him but I'm trying to force the situation and he's having none of it. He holds off, and holds off, his lips finding their way up my neck, my jaw, my cheek, softly kissing the corner of my mouth, and then he's looking down at me and he pauses.

"Are you sure you want this?" He's grinning, teasing because he can feel me wriggling with pleasure under him, and I answer, in all seriousness,

"Do you?" His face darkens for a moment, it's not too late I think, it's not too late and he could still back away but then his lips meet mine in a hard and passionate kiss as he claims me. I wrap my legs around

172

him as he enters me, filling me with each thrust. Then he stills.

"Hold tight," he whispers, his lips against mine and he rolls us over until I'm looking down on his beautiful face. "This will be better for you." He smiles and I lean down to kiss him and as I start to move, his hands are restless on my body, caressing my back, hips and thighs. I'm close already, the exquisite foreplay bringing me swiftly to this point and I turn my head away, unwilling to meet the intensity of his gaze but he says, "Look at me," and I do. Like deep pools linked straight to his soul his eyes absorb me and immediately there's a connection, and it's so much more than a physical one, but as pleasure builds, as I get closer to the edge it's too much, it's too intimate and I have to close my eyes. I feel the heat radiating off him and I know he's ready, that he's waiting for me and as I peak I cry out, crashing down the other side as waves pulse through my quivering body and he drives into me groaning as he releases then holding me tightly to him, as the aftershocks rock me and our jagged breathing calms.

I roll off him, collapsing onto the bed at his side as I take a few calming breaths and he turns towards me, leaning his head up on his hand as his other one rests on my stomach.

"Alright?" he says.

"Totally, and you?"

"Brilliant," and his grin is so broad I feel a small thrill of satisfaction deep inside. He kisses me lightly on the temple. There's something I should say to him, that I should actually have said before we got into this but it feels awkward now and I dodge the situation by offering him something to eat. It's still early.

"Please, I hadn't got round to that before I found myself accidently passing your door." I laugh but love the fact he came and sought me out.

I grab my bath robe, wrapping it around and securing with the tie, and he follows me downstairs having pulled his jeans on.

"What do you fancy?" I say as I peer into the fridge. His arms come around me and he nibbles my ear which makes me giggle.

"Just you," he says, and I twist in his arms until we're face to face and we begin kissing again until I break it off and say,

"I thought you were hungry?"

"I am," and he grins wolfishly at me.

"Well, Mr Travers, you're going to need to keep your strength up with what I have planned for you. So you'd better eat while you have the chance." He raises one eyebrow at me.

"That sounds like a challenge, Ms Ross. What do you suggest?"

"I'd like to sound knowledgeable and suggest some carbohydrate and protein or whatever that will give you the slow releasing energy you're going to need, but I know nothing of such things. So I suggest pizza."

"Why?"

"Because it will be ready in a few minutes and then we can get back to the good stuff." He laughs and agrees. While I get a pizza out of the freezer and put it in the oven he takes a browse around my kitchen and marvels at the stacked contents of my cupboards.

"How many people do you feed here?" I'm immediately anxious that he thinks there's a constant flow through the cottage

"Only me," I say quickly. Then I elaborate. "I like to know I've got food in, that's all. In case of being cut off by a snowstorm, or flooding. Actually, you are the

174

first man to ever be here, for this," and I gesticulate between the two of us, "just in case you were wondering," and my voice tails off.

"Oh, I didn't mean anything by that," he explains, picking up on me immediately, "although I am honoured."

"Okay. Well as we're on that sort of subject, you should also know there isn't anyone else. Not now."

"It's alright, Maddy, I realised it was horribly possessive of me to expect you to change your way of being. I was just hoping I'd be different, that's all, and yes before you say it I do realise that is pretty arrogant of me." He closes the distance between us, takes hold of the tie around my waist and undoes it, my robe falls open and he reaches his arms inside and around me, holding me close.

"You are," I murmur, "different, that is, rather than arrogant," and we kiss, the temperature rising in the kitchen until we are interrupted by the pizza being ready.

I eat one slice, he devours the rest and we top up our drinks.

"Does that often happen?" he says as he finishes eating.

"What?"

"You being cut off by snowstorm or flood."

"Well it hasn't happened yet, but you can never be too careful, and as you know I do like to be prepared."

"Okay," he says, and he's looking at me as if I'm a bit bonkers.

We return to bed soon after and enjoy getting to know each other over the next few hours.

It may seem strange but with all my experience of men I've never had someone sleep with me, I mean actually sleep with me. For me that is the real commitment, not the sex, anyone can do that. It's the after bit, the lying with someone, the holding them, possibly, depending on if you like that or not, but it's definitely the being there thing that makes the difference, that makes them a keeper. Although I have to admit that tonight the sex felt different too, it was intense and it had that connection, the way it's truly meant to be I guess. But for someone to want to stay beyond that? It's not what I'm used to.

The only proper boyfriend I've ever had used to come to my flat, or I'd go to his. We might spend a bit of time watching the telly or something but we'd always have sex and after we'd go our separate ways again. When my mother was there I'd understood his reticence about staying but when she wasn't, I didn't get it. He'd said he liked his own space and I didn't think it was that strange at the time so put up with it, and the loneliness after. Now I realise it's not right, it's not normal to want to be apart if you care for someone, however although I long for Dan to stay, I expect nothing.

I'm not sure when the loving stopped, if we consciously decided to go to sleep or if it was just a natural progression but I remember the warmth of his body curled around mine, of being aware of every breath he took, of feeling content and safe, of my body satiated as I drifted off.

I wake in the morning, more unfurled than I have been in years, my muscles are relaxed, my jaw unclenched and he is still there. This is a first.

Chapter 18

I've been self-absorbed over the last few days, I know I have. I've been buried in a level of introspection I've never wallowed in before, and now faced with the reality of a brand new week I realise I've forgotten about Mike. I know I will have to tackle him today, because he is unaware our arrangement is at an end, and this irritates me because in my head I've moved on.

Everything is bright and sparkly in my new world and I thought this previous life of mine was well and truly in my past. This is the main issue occupying my mind as Dan and I get ready for the day ahead, a little awkwardly. I have no idea how to deal with having a man in my cottage in the morning so I press on with my usual routine and hope he falls in with that. As he takes a shower I use the opportunity to slip my folder back into the hidey-hole.

He'd greeted me with a 'Good morning' muttered from the other pillow, which seemed strangely formal, but I'd smiled and responded with the same. He'd kissed me, and more, and although I'm a little tired after the night's antics I'm amazingly perky and feel totally set up for the day. But then for two people who have had no difficulty in sharing intimacies we become strangely quiet around each other as we get ready.

Dan tells me he is coming to the gym, with me, first thing. He's got the morning off apparently, which is great, of course, but it makes me anxious that I've now got to deal with Mike while Dan is in the vicinity.

I share my concerns with him as we're drinking tea and eating toast in the kitchen.

"Don't worry," he says, "I won't get in your way, you just do whatever it is you have to do."

"Oh, okay." I feel a mix of relief and surprise, because he genuinely seems alright about it.

We leave a short while later in separate cars, and as I follow him up the lane I see Diane perfectly placed to see us pass. I slow my car and wind down the passenger window as I reach her.

"Is that him? The new man?" she says, as she leans in through the window.

"It is," I say, and I can't keep the smile from my face.

"He is gorgeous. If only I were forty years younger," and then she sighs.

"Well if you were you'd have to fight me for him, and I don't fancy your chances much."

"You had a good night then?" There's a twinkle in her eye as she asks and I shake my head.

"Yes, thank you and no, you're not getting the details."

"Oh go on, I might as well live vicariously through you, it's the only chance I get nowadays." I laugh because I doubt that very much, then remembering that time is getting on I make my excuses and continue with my journey to work. I stop off briefly to see Sidney and although it's impossible to ignore the terrible cough wracking his body, there is such a spring in my step this morning I barely notice his lack of interaction as I continue on my way.

I'd told Dan that morning about Sidney and he'd thought it was hilarious that I was even getting a physical paper. He'd asked why I didn't get it all online and I'd started to explain about my aversion to any web-based activity then thought better of it, dodging the subject instead by muttering that I preferred it that way. He must realise my lack of interest in such things anyway, he only has to look at my phone. It makes and takes calls and texts, and that's it. As far as I'm concerned his is fundamentally a tracking device, its secondary function being a phone, and that would never do for me.

Even now, even with the new life I have in Crowbridge, I've spent a lot of time covering my tracks and building a fresh story, so what would be the point of all the efforts I've made if the slightest slip up, such as me appearing on some social media post, could lead someone from my old life straight to me.

With the stops I made Dan is already running on the treadmill by the time I get there, and he gives me a smile that reaches right to my core as I pass by the wide expanse of glass. I see Mike lifting weights at the back of the room and gird myself to deal with him first. By the time I get in there he has moved on to the rowing machine and I crouch down in his eye line and say I want to speak to him.

"Just give me a moment can you, I need to finish this." *Of course*, I think, *first things first*. I'm warming up on the cross trainer when he comes over. He has a towel slung round his neck, using the ends to wipe sweat from his face. I know he doesn't interact much with the others in the Centre so if there is talk about me the chances are he won't have heard it.

"What's going on?" he says. I slow down again to talk to him.

"I just wanted to let you know I won't be coming round to your place."

"Oh, okay. That's no problem." My spirits lift for a moment then he says, "I'll see you next week." Damn it.

"Ah, no, sorry. I didn't make myself clear. I'm not coming round *again*."

"And why is that?" I note the terse tone that's crept into his voice. He'll hate having his routine messed with, I know that.

"I just don't want to be doing that anymore. I want a more permanent relationship."

"Oh." It occurs to me that maybe he hasn't realised that while I've been seeing him I've also been free and easy with my charms elsewhere. It's not something we've ever discussed but as Monday is the only time I see him here perhaps he hasn't been aware and that for him this was a permanent relationship, which could now make this all a bit awkward. "You're finishing with me? I thought we got along great." His reaction furrows his brow.

"We do, or rather we did, but I want more than only having someone's attention on a Monday afternoon." He considers this for a moment, his expression darkening, and I wonder if he's thinking about cutting something out of his life in order to fit more of me into it, but then I remember how obsessive he is and I know I'm safe and that my decision will come as more of a terrible inconvenience rather than that much of a loss. But it seems I misunderstood our relationship, at least his view of it.

"No," he says, firmly, moving closer to me, "you can't end it like this. We should spend more time together."

I am totally taken by surprise. Never in a month of Sundays did I expect this reaction from him. There's no one else near us but he speaks quietly as he continues, "Come round this afternoon and we'll talk about it."

This is proving to be more challenging than I was expecting but there is no point in building false hope and I know I need to be definite. "No, Mike, I'm sorry but we're done." He grabs hold of my forearm and as I try to pull it away he holds it tighter.

"Give me a chance, Maddy, I don't want you to go."

My voice is louder as I say, "You've already had a chance and you wanted the relationship we had but it no longer suits me."

"But we could change it." There's an edge of desperation to his words now and I really hate to do this but in my need to bring this to an end I blurt out,

"I'm seeing someone else." He stops and stares at me.

"Who?" and he looks round the gym to find that with our raised voices several people, including Dan, are now looking back at us. He has moved closer and I can see his concern but I give him a warning look and hope he'll keep clear.

"That doesn't matter, Mike," and on hearing his name he focuses back on me but I'm alarmed at how badly he's taking this. There's a wild look in his eye I've not seen before and for a moment I'm concerned about what he's going to do.

With some relief I find Steve at my shoulder and he says, "Look, mate, perhaps you need to go and cool off for a bit?"

"I'm fine," Mike says with a snarl, not taking his eyes off me for a moment, and I feel his grip tighten on my arm. He makes a decision and says, "You're coming with me, we need to talk about this," and he pulls on me as he takes a step away. I don't want to make any more of a scene than we're already creating but he's stronger than I am so I know the only way to stop him is to disable him and the only sure way of doing that is to kick him right in the…

And then Dan's there beside me and although he appears calm, blocking the way to prevent Mike from moving anywhere, easily, I sense his anger, the tension rippling through him. They're about the same height and I wouldn't like to bet on who'd come out on top if this thing escalates.

Steve looks between Dan and Mike and knowing this is heading for trouble says, "Let go of her." His tone is uncompromising and I know he won't take any nonsense. Mike knows this too and I feel his grip on me loosen then release completely, and I pull my arm back and towards my chest protectively.

"Mike, please," I plead with him because I want this to end peacefully, "just go." He takes a long look at me as if contemplating his options then turns away, and before Dan can move aside he pushes past him and storms out of the gym.

"Thanks," I mutter at Steve, who pats me on the shoulder and says it's alright before turning back to his duties. I look up at Dan. "That could have gone better." I'm a little shaken and could use a hug but we've agreed to keep our, whatever this is, on the down low for the time being.

"I don't know why you're that surprised he's developed feelings for you," he says, and although I realise how difficult he's finding this when I see his jaw clench, he shrugs as though it's just a passing remark and we drift back to our separate workouts.

But I am surprised, and even more so that Mike's never indicated that he has. I carry on with my routine, unsettled about what's happened until eventually we finish and head for the showers.

After the difficult ending of things with Mike I feel an inexplicable rush of happiness when I find Dan waiting for me when I come out of the changing room; apparently the 'down low' bit doesn't count out here as he takes my kit bag from me and my hand in his, threading his fingers through mine and squeezing them as we grin stupidly at each other. I wonder how differently my life might have been by now had I met a good man like this years ago. As we turn to leave I hear the whoosh of the automatic doors opening, feel the delayed blast of bitter wind from outside as it eventually reaches us, and as I look up to see who's entered my blood turns to ice in my veins.

He has found me.

Tag.

The 'someone from my old life'.

Chapter 19

His black hair is as unruly as it ever was and the white sleeveless tee-shirt he wears shows to full effect the tanned sculpted muscle he's always liked to display, whatever the weather.

Once upon a time my poison of choice, there was never going to be a happy ending.

My throat constricts as he says, "'ello, Red," and glances at, then ignores, our interlocked hands before fixing me with his piercing gaze. And I know I'm in trouble.

"What are you doing here?" My voice is quiet though I'm surprised I can get any words out and Dan's hand tightens on mine as Tag grins.

"Searchin' for you. Why else would I be 'ere?" He pauses, his expression serious and I detect the edge in his voice as he says, "Four years, Red. You've 'ad me lookin' for four years." He stops and with the merest tilt of his head in Dan's direction but without losing eye contact with me he says, "Who's 'e?" Dan goes to speak but with a squeeze of my hand I silence him.

"Dan, a friend."

"I see. Very cosy."

"What do you want, Tag?" I cut straight to it and he laughs lightly but I know it's not because he's happy and there's a twist in my gut at the sound.

"All in good time, Red, all in good time. Now I know where you are I'll see you around," and with that he leaves and my legs feel like jelly beneath me.

It was four years since I had run. Six since I'd started planning my escape. I'd been careful to cover my tracks as I'd walked out on him and the life we'd had together and I'd never looked back. But now it seemed I'd not been careful enough.

My disappearance wasn't perfect, but it was the best I could manage, however I had one thing in my favour. There was no one who would report me missing, apart from Tag, and I knew he wouldn't go to the police. He would never risk them taking a closer look at his life. I imagined he would ask around, search everywhere he knew I hung out for a while and then go and get on with his life, and because of that as the intervening years had passed I'd started to think that today would never happen.

Until it did.

I'd never doubted Tag had loved me but our relationship was toxic because he had wanted far more from me than love and deep down I thought he'd wanted that part of me more than the actual being in love bit.

It appears I was wrong, because here he is and he's been looking for me.

All. This. Time.

And I can't imagine, not for one single moment, that finding me is going to make him a happy bunny.

Although of course, it might not actually be me that he is after.

I'm frozen to the spot, staring at the place where he was standing only a moment before. Thoughts tumble in panic through my mind as I wonder how long I've got before he makes his move.

"Who was that?" Dan's voice, though quiet, brings me out of my state of shock, and although that seems too strong a word for what's just happened it's the only one I can come up with that does sum up how stunned I'm feeling. I'm weak, my legs barely able to hold me up, and that won't do at all, not now. I mentally shake myself and turn to look at Dan, all bright and breezy.

"Just an old friend," *tell the truth*, I chide myself, "an old boyfriend actually, I haven't seen him in a while."

"Obviously." I don't miss the tone in his response and I put my feelings aside for the time being; I'll have to deal with them later because for now there is only the need for action.

"Come on, let's go, you've got to get to the office, haven't you?"

"Yes, but I can cancel that if you need me to." He gives me a searching look. "You seem tense."

"I'm fine, honestly." We're walking out of the door by now and I scour the car park for any sign of Tag. There is none.

There is however, Mike.

"Oh bloody hell, what now?" I mutter as he strides towards us. I suspect he was watching from his house just waiting for me to appear. And now he knows who it is I'm seeing.

"I'll deal with this," Dan says in all seriousness, and right at that moment I am so tempted to let him, but I need to try to get through this encounter without a punch being thrown and the likelihood of that happening can only be down to me.

"Thanks, but I'll handle it, it's my mess after all."

"Okay, but don't worry," and he squeezes my hand reassuringly, "we're in this together." I've never had anyone say this before to me and I draw strength from it.

Mike stops in front of us, waves of fury radiating from him. I can see a vein pulsing in his temple and I let go of Dan's hand.

"So this is who you've been seeing behind my back!" His voice rises in pitch as he speaks.

"It wasn't like that, Mike." I try to calm him but have no idea what he is hoping to gain, and to be honest

I could do without this confrontation coming hot on the heels of Tag's reappearance in my life. I move away from Dan, dragging Mike's attention with me.

"I want you to reconsider, Maddy." He glances at Dan but other than lowering his voice a little doesn't seem to care what he says in front of him, as he continues, "we had a good time, didn't we?"

"We did, Mike, but that's over, I've moved on and I'm sorry if I've hurt you, it wasn't my intention." I've always known how uptight and controlled Mike was but I hadn't fully realised the implications of my actions. If he didn't accept the situation and calm down it was going to be awkward using this gym from now on, what with him living so close by, and I could do without the hassle.

Dan has considerately moved further away, giving me some space to talk to Mike with a bit of privacy. I know he is keeping a close eye on us and I can feel his presence but I don't want him crowding the situation and antagonising Mike further.

"It's just taken me by surprise," Mike then says quietly, and I sense the fight go out of him a little.

"I know, I'm sorry." He lets out a deep breath and I feel for the first time he's taking control again. "I should have been more thoughtful with you, Mike, I didn't realise you cared quite so much."

"Not care? After all that time we spent together." He obviously had far deeper feelings for me than I'd ever given him credit for, it's a shame he didn't show that side of him earlier.

"I never meant to hurt you."

"But you have." There's a finality to his bitter words but he manages a weak smile, then glances over at Dan. "I'd best go back to my workout, if Steve lets me back in." I nod, it would do him good. "I'll see you around, Maddy."

"Yeah," I say, although I think it would be best if we kept clear of each other for a bit which means me missing my Monday mornings. A small sacrifice in the circumstances.

Ignoring Dan's presence completely, he moves past me and heads towards the Leisure Centre doors.

I breathe out a sigh of relief and hope this issue is all over because I have other stuff to deal with. I walk over to Dan and smile at him.

"There's never a dull moment with you, is there," he says, "Are you okay?" and I nod.

"Now, where were we?" I say. I'm keen to get my plan of action back on track, and pushing the situation with Mike to the back of my mind for the moment I need to focus on Tag.

"You could come to the office, hang around a bit then we could do something later?" He's being protective, wanting to keep me near him with everything going on but that won't do at all. I need to keep as much distance as I can between him and Tag. I don't want them meeting up again and I certainly don't want Tag telling Dan all about my past. On the spur of the moment I say,

"I can't I'm afraid, I'm meeting Chris this evening."

"Oh, you didn't say."

"No, sorry, I only just remembered. Is that okay?"

"Of course, I'm out all day tomorrow though so perhaps see you tomorrow evening?"

"Absolutely, yeah that would be great." I lean in to give him a kiss and he responds, his arms close around me and for a moment, while I'm wrapped in the warmth of his hug, I can almost feel my broken pieces coming together. I smile at the memory of what Cubby had said and indulge in the momentary feeling of safety while I can.

"Can I ask you something before I go?" His voice is soft against my ear.

"Of course," and I stay buried in his arms, waiting for what is coming.

"Red?" I pull back a little then so as to be able to look at him.

"That's a nickname." I pause, knowing I'm going to have to reveal something of my past, "because my name was Scarlet. My mother was obsessed with *Gone with the Wind*, our surname was Butler so Scarlet was the obvious choice." He says he likes the name but asks nothing more about why there was a need to change it, for which I'm grateful and I smile. "I guess I should be thankful I wasn't a boy. Rhett would have been so much harder to live down at my inner city comp."

He chuckles, "True, and what about Tag, what's his real name?"

I know I'm frowning as I say, "He's just Tag." I find myself questioning why he wants to know because I don't want Dan checking him out, or tracking him down.

"No surname?"

"Smith," I say, reluctantly.

"Really?" He fixes me with a steely gaze, "Tag Smith. Sure it's not Jones?"

"I'm sure," and as I don't look away, he smiles and the intensity of the moment is broken as he continues,

"Tag's probably a nickname, Maddy, just like Red. You'll be telling me next you think Cubby is a real name," and he chuckles again.

"Isn't it?"

"No, of course not. Bloody hell, Maddy, you're not very curious, are you?" I assume he is not expecting an answer to that as he sighs before continuing, "Now, as much as I never want to let you go I have to be getting to work." He kisses me and it's a mixture of tenderness

189

and longing and while I want to stay in that bubble forever it pops as he pulls away, although he gazes at me a moment before he says, "Bye," then lets me go, though I wish he wouldn't.

"Bye," I respond, my voice sounding forlorn as I watch him walk away to his car.

He drives off and I check round again before I get in mine and take a deep breath. I have to buck my ideas up. I need to focus, I need to be alert and I need to get home, but not before taking a few precautions first. I have no idea what Tag knows already, and whether he's spotted my car but knowing him I have to assume he does, therefore as I set off I keep a careful watch on the cars around and behind me. I don't go straight home. I take a tour around Hartleigh first, turning down side streets and back roads, checking each time I do that no one is following. Satisfied at last, I leave the town and head for Crowbridge.

Chapter 20

I have heard it is difficult to disappear but I didn't find it so at all. Although I imagine some would consider it sad that I had no one who would notice my absence, I found it useful because it meant no police involvement. If the police start looking for you the chances of you staying missing diminish, rapidly. They have the resources, the contacts and the reach to spread the word and hunt for you in ways an individual can't. They can get CCTV footage, track mobile phone use and check on bank account transactions which could easily spoil your escape plan. Unless you are careful. As it was I was extra careful, so that if it came to it even they would have had a hard time tracking me down.

Everything changed for me the day I turned eighteen. I won't go over the tedious details but without warning I found my eyes abruptly, and brutally, opened to the reality of my situation. Up until that point I'd been drifting, the decisions I'd thought I was taking I realised were made at the whim of someone else, and I looked at my life and found it wanting. I didn't like what I had become and was fearful of what my future held, so I'd decided to make a different life for myself, and I knew I could only do that alone.

I didn't know how long my departure was going to take and in the end it was two years in the planning which may seem like a long time but I was determined that if I was going to do it then I was going to do it right. I needed the time to set things up properly and carry out my research. I'll also admit that I dawdled a bit as well, blinded as I was by my love for Tag, not wanting to go but all the while knowing I had to.

I'd made my life look as normal as possible. I'd got a job as a pot washer for a nearby hotel, real dogsbody stuff. Tag wasn't happy, thought I was an idiot for doing so actually, but I didn't want to be signing on and when I explained my reasoning he allowed me to carry on with it. Right there at the Job Centre is a place where your absence might be noticed. I say might because the likelihood is that I would have merely become a statistic that nobody followed up on but it's a loose end and as you might have gathered by now I am particular about my planning, and I do dislike a loose end. The job was hard work for minimum wage. The hotel was large, the staff turnover rapid and the management uncaring as to who came and went, as long as someone was around to wash the pots. But the main point of it was that it provided a supply of legitimate money coming into my bank account. If anyone had taken a close look at my life they would have soon realised that I was living beyond my means but I'd hoped to be long gone before there was a chance of anyone doing that. With no housing benefit to pay my rent and my earnings too meagre to afford it, I had to supplement them with cash from my illicit activities and put my trust in the silence of those who had helped me before.

Because of the circles I moved in with Tag I knew all the wrong people so I had contacts, and by listening to whispers and concentrating for a while I found someone, who knew someone, who knew someone who could get me a new identity. I arranged this as far from Tag as possible but even then I never met that contact in person although I couldn't avoid them having the required photo, of course; however I made it crystal clear how badly I would damage their reputation should they ever breathe a word of our transaction. I can be tough, believe me, when I need to be.

Once I had my new identity in the form of a birth certificate and passport I was in a position to escalate my plan. I worked out where I wanted to live by doing my research on the internet. Unlike everyone else I have ever known, and as far as I am aware, I have no digital footprint. Apart from the pay-as-you-go phone I've already told you about, I don't own a laptop nor any type of tablet. I have never been on any form of social media and as far as I can be certain I don't appear on anyone else's. I actively discourage photos, so there will be no selfies with me, thank you, and I do not wish to be tagged anywhere.

There have, however, been occasions when I've needed to do some research for a job. For that I used to go across town to an internet café and use a fake ID, provided by one of Tag's boys, to get the information I needed. I obviously couldn't use the same ID, or source of one, on this occasion but the beauty of leaving yourself plenty of planning time means that you can make the most of opportunities when they land in your lap.

Mine arrived in the form of a group of drunken girls on the underground late one night. They filled the carriage with their screeching laughter and inane chatter and it was a blessed relief when they got out and left me alone to the silence. When I approached the doors to get off at my stop a while later, I realised a small wallet had been left on one of the seats they had occupied. As I travelled up the escalators I flipped it open, slipped the driving licence into my back pocket and, after wiping it of prints, I pushed the wallet through the letterbox of the local outreach police station that was closed at night because, apparently, bad things only happened around there during the day.

Now I had another ID I used a different internet café, of course, and started investigating online. I knew where Watson & Grove had their offices and I worked out where I needed to live to ensure I could keep my home and the 'work' life I had planned separate.

Despite the physical relationship Tag and I shared, as I've already said he never stayed over at my place and the fact he was selfish with his time worked well for me. On my chosen date I did the lunchtime shift at the hotel and returned to my flat. I called Tag to suss out whether or not he was expecting to see me that evening, but he had other plans. I packed everything I wanted to take into a suitcase and spent the evening watching films and dozing.

At four the next morning I climbed out of my bedroom window and onto the flat roof of the storage rooms of the shops below – it was a familiar route as I had come and gone this way before. The night was dark, the moonlight muted by clouds, and I remember crouching in the shadows, my senses on high alert as I checked I hadn't disturbed anyone in the flats around me. When I was sure all was quiet I crossed the roof, and dropped my suitcase over the side where it landed on the pile of cardboard packaging stacked by the back door, before following it by lowering myself as far as possible and jumping the rest. I did all this to avoid the CCTV cameras that watched the front of the precinct. I disappeared into the estate maze of high-rises and terraced housing and appeared again at a railway station a couple of miles away, where I knew I would be caught on a camera. There was no avoiding it. However, all that would have recorded was a woman with a blonde bob wearing high heels and a sharp business suit pulling a suitcase and boarding the first train of the day, like so many others. By the time I left that train I was a beanie-wearing brunette in jeans and a sweatshirt mingling with all the other student types arriving in the city.

It goes without saying that from the moment I left the flat I paid in cash. I turned off then took the battery out of my phone, destroyed the SIM, along with my bank card, then scattered the remains like confetti into several bins along the way.

And just like that I disappeared.

I lived in a grotty, but necessarily cheap, bed and breakfast for the next six months or so while I learnt to drive and I spent a lot of time in cafés listening to the locals, mimicking their speech, ironing the London out of mine. Then once I got my driving licence I bought a car and was ready for my move to the country.

Of course, it's one thing to go missing, it's entirely another matter to remain so. There are three main reasons why most people fail to disappear successfully. The first is because of the emotional pull. Going missing can be a lonely business and human interaction is a powerful driver. Many think they can leave but find they cannot completely let go of family and friends and, even if they start out with the best of intentions, they end up needing to make some sort of contact. Calling repeatedly to listen to an answerphone message. Ringing, then hanging up the phone when their person answers. Eventually they may even risk everything by returning to the area in the hope of catching a glimpse of those left behind.

The second is not managing to build up and maintain a convincing backstory. The trick here is to develop parallel lies. Making up a new life for yourself may initially seem like an exciting prospect. As an example you may decide to invent a whole new family, giving yourself brothers and sisters you've never had. This is a mistake, for you will find yourself in an increasingly tangled web of deceit when you start having to develop their lives and backstories as well. Keep the lies you're going to be telling parallel to the truth of the life you previously led. Then you will recognise it and it is easier to stay on track. I am the only child of an absent father and disabled mother, which explains why she never visits and why I sometimes disappear for a few days at a time to look after her. Simple.

The third reason, being weak spots and patterns, is my Achilles heel. Ideally you should live much as you did before and in the same sort of surroundings as you will understand them and not stand out. But at the same time you should not *do* the same things as before, so you need to change your habits and routines. I broke both these rules, but I did so knowing the risk I was taking, and, because I rather arrogantly believed I could get away with it. Firstly, I come from the city but moved to the countryside because I wanted to experience that way of life, and I've had to work hard to blend in. Secondly, I am a creature of habit, and although I have changed most of what I did before, for example I never used to get a paper so Sidney's is a new routine, there was one thing I couldn't change. In both places I was and still am an active member of a gym. And this has been my undoing.

When I get to the exit to Crowbridge I drive straight past and keep checking the rear view mirror. I take the next slip road and double back cross country from the first village I come to. The lanes between the two are narrow and winding so there is no way a car can inconspicuously follow me down there without me knowing about it. I am relieved when I eventually make it back to Crowbridge and turn down between the pub and church.

I leave the engine running as I get out of the car, open the wooden doors of the garage then drive the car in. Closing them up behind me and therefore hiding the car from view, I'm satisfied I've done all I can to cover my tracks.

I open the front door, longing to get into the sanctuary of my cosy home but the minute I step into my sitting room I'm hit with the realisation that all my efforts have been in vain.

He has already been here.

I know it, I can feel it, and my heart sinks.

On the coffee table, instead of where it lives on my bookshelf, is my copy of *Oliver*. In our early days when everything was a lark and a bit of fun I'd once likened Tag to Fagin. He didn't know who I was talking about, he didn't do books, but we'd watched the film together and he'd corrected me and said he was more like the Sykes character. We'd joked about it then, until it became something not to be laughed at.

I hate the fact that he has been in here, in my home, in my safe place.

I do a quick lap of the cottage to check he's not lying in wait for me, as with the detours I took getting home he could easily have beaten me back. Once I'm convinced the house is empty I bolt the front and back doors, top and bottom. I check all the windows and make sure they are closed. But all the time I do this I'm fully aware the efforts I go to are pointless because I know that if he wants to get in he will find a way.

I go back to my bedroom and open the wardrobe door, getting on my knees to make sure nothing on the floor has been tampered with. I always leave my shoes in a precise pattern and I would know if they had been moved, but everything is in place and I'm satisfied no one has found my hidey hole. Then I keep checking out of the windows. Between the ones upstairs and down I can see in all directions around the cottage and I move between them all, checking and rechecking. It's early evening by now and I see Diane's lights go on. I imagine her busy in her homely kitchen and I wish I was there with her but I don't want to bring anyone else into this.

As I check out of the kitchen window a yowl startles me and I curse and jump back and my hand, clutched to my chest, feels my heart racing as adrenaline spikes through my veins. I take a couple of deep breaths to settle myself and wonder what the hell is making that noise. It's coming from outside the kitchen door and I peer back out of the window over the sink, squint sideways and manage to catch a glimpse of Cat's tail twitching in the air. He never comes round and I don't know what he's doing here now but the noise is not letting up and I can't put up with it for much longer. It's unsettling, and my nerves are already on edge. I can see no one else around so I quickly undo the bolts, unlock the door and let him in. He enters in a rush, like he's the one being hunted, then as I lock up again he rubs up against my legs purring as he does so, but I push him away.

It's getting dark but I don't want to draw the curtains to show anyone's at home so I take a large knife from the kitchen drawer and go upstairs. Between my bedside cabinet and the corner of the room there is a gap. It's currently filled with a couple of piles of books I've yet to read but I pull these out, sliding them along to lean up against the wall instead. I then get into the space that's left. There is nowhere to hide in the cottage and here I'm as protected as I can be. I have walls to my back and one side with the cabinet on the other, and I'm behind the door so I'm alerted to someone coming in before they can see me. I sit with my knees pulled up in front of me and I have the knife which I place on the carpet to my side. I'm as ready as I can be but fear it will be a long night ahead.

I left Cat to do his own thing but he has followed me upstairs and stalks towards where I'm trying to be invisible. He's like a shadow moving in the ever deepening darkness with only the fading light from the window glinting across his eye to distinguish him. He's purring the moment he reaches me and rubs his face against my leg again.

"What are you doing here?" I say, "Go on, scram," and I try to push him away but every time I do he comes right back and he's more insistent than ever. Eventually I give up and he squeezes his way into the space created between my bottom and my feet, curling around and settling down I assume to sleep but the purring doesn't stop.

"Shhhh…" I try to quieten him. He's so loud I'm convinced anyone will hear him the moment they set foot in the place. "If you stay you'll have to be quiet. I shan't be letting you out, you know? Or getting you food. We're here for the duration." I don't know why I feel I have to tell him the rules of him remaining with me but strangely, like having him close, it feels calming. I don't feel alone after all and I put down a hand, my fingers burying into his soft fur and his purr deepens as I do. It sounds contented and relaxed and I find the action of gently kneading him comforting. Maybe Diane is right in her assertion that he goes off helping people, he's certainly doing so now and I wonder how he knew I was in trouble.

The night darkens and there is nothing to hear other than the occasional rumble from Cat. I don't know if he's asleep and doing this at the same time, or if like me he is awake and intending on staying so throughout the night.

I have a banter by text with Dan late evening. He asks after my meet up with Chris and reminds me he's off out tomorrow, and though I express disappointment I'm secretly pleased as it helps in my need to keep him as far away from Tag as possible. I tell him dinner with Chris was terrific and that I'm planning an early night. I'm saucy with it too, telling him I need to catch up on some sleep after he'd kept me awake for so long the night before, and we're flirty and for a few minutes it's fun, it takes me away from my current predicament, and I hope my past is not about to bollocks all this up.

When I eventually send Dan off to bed there are hours ahead of me, and while I've successfully managed to block nearly all thoughts of Tag from my mind in recent years, him reappearing out of the blue has brought back a rush of memories that I could do without.

He'd looked good today, there was no doubting that. I'd often wondered how it would go if we ever met again but I'd never imagined it would be like it was today. I'd thought if it ever happened he'd be furious and aggressive with it, letting rip at me in his need for revenge. I'd definitely never considered he'd be so calm. That he'd merely mention that he'd been looking for me, as if *that* was what was important to him, and that then he'd leave. He'd learnt some control, I realise, or some patience perhaps since I'd seen him last and I ponder on this and realise that this Tag is potentially a far more frightening prospect than the younger version I'd known. He would be thirty-four now, a less inappropriate age gap than when we'd first met and become lovers when I was fifteen.

I'd come to his attention when he saw me giving out my favours to a school mate behind, that cliché of all things, the bike shed. He was passing along the alleyway that ran round the back of the school and intervened like some bloody knight in shining armour, although I didn't exactly need saving. I'd been pleasing the boys for a couple of years already and knew precisely what I was doing.

Want me.

From then on he'd stopped me from seeking attention from the boys at school. Attention that I now know I'd used to prop up my flagging self-esteem, and he'd changed me from being the plaything of many to becoming the partner of one. And we were partners in more than one way.

Tag had led me astray and drawn me into a life that, given enough time, would eventually only ever have ended one way. Although at the start it was all a game. We'd be out in town and he'd dare me to lift a couple of small items from a shop and when I did we'd run breathless and laughing up the high street, exhilarated by our success. It was a bit of fun, that's all, but we soon gave it up. No use getting ourselves marked, he'd say, not for nothing.

In hindsight I know I was gullible and that at his age he should have known better but I was smitten and, blinkered by that, did anything he asked of me.

I naïvely thought that I was special, that I was some sort of chosen one, that it was just me, just him and me. How wrong I was. For I soon found out that I was one among many of his supporters.

It was a while before he introduced me to the others in his network. The 'disciples' I'd call them, his gang of admirers. He had the young kids doing small jobs for him, picking pockets, lifting wallets, purses and the like from the unwary, bringing back the goods for which he'd see them alright. Training them up, he'd call it. The older ones he organised into robbing from houses, taking stuff easy to shift and I'd meet the girls, a unique brand of devotee, and know immediately he'd slept with them all. Their bitter bitchiness gave them away in an instant.

Need me.

And then there was me, and I was flattered into believing I was different from the rest because he had other plans for me, he'd said. Big plans. It was time for him to move on to bigger and better things, he'd told me, and I was going to go with him. And I'd loved him and gone along with it because I'd wanted to please him, no, it was more than that, I was eager to please him.

Like me, please like me.

We'd left the others to the petty larceny while we concentrated on the longer game. It all revolved around the undisputable truth that people with too much money often tend to be careless with their possessions. We planned carefully and we took what we knew we could move on, expensive jewellery and flashy watches, mostly. I couldn't believe how much people spent on this stuff and if I ever faltered in my reasoning for doing this Tag would reassure me that it was all insured and everyone would get their money back. So that was alright then.

And we were professional with it too. We only drank occasionally and although I knew he sometimes smoked a little pot he kept me clean and well away from drugs because that's where you get the screw-ups, he'd tell me, and we were at the top of our game with the money rolling in and couldn't risk it. My world had revolved around him during that time and I'll admit I was in awe of him, an older man controlling so much.

He was good to me too, although occasionally I'd seen what he'd done to others, the beatings he'd handed out, sometimes even to those who followed him. For that was what we were, followers, doing whatever he wanted with almost slavish devotion. I'm not sure what the hold was that he had over us acolytes but he most certainly controlled us and like a lion protecting his territory he'd bat down those who stepped out of line or challenged his authority. But he was never violent towards me, I'll give him that. Never even lifted a finger in my direction and I genuinely believed he loved me, at least I did back then.

However, despite all the love he gave me, and all the times he told me I was special, I didn't believe, not for one second, that he would simply let me walk away unscathed if I told him I wanted to go, and that is why I did what I did.

I *was* in love with him, I really was. It was intense and red hot and over the years with him that had never diminished, not one jot. He couldn't keep his hands off me when we were together and it was an all-consuming, passionate love. Although looking back I see that while it was all those things, that was only when it suited him.

I left while I still loved him, which was the hardest thing I have ever done, but I did it because I knew the way I was living was no good for me. When everything changed at home I realised that I wanted more than the grubby flat I rented and the seedy world I inhabited. I just didn't want to get my new life the same way Tag wanted to.

The two years of planning had helped me to gain much needed perspective on my situation. It enabled me to stand back and look at the life I was leading with clarity then ruthlessly calculate the way forward. I worked on my independence, becoming less needy, less reliant on having Tag around. I guess I grew up but if he ever noticed he never mentioned it and with his mind set firmly on his own desires he remained completely unaware of my plans.

And I wonder where we stand now. He may have appeared calm but there is no way he won't be pissed at me, that he won't see what I did as a betrayal, and I have seen what he's done to others who betrayed him, and I'm afraid. What I did was so much worse and for a while I mull over the possibility of just packing up and running again. But something tells me that now he's found me once I'll never get far enough away. Plus, this time my money is tied up in the cottage and I have nowhere near enough to buy another identity and set myself up somewhere else. I know I'm going to have to face what's coming and that it'll be exactly what I deserve.

I fret through the hours of darkness, trying to plan a course of action but my nerves are frayed and my mind jumps from one train of thought to another with nothing coming out that makes any coherent sense. I keep telling myself he is the past, that the feelings I once had for him are gone and that as we both have new lives he no longer has any hold over me, but I sit in fear, my knife ready, wondering when he'll make his move and jumpy in my expectation of him appearing at any moment.

The emotional expense of energy takes its toll on me but the sky is already lightening by the time Cat stirs and the purring starts again, its soporific effect finally too much and under its hypnotic rhythm I eventually drift off to sleep.

What feels like only moments later, I'm startled awake by the sound of someone hammering on the front door.

Chapter 21

Shaken by the abrupt awakening, it takes mere seconds to remember why I am where I am and I pick up the knife and stand. Cat, disturbed in the process, stretches himself out across the carpet baring his claws, a handy weapon to have concealed.

My body is stiff, I'm in yesterday's clothes and feel dirty and tired. My mouth is dry and rough like the sandpaper at the bottom of a budgie's cage and my pounding head reminds me that I can't remember the last time I ate or drank anything.

The hammering starts up again and I gingerly make my way down the stairs, keeping my back to the wall as I approach the door. My phone starts up in my pocket which makes my shredded nerves jump and as I take it out I see it's Kourtney. I answer, my voice quiet though whoever is outside will have heard the ring tone and know I'm here.

"Hi," my unused voice croaks.

"Oh! You *are* there," is her perky response, "I've bin knockin' for ages, 'cos I can't get in."

I don't respond but end the call and relief floods though me as I reach to unbolt the door and open it to my eager cleaner.

"Christ! You look like shit, where's yer car?" is Kourtney's unguarded reaction when she sees me.

"I overslept," I mutter, and drag a hand through my knotted hair then wave vaguely in the direction of the garage, "the car's in there."

"You're in yer clothes." She sounds surprised and when she catches sight of the knife I'm now holding by my side she adds with suspicion, "What's goin' on?"

"Nothing for you to worry about, come in," I say as I stand back and wave her in with the knife, although her curiosity is not that easy to deter.

"What're yer doin' with the knife?" Cat has followed me downstairs and I pick him up and put him outside, giving him a quick stroke as I do so.

"I was about to chop an onion." She puts on a don't-give-me-that-nonsense look but I ignore it and re-bolt the door. "Don't let anyone in, I'm off for a shower," I say, and I leave her to the cleaning. She's good, she really is. It's a pleasure not to have to do the housework and as I stand under the hot water this thought makes me smile which feels strange on my face after the last few hours. With the blast from the past I've just had I can't help thinking how things have changed for me. From the poverty stricken childhood in the dingy nicotine-stained flat looking after my mother and seeking comfort anywhere I could, I now have my own place in the country, that came with its own gardener, a car, a job and a cleaner, what would my mother have made of that? I might even have a decent bloke in my life for the first time and I wonder how much of this new life will still be in place after Tag has done whatever it is he is going to do to me. I realise I've been standing deep in thought for far too long letting the water stream over me, and I turn it off and reach for my towel.

I dress in fresh clothes and grab a bagel to eat in the car but pass on the coffee, I'm far to wired already for that. Kourtney is watching me carefully as I get ready to leave and I try to behave as normally as possible and ask her how she's getting on and if she's had any more trouble with the bloke from the pub. She scoffs at that and says she has no time for all that nonsense and yet again she impresses me. She is so much more mature and together than I have ever been with men.

Leaving Kourtney with strict instructions to let me know if she sees anyone around, I leave wishing I didn't have to step outside my home. However, I know if I don't make myself available to Tag he will come and find me here when he's good and ready and I don't want whatever is going to happen to ruin my safe place for me. Because amongst all my muddled thinking there was one thing that did become clear for me last night. Whereas I'd always thought my real self was the one I displayed in Hartleigh, it's not. Not anymore. This is my home, I really have moved on and this is the life I want to live, the person I want to be and I know I have to protect it by keeping the past well away.

I see Diane and Joe in the garden of her cottage as I pass and I return their waves but I don't stop, feigning being late by tapping my watch, and I see Diane glance at hers in my rear view mirror.

I keep checking about me as I drive to Hartleigh to make sure I'm not followed then pull in as usual outside Sid's. Although I can hear he's wheezing and his cough is no better I barely acknowledge his presence as, preoccupied, I pull out the papers I want. I catch him looking over at me and frowning as deeply as if I'd asked him to multiply fifty-eight by two hundred and sixty-four.

"You okay?" he mumbles, his voice growly and rough, I assume from lack of use. This is a breakthrough and an opportunity that at any other time I'd have grabbed with both hands at the same time as cheering my success at eventually getting him to speak, but right now I'm mentally unfit to capitalise on this utterance other than to say,

"Yeah, fine," the way all British people do, whatever state they're in, and I pick up my papers, then hesitate a moment. "You?"

"Mustn't grumble," is his equally British response that sends him into a paroxysm of coughing that I can still hear once the shop door has closed behind me.

I flick through the papers and see an editorial piece combined with an advert for the forthcoming attraction at Danewright House of the Duchess de Havilland's Jewellery Collection which will be on display for a couple of weeks.

I drive to the gym and circle the car park, checking all the vehicles in there before reversing into a parking space in case I need a quick getaway. As I walk towards the doors I rotate each of my shoulders trying to release the tension that's built up in them. The usual crowd for a Tuesday are in and rather strangely, given how long we've been together I am missing having Dan here, which is odd particularly when it's as well he isn't around today, with what I've probably got to tackle at some point. I briefly wonder where he is but dismiss the thought as he'll no doubt fill me in at some point when we catch up later.

I return the greetings as I walk in then enter my personal zone by putting my earbuds in and my iPod on shuffle as I start my workout. I feel better as soon as I start the familiar routine and my confidence grows. I manage to concentrate purely on the physical actions at first but as I relax bad thoughts creep back in to disturb me about what's going to happen to me when Tag eventually decides to show his hand. I thought through what Tag might want of me and what sort of retribution he would take and as the worries pursue themselves through my mind along with endless what ifs and how abouts I almost wish Tag *would* put in an appearance. The anticipation must be worse than the reality, surely?

So deep am I in my thoughts that I change from the cross trainer to the running machine without thinking and focus on picking up the pace for a few minutes. There's a television screen visible from where I am and I catch the headlines of the news, reading as it scrolls along the bottom of the screen. When it ends I turn my attention back to the space in front of me, look out through the sheet of plate glass, and see Tag sitting on a bench directly opposite. My breath catches in my throat but I carry on running, not wanting him to see me falter. Not wanting him to see he's got to me. He's only twenty feet away and I wonder how long he's been there. We don't acknowledge each other in any way but we make and maintain eye contact until it feels far too intense but I can't break the contact and be seen to back down, and I'm glad when I get to the end of my run and can legitimately walk away.

I've finished my routine and although I was planning on adding a few lengths in the pool I know I need to get this meeting over with. I pick up my stuff and go to shower and dress and as I do my nerves build. I have no idea how this is going to go but my main aim is to somehow keep Tag away from Dan and Crowbridge before he destroys the life I've built.

When I walk outside he hasn't moved but he has lit up. It had always astonished me that considering he spent so much time looking after his body, he had never quit smoking. I suspected it was vanity that kept him addicted to the habit because Tag was the type of guy smoking was invented for.

I head over to him and, reminding myself that I am perfectly capable of dealing with this, I sit down deciding to let him run the game for the moment, just to see where it leads. He inhales then lets tendrils of smoke trickle out through his lips. It drifts up and he squints as it reaches his eyes, his messy hair falls over his brow begging to have fingers run through it to sweep it back and I know he knows this. The creases at the corners of his eyes deepen and the dangers of smoking aside he looks as cool as fuck and I'm alarmed at the arousal he inspires in me. Nothing has changed there and the fact he's had this effect on me is concerning. I feel that distinctive familiar pull, bizarrely still finding myself drawn to him after all this time. He reaches his arm out along the back of the bench; his hand would have touched me but I pull back in time to escape it and I see a brief smile come to his lips as he notices. I can't have him touch me, I know that. But I am strong and as I repeat this over and over in my mind I show nothing, waiting for him.

"Loverboy not around today," is his opening gambit.

"He's got work issues." I'm noncommittal.

"Yeah, the insurance industry must be a demandin' occupation." He's having a dig and I don't rise to it but clock the fact he's done his homework.

A movement catches my eye and I look past him to see Mike coming in our direction. *Shit*. He has his kit bag with him and I hope he's going to ignore me, but no such luck.

He stops right in front of us, tilts his head towards Tag and says, "This another one you've been shagging?"

"No." I shake my head and note that while Mike has not directly looked at Tag once, Tag is studying him with some curiosity. "He's just a friend, Mike. Why are you not at work?"

"What's that got to do with you?" There's animosity in his words and I hold my hands up in defence; he's right it is nothing to do with me but I was only trying to make polite conversation, now I wish he'd just move along.

At that point he turns to Tag and says, "You want to run from this one. Don't say you weren't warned." I see Tag's eyebrows rise but he gives no other indication that he's even heard Mike who, disgruntled no doubt at the lack of response to his dire warning, walks off. I watch him for a moment, turning back when I hear Tag's soft chuckle.

"Still making friends I see, Red." Then dropping his cigarette on the ground he grinds it out with his foot and changes tack. "Come on, let's go get somethin' to eat." He stands and I suggest The Bull on Market Square and say I'll lead the way.

He's parked next to me and I mentally note the make, model and number plate then we drive down from the gym and back towards the centre of town. As I pass through the streets heading towards the square I mull over the physical changes in him. The years look good on him, there are a few more lines and a hint of grey at his temples but his eyes are as vibrant as ever and I know they miss nothing.

We pull into the Square and park. I particularly like this part of town. The Square is surrounded by an eclectic mix of old buildings, some brick, some rendered and painted, the colours subtle and blended well together. We walk over to The Bull in silence. I want to run, to not face the conversation that is coming but I know, I have known since last night that I'm resigned to having to face this at some point and therefore I cannot be a coward.

I am strong, I tell myself, *I can do this*.

The pub is quiet and we slip into a booth made for four which gives us some privacy. My stomach is churning over with nerves and I don't think I can eat a thing so choose a salad while Tag decides on ribs.

"D'you want a shot of Jack to go with that?" he asks, "I assume that's still your favourite."

"I'm driving, Tag, a coke will be fine, and make it diet."

"Well aren't you the sensible one, a salad and diet coke coming right up." He disappears to go and put in the order and I gaze out of the window. Our table is at the front of the pub though the glass only starts at my head height and even then the view is obstructed. This building is hundreds of years old and listed. The windows are made of small leaded panes and running along the bottom, and in the bit I'm looking out of, there is an additional pattern of small leaves, the colour of deepest emerald, in intricate leaded shapes with the occasional splash of a ruby red flower. I've always loved the richness of the colours in this beautiful window and the ambience of the pub in general. There's warming wood panelling throughout, the bar is tiled in dark green rectangular tiles that remind me of the older stations on the Underground and the partitions for the booths are ancient and ornately carved in a darker wood.

Across the square is the only hotel in town, The Cromwell, an historic coaching inn. I have no need to ever go in there and probably couldn't afford to anyway. Its only competition is from a low budget multi-room affair on the outskirts so for anyone looking for a touch of luxury The Cromwell has the market all sewn up. There are only a few people out and about on the streets but as I watch I see a couple cross the square heading for the hotel. His arm is around her waist, her blonde hair a mass of tumbling curls coming halfway down her back but what stands out, what catches my eye is the peacock blue checked jacket he is wearing. You don't see many of them around here. I watch them disappear into the doorway of the hotel and ponder on this for a few moments but I have to put that out of my mind because as soon as Tag returns to the table I'm back on guard.

He puts the drinks down then sits opposite and again I let him lead.

"So how've you bin, Red?"

"My name's Madeleine now."

"I know, classy, innit…Madeleine," he tests it out then says, "It goes well with the posh way you talk now an all, but I think I'll stick with Red," and he repeats his first question.

"I'm fine, and you?" This feels so ridiculously formal, so terribly English, it's as though we're about to sit down to a nice pot of Earl Gray and afternoon cakes.

"So-so," is his blunt response and now we've got to this point it seems he has little to say and he downs a quarter of his pint and I wonder if it's for courage. He's never been lacking in that, however I can sense an agitation in him that's unexpected. I remember him as being laid back before, confident and a little cocky, because it used to be a source of worry for me but now there's something different about him, something I feel lurking beneath the surface. I park that thought though as one question has been on my mind, and as our conversation has lulled I think I'll ask it.

"How did you find me?" He puts his pint back down before answering.

"I knew you'd still be using a gym somewhere so I've been checking each one in ever increasing circles out from 'ome."

"That's a lot of gyms."

"I've 'ad plenty of time." He looks away and out of the window. I see indecision in his expression and wonder what's going on with him.

I wish he'd get to what it is he wants but like a cat with a mouse he's playing me. He takes another long draught from his glass and as he puts it down again, straightening the beer mat under it so he lines up the glass dead centre, it seems as if it's galvanised him and he cuts to the chase as he looks up at me.

"Why d'you leave without sayin' anything, Red? That's what hurt most." I'm surprised and I know that shows, disbelief in my arched eyebrows.

"Really? That's what hurt the most?" Incredulity is etched into every word and I look at him carefully; he seems genuine but I know I need to tread cautiously. At that moment a waiter arrives with our food and it takes a few moments to get ourselves sorted with cutlery and dressings then we're alone again. I decide to answer him straight. "I didn't think you'd let me go."

He shakes his head. "If you'd wanted to go, I'd 'ave let yer."

"Are you sure about that, Tag?"

"I loved you." I'm surprised by his candour. "I'd 'ave done whatever would've made you 'appy." An admirable statement, but one that I believe he is only making given the luxury of the distance of time from which we are now viewing my departure.

"I loved you too, Tag, but that life was bad for me. We both know that. Where we were heading I didn't want to go, I didn't want to end up in prison." I had never doubted my decision but after what he's just said I briefly wonder if I'd misjudged him. "I didn't think you'd let me go so I did what I thought I had to do and, well, here we are," I finish helplessly and for something to do as much as anything I take a forkful of salad which I instantly regret because on his next words it turns to ash in my mouth.

"Or, did you do what you did because if we 'ad just broken up and you'd gone on your merry way you wouldn't 'ave 'ad my money to set yourself up with?" Oh. Now we are getting it, as I'd suspected he'd come for more than just me, and I watch him closely. He spoke evenly enough but as he looks up from his plate at me I see his tell, the smallest flare in his eye and I know the anger isn't far away. However, I don't appreciate his accusation.

"It wasn't your money, Tag, it was *our* money, and I took my half." He shrugs but I'm determined to assert that I've been fair in at least some of what I've done. He's eating, picking the ribs up in his fingers and gnawing at them, as if he hasn't a care in the world while I feel like I couldn't swallow another mouthful of food if I tried and I reach for my drink instead.

"I didn't see it like that." *No, I bet you didn't,* I think. "'Owever," he goes on, "there is something you can do to make amends." *That rather depends on whether or not I think I have something to make amends for, doesn't it?* His assumption is making me bristle. However, I'm intrigued enough to see what's on his mind.

"Really, and what would that be?" He's busy finishing off his ribs and holds up his finger to indicate patience, and I carry on the lame efforts I'm making at eating my salad while I try not to appear too inquisitive or show he's getting to me, but he is. He licks his fingers then says he's off to wash his hands and although the suspense is killing me I finish what I can of my salad by the time he returns so that I'm ready and waiting.

He comes back with another round of drinks and once he's put them down he pulls a piece of paper out of his jeans pocket. It's been torn from a newspaper and he places it on the table then slides it purposefully towards me. It's the cutting that I'd seen that morning, the editorial on the jewellery collection coming to Danewright House, and my heart sinks.

Shit. Shit. Shit.

Now I know why he's here.

Now I know how he found me.

I look up at him and he sits down, but not opposite like before, right next to me and I move as far back along the bench seat as I can as I say, "You've got to be kidding!" He grins mischievously and flashes his eyes at me in the way he used to back in the days when our lives were built recklessly on dares and challenges.

He leans closer and, conscious of our surroundings even though there is no one within earshot, he whispers, "Our biggest job yet."

I ignore that and instead raise my own question. "So you've been searching every gym for me, have you?"

"Absolutely," he says, and there's that grin again.

"I don't believe you." He holds his hands up in mock surrender.

"Okay," he says, and he's back to being serious. "I did look, as far as I was able to, but I 'ad no leads to go on, you did a good job there," and I bow my head in acknowledgement of the unexpected compliment. He turns towards me, and stretches his arm out along the back of the bench and this time I can't move any further away. "So thinkin' it was unlikely you'd change your spots entirely I kept an eye on anything around that looked like somethin' you'd go after and I'd go and scout out that area for a bit to see if you'd surface." He then prodded the newspaper article with his finger before finishing, "and this fits the bill." His fingers stroke my shoulder. I try to ignore their heat, and twist in my seat to move out of his reach as I reply.

"Hardly, it's a bit rich for my tastes isn't it? How would I get rid of that quality of merchandise?"

"I've moved on, Red, I thought you might 'ave done too. I 'ave someone who can break these types of goods down inter stuff you can pass on." He must have expanded his enterprise considerably if he was now capable of that and I know it's time to knock this on the head.

"I'm not in the business anymore, Tag, I told you I didn't want to end up in prison so I've gone legit and I'm not having anything to do with it." I hold on to the hope that if I'm negative enough about it he'll be dissuaded from continuing with this folly. But from the look that comes over his face, I don't think that's likely. He shifts in his seat, leans towards me, and brings his hand over to rest casually on my shoulder. I ignore its touch.

"I'm not askin', Red, you don't 'ave an option. You owe me, an' this is 'ow you're gonna pay me back." The way he looks at me as he says this fills me with dread; this is the old Tag, the one that never took no for an answer, but I am stronger now, I can resist his influence and I stand my ground.

"I don't owe you anything and anyway it's too big a job. Too big for either of us."

"I told you, I 'ave someone who'll deal with stuff like this."

"That's beside the point, how do you think you going to get in there in the first place?" His fingers trail to my neck and I feel his thumb stroke my cheek.

"In your job I'm sure you've assessed the place for any security weaknesses?"

How the hell does he know about my job?

"Sorry to disappoint but I haven't!" I lie, taking hold of his hand and placing it firmly on the back of the bench, "this is at a much higher level than I'm usually involved in."

"Really?" He looks puzzled, then leans closer as he whispers conspiratorially, "are you telling me that it was just an 'appy coincidence that you were there the other day then?"

How long has he been watching me?

"Absolutely, Jeez, I was just enjoying a day out." I aim to convince but feel my act falls short of what's needed. I'm struggling with being this close to him, I'm warm, can feel my face flushing and have a sudden need for some fresh air.

"With loverboy." A statement, not a question, but I answer anyway.

"He wasn't, then."

"Oh, so that really is a new thing?" *Do I detect a hint of jealousy?* I'm pleased to note at least something in my life is coming as a surprise to him. Presumably he takes my silence as agreement as he continues, "well we don't want to ruin that for you now, do we, sweetheart, 'cos I reckon if he finds out all about your dirty little past, it's gonna to put your job on the line as well, ain't it?"

The contents of my stomach clench into a ball with this threat and I know I have to try and put him off.

"There's no point going after those jewels, Tag, the ones on display are going to be imitation."

"Bollocks. Don't think you're the only one who can do their 'omework, Red." I wonder who he has got doing that for him now, as I know the planning part has never been his forte. His boredom threshold was always far too low and in the past if he hadn't had me to prepare things properly he would have just winged it. "I'm not intendin' on takin' the whole collection, just the centrepiece, the necklace. That's all I want."

"Oh right," I say, as if that is totally fine then. "Well don't say I didn't warn you." I fix him with a stare that I hope makes him realise I mean business before saying, "I'm leaving now, Tag. Keep away from me and Dan, and give up on this stupid idea." The table is bolted to the wall and I have to get up at that slightly awkward angle because of it. He makes no effort to move out of my way.

"You wanna get out, you're gonna have t' climb over," and he grins like he's looking forward to it. But there is no other option if I want to leave and if he is going to fail to be a gentleman. He shifts in his seat and I have to lean towards him as I lift one leg over his lap, planting my foot firmly on the floor the other side. I'm uncomfortably close and don't want to meet his eyes but then as I go to lift my other leg he grabs my wrists, his hands like vices clamping around them. He pulls me near. My face is in his and I see the anger in him as he glares at me, and I'm surprised, he's edgy, his emotions playing closer to the surface than I was expecting, and as I try to pull away he grips tighter.

"Let go of me," I say through gritted teeth.

His tone is threatening, his voice low as he speaks. "Listen carefully, Red, I'm goin' in there anyway so think carefully about whether you want me tramplin' all over whatever it is you 'ave planned or," and he pauses for effect, "maybe it'd be better for you if you just took me along. Wouldn't want word getting out about you now, would we? What d'you think they'd all make of what you are in that village of yours?" I try to shake this off, to show I'm unaffected but I'm surprised by how much it concerns me.

"Let. Me. Go," I say again, making more of an effort to pull my hands away. This time he releases me and I finish exiting the booth with as much dignity as I can muster. I don't say another word, I can't, not trusting what might come out of my mouth next.

"See you soon," he calls after me and I can hear him chuckling as I fling the door open and step outside, relieved to be able to suck in a cold, fresh lungful of air.

I'm shaking as I cross over to my car, shocked at how much I'm affected by him, even after all the time and distance I've put between us and I have no idea how I can get out of submitting to his demands. I know he will carry out his threats. I've never known him back down and my head is spinning with all I've got to think about.

I sit in the car and give myself a moment before starting the engine. It's typical, isn't it? The first time I have a glimpse at what could be a happy future and it's all about to be snuffed out. This is karma, this is. Retribution for all my past wickedness and I know I've earned every bad thing that is coming my way.

Chapter 22

You've travelled down to the northernmost outpost of the capital city, and although still part of the whole, the rundown streets you're now driving along could not be more different from the affluent centre, or anything you've experienced in what you're now realising has been a rather cosseted existence. This is the third short row of shops you've come across amidst the blocks of high-rise flats and back to back terrace buy-to-lets, the host of agents' boards that litter the frontages advertising the fact. Someone has the money around here and it sure as hell isn't the occupants.

You were right, she wasn't happy at all when she found out about the role you're going to play in her life. You could see how much she hated the idea of you becoming her boss. But things have moved on and you believe she's mellowed, at least you hope she has.

You're here because you feel compelled to find out more about Maddy. You know there's stuff she's keeping to herself and while Cubby seems happy with the scant, and mostly untrue, information he has on his files, he's not the one sleeping with her and you need to know more. You would have left it, probably, been happy with discovering things about her as you'd gone along but then yesterday happened and he turned up, Tag. And you know, you just know that there is something very wrong there. You were jealous, you realise that, you recognised the sensation, that twist in the gut, and you hate that you feel possessive of her, after only one night for God's sake. It's pathetic. But beyond your feelings you felt something else in her, you felt it as fear and you didn't like that, not at all.

You doubt she will tell you what's going on, she clammed up pretty quickly after Tag left and she's clearly been living a lie for the last few years so why would she start sharing now? No, you need to find out the truth for yourself and that is why you are here. And you try, somewhat unsuccessfully, to put aside the gnawing sensation that should she find out what you're doing it is highly likely that you won't be sleeping with her for very much longer.

There's little traffic and you slow down in the granite grey shadow of a depressing Sixties-built tower of stacked housing. On the other side of the road there's a wide expanse of paving in front of the shops. This is being made full use of by a discount store whose goods have exploded out of the front door, stacks of general tat displayed so as to encroach onto the pedestrian area. This arcade is not much different from the others that have been dead ends in your investigation. Rundown, flat-roofed and ugly, the second storey sags onto the first, the frontages are dirty, the signage garish and cheap. One of the units is empty, the shutters down and padlocked, a weathered board advertising it for rent. There's a low-end own brand grocery store well-stocked more with alcohol than with vegetables, a Chinese, currently closed, a launderette; and, exactly what you're looking for, a fish and chip shop. You pull into the side of the road and park.

A kid appears as if summoned from the kerb as your tyres brush against it.

Watch yer car, mister? he says as you get out. He looks about ten, pale, the remnants of a bruise to one cheekbone and skinny inside his scruffy clothes.

Not necessary, thanks, you reply. I'm only going over there, and you jerk your thumb over your shoulder in the general direction of the precinct.

222

Your choice, mister, dodgy area tho', anyfink could 'appen to it. He fixes you with a beady eye and an expression so unfathomable you know he'd be a bugger to play at poker.

How much? And he sniffs.

A tenner.

You've got to be kidding. I'll give you a fiver, when I get back, if the car's untouched.

He stares at you for longer than you'd like then says, done, and you think you probably have been but he spits into the palm of his hand and holds it out to shake yours. You don't want to but you do, then he turns and goes to lean up against the wall of the block the other side of the pavement, crossing his arms as he does so. You've parked behind two other cars and wonder if they are similarly protected.

You turn to look at the fish and chip shop, then up at the window above. This fits with what you know, what she let slip. There's a door sandwiched between the chip shop and the launderette and you wonder if that's the entrance you're looking for. It's late lunchtime and only a couple of customers are waiting to be served. One is just leaving and he enters the launderette, taking a seat in front of one of the machines before unwrapping his parcel on his lap. Your stomach growls as the aroma of the shop's fare wafts towards you and you cross the road.

There are plastic-covered tables pressed up against the window and once you've placed your order you take a seat at one of these. You watch the couple behind the counter. You think they're married and you know neither is a stranger to sampling their wares. Cooking fish to order now the rush has died down, he's a big bloke, rugby player size, but he's gone over, muscle turned to fat and now so unfit he's a heart attack waiting to happen, the buttons of his shirt straining around the belly within. It's a hot job and he uses his lower arm to wipe his forehead, the dark hair that sticks up in front shiny from sweat, or grease.

The chips are ready and although nothing appears to pass between them, subliminally she knows when to start putting together the package. She's shorter than him and plump with huge breasts that are barely contained by the tee-shirt she wears and rest on the rounded stomach below. They jiggle as she puts together newspaper, greaseproof sheet and a bag to house about a third of the chips she's doling out and you try not to stare at what must be a main attraction around these parts, but you're largely unsuccessful. She calls over.

Salt and vinegar?

Just salt, thanks, you answer and you're on your feet and approaching the counter, keen to give your stomach something other than itself to digest. He's just laying the still sizzling battered fish on top, and you carry the whole lot back to your table.

It's quiet as they set about clearing up behind the counter, moving between that and a room that leads off to one side as they restock and prepare for later, and you concentrate on eating. This place is no frills and you eat out of the paper, using your fingers. You break off chunks of soft fish, firm white flakes visible inside the coating of crunchy salted batter. The chips are well done, the perfect combination of crisp outer shell and fluffy inner potato. You are ravenous and the delicious staple of many a diet disappears quickly. As you finish you lick your fingers and scrunch all the wrapping up into one ball. You check over the road to see that your security is still in place, pleased to find the minder is taking his responsibilities seriously.

Looking over at the counter, you see that although he has disappeared she is watching you so you get up

224

and wordlessly she holds out one hand for the rubbish while passing you a cleaning towel in a hermetically sealed package.

That was great, thanks, you say, as with greasy fingers you struggle to release the citrus scented cloth from its wrapper.

Yer welcome, she replies. Ain't seen you around 'ere before. She's curious and is seeking information which is just as well because so are you. You wipe your fingers thoroughly before throwing both the used cloth and its packaging into the bin near the door.

No, I'm looking for someone, you reply, then correct, actually I'm looking to find out about someone.

Oh yeah? She's immediately wary, you see it in her eyes, but though guarded her natural curiosity makes her ask, who's that then?

You don't answer directly but gesticulating upwards with your head you ask; do you own the flat upstairs? She nods.

I think someone I know may have lived there once.

Her interest is piqued, you see the change in her, the next word coming out almost as a whisper; Scarle'? You nod.

'Ow is she? She softens and there's a genuine warm feeling coming from this woman like she truly cares, and you're intrigued to find out more.

She's fine, you reassure, and you introduce yourself and tell her you're a friend of Scarlet's. You find out her name is Bet.

Could I ask you a few questions about her? And I'll have a coke please, you ask, and putting your hand in your pocket you pull out a handful of change, pick out the coins you need and put them on the counter as Bet turns to reach for the can from the upright fridge on the back wall. You've given her a moment to think and when she comes back she shrugs and says there's not much she can tell you.

Can you come and sit with me a minute? And you incline your head towards the table before heading back to your seat. After scooping the coins up and adding them to the contents of the till she lifts up the hinged section of the counter, leaning it back so it touches the wall and pushing the door below open she waddles through, and all at once you fear for the chair opposite you. It is plastic, it has arms and Bet's ample backside is going to be a challenge for it. She hesitates and clearly thinking better of her actions returns behind the counter. You think she has changed her mind about talking but she reappears with a stool which she places up against the table, plopping herself down on it with a wobble and a sigh of relief at the chance to rest her feet for a bit.

Wha' d' yer wanna know? She abrupt but doesn't appear unfriendly and you realise she's clearly someone who likes to get to the point.

What can you tell me about her? Did she live here long? Did she live here alone or with her family? She takes a deep breath and gazes upwards as if gathering her thoughts.

We took on this place abou' twenny years ago and they were tenants then, she recalls.

They? You prod.

Yeah, Scarle', 'er mum an' dad. Tho' 'e left, and she pauses, thinking for a moment, then shrugging continues, a few years later not sure exactly when but that poor kid weren't even ten. Terrible rows tho', we used to 'ear 'em, goin' at it, so I guess it weren't no surprise.

So then it was just Scarlet and her mother, you clarify, wondering if another man appeared on the scene.

Yeah, that's right but 'er muvva went right down 'ill after that. Never did nuffin' for the girl. Scarle' 'ad to do all the shoppin' an carin' for 'er.

That's very young to be caring for someone, you say.

Yeah, she never 'ad much in the way of shoppin' to carry neither. Couldn't afford much of anythin' I don't suppose.

How did they cope for money? you ask, it's really none of your business but you're intrigued as to how people survive in these situations.

Mostly got it from the state I suppose, an'— She stops, looking shifty, like she's uncomfortable about continuing.

Go on, you encourage.

Well, there was men, weren't there. Bit of a revolvin' door up there actually. Comin' and goin' a' all 'ours. We don' pry, she adds as clarification, as if all at once she's concerned you're judging her, and you shake your head in total sympathy hoping she'll continue. But the door's righ' there next to ours, she explains, pointing to the exit as if I might not be clear as to where it was, yer see it all.

So these were boyfriends? you seek to clarify, thinking that at least they would have helped out Maddy and her mother. But even as you think this you feel an unease creeping over you.

Bet shakes her head, no doubt at your naivety. None ever stuck around long enough to be a boyfriend, she says, and she gives you that look that nudges your thought process along a bit, until it clicks.

Ahh, her mother was a prostitute. Well I guess that must have brought them in a bit more money, you say, as you try to spin this into a positive, you know, people have to do whatever's needed to get by.

She nods before adding, yeah but she weren't no business woman. I got the feelin' she were paid more in booze an' fags, probably other stuff an' all, drugs an' that. The stuff Scarle' couldn't get for 'er. I doubt much money changed 'ands, and she pauses, a look of pain coming over her face.

What? you say, knowing immediately there is more.

Her voice drops to a whisper; we was worried for Scarle', we din't know what was goin' on up there an' hated the thought that... and she stops and looks away but not before you see the tears well in her eyes.

Oh my God! The penny drops and you feel the slow burn of fury, of acid, rising like bile, as revulsion turns your stomach. All you want to do in that moment is find Maddy, hold her tight and never let her go. You clear your throat.

So things never improved then? you ask, feebly hoping for an upturn in their fortunes.

Not judging by the state of that poor mite. We'd call Scarle' in sometimes, get 'er to sit down an' give 'er fish 'n' chips. Always ravenous she was, ain't never seen anyone demolish a servin' so quick, and she smiles at the memory.

That was kind of you, you say, though your heart is sinking at the poverty Maddy had endured. Now you understand her need to overstock on food. What happened as Scarlet grew up?

Bet stretches her pudgy arms out across the table before crossing them where they lie resting on her impressive chest. She sighs then sounds resigned as she carries on; she got the attention of the boys far too early, that's what 'appened. She were runnin' with the crowd around 'er and then took up with an older guy, she were only about fifteen, and she shakes her head in disapproval, her chins wobbling in unison.

This must be Tag, you think. Did you see much of him?

Nah, at least not then. He'd come an' stay for a bit, or pick 'er up, he 'ad a car an' all but never hung around.

When did you see him then?

What? She looks puzzled so you clarify.

You said you didn't see him then, so when did you?

Ah, yeah that was after. After she'd gone. He kept comin' round, got righ' bolshie an' all. Vince ended up havin' to have a word, know what I mean? Seemed to think we knew where she was. His name was weird an all, Tag, I think it were. Nasty piece.

At that point the man you thought was Bet's other half shuffles back through from the another room to behind the counter, and Bet looks over. He doesn't appear surprised to see her sitting the wrong side, and with a strange man.

Vince, she says, Dan here is asking about Scarle'.

Oh yeah, nice kid she were, at least mostly, shame about the mother, he replies.

Yeah, I've told 'im all about ''er. What else d'you remember about Scarle' tho'?

She did a runner, I know that much, Vince says. Bugger, you hadn't thought about that possibility and you feel you should offer to make amends.

I'm sorry to hear that, you say and you reach for your wallet. How much did she owe?

Oh, no, no, no, nothing like that, Vince replies, like I said she were a good kid, not like that waster of a mother of hers. Scarle' paid everything up to date plus she left us with three months an' she didn't need to. Her note said she was off an' asked us not to say nuffin about it to that bloke of 'ers. An' we never did. No, what I meant was that she never said a word, did she,

Bet? One day she was 'ere right as rain and the next, gawn. Never said a word.

And her mother went too, I assume? you say.

Oh no! says Bet. 'Er mother was dead well before then. Dreadful business that were.

What happened? you ask, as you're reminded yet again of Maddy's really shit start in life.

Well she killed herself, didn't she! Right up there, and she points to the ceiling. Poor Scarle' was the one what found 'er. You close your eyes briefly and wonder if this could get any worse. But Bet's in full flow now and you don't want to interrupt.

Scarle' weren't at school no more, she was earning a bit of money somewhere or other and had started to smarten 'erself right up. But she came 'ome one day and found 'er dead. She'd OD'd, we was told. Scarle' came right down 'ere to wait for the ambulance. Sat where you are now and she's rocking in shock like and saying over and over how she'd done it for 'er. I didn't understand at all till later. Bet stops as if that is the end of the story.

And? you question, then at Bet's bemused expression you say, what did you understand later?

Well, it were the date weren't it? She'd only gone and killed herself on Scarlet's eighteenth birthday.

Jesus Christ! Happy bloody birthday!

You're quiet for a moment, thinking this over, then it dawns on you. Scarlet was an adult, she could take on the rent of the flat and not face having to go into child services. You voice these thoughts to Bet, who nods in agreement.

It were like she were just biding her time, she adds, which sends a shiver down your back.

Scarle' carried on as our tenant for another couple of years, Vince confirms, having remained silent throughout Bet's explanation. *We ain't let it since though, keep it for storage now. You imagine therefore that probably not much has changed in it since she lived there.*

You think your time is about done here, and as you ask Vince to make up another serving of fish and chips you thank them for their time. You had intended on asking if you could go and have a look at the flat but now you feel you've intruded enough into Maddy's past and the thought of gazing upon the place where she barely got to be a child feels like a step too far.

Where's she livin' now? Bet enquires, and that has you thinking for a moment. You don't think it's for you to share and you don't know who else might be keen on gaining that information around here.

I can't tell you that, I'm afraid, I don't think she'd want me to for fear of Tag catching up with her, you reply. She's not to know he already has, you think. I can tell you, you continue, that she's happy and settled, living in a small village.

Good for 'er, Bet smiles and seems satisfied. If you get the chance pass on our love to 'er.

I will do, you promise as you hand over the money for the takeaway.

Your security watches as you cross the road, and pushing himself off the wall he walks towards you so you meet at the kerb. You hand him the package and his face drops.

I can't be paid in chips, mister, he says, and you wonder what he wants the cash for.

Of course not, you confirm as you reach for your wallet and take out a tenner. Here you go.

Fanks! His face brightens, an' fer this. He indicates towards the aromatic parcel in his hand. I'm bloody starvin'.

Chapter 23

I'm home when Dan calls; he's just got back and asks if he can see me. I'm shattered and say I'm planning an early night which he says fits in with him perfectly. Part of me wants to keep him away, just in case Tag comes round, although I know that's less likely now we've met and I know what he wants, but I have no idea how I do this without him getting hurt, or suspicious as to my motives. So I give into the other part, the larger part that wants to welcome him with open arms and longs to feel safe in his warm embrace.

He arrives within twenty minutes, by which time I've hidden my knife under the mattress, and once he's in I bolt the door behind him. He doesn't comment on this and as he's brought beer and neither of us appears to want to talk much about our day, we crack open a couple of cans, curl up on the sofa and watch the television as happy with the silences between us as when we chat. I enjoy the evening and it crosses my mind that this is what other people take for granted when they are seeing someone, and I wonder if I can do this, if I can have a normal relationship. I'm not sure what one of those even looks like but I hope we have the chance to find out together. As promised we go to bed early and when I eventually get to go to sleep I do it soundly, due both to the exhaustion of the last couple of days and the presence of Dan. I could get used to this, although even as I think that I feel my stress levels rising with the worry of how to make sure Tag doesn't ruin it for me.

When I wake it's to a surge of anxiety for the day ahead. The jewellery is arriving at Danewright Hall on Friday, and will be on display in the library from

Saturday. I plan to try to steal it Saturday night but because of Tag's appearance I'm already eaten up with nerves, and it's only Wednesday. I try to cover but Dan notices I don't eat and makes some comment about exercising on an empty stomach, so to mollify him I grab a bagel on the way out, but it lies uneaten on my passenger seat as I drive to Hartleigh. I skip going to Sidney's, wanting to keep close to Dan to try to ensure there's no opportunity for Tag to make an appearance and be alone with him. Both of us do our workouts and I spend much of my time looking through the glass window trying to catch first sight of Tag so I can head him off, but there is no sign of him. By the time I'm finished I'm tense and so on edge I know I can't go on like this.

Dan insists on us having an early lunch in the café and I sit and tune out the chattering women around me for whom this is a social occasion. I can feel Dan watching me and he asks if I'm alright and I tell him I'm anxious about the weekend. I'm not sure he believes me and I don't meet his eyes for fear he will see straight through me, so I make a decision and say,

"Actually, would it be alright if I didn't see you again until this job is over?" His eyebrows rise in surprise and I'm quick to continue, "This is great," and I indicate by moving my hand back and forth to whatever it is between us, "I'm loving spending time with you but it's distracting me and I need to have my mind in the game."

"Oh," and his expression darkens as he says, "are you sure that's necessary?"

"It'll only be until Sunday," I clarify, as small frown lines gather between his eyes.

"We've only just started seeing each other, Maddy. I want to be with you more, not less." I feel a slight flare of irritation that he's questioning my decision.

233

"This is business, Dan, I need to be able to concentrate," I say, and I'm as direct as I can be without, I hope, coming across as too arsy.

He hesitates for a moment then says, "Okay, whatever you want." He sounds resigned and while it's not quite the level of enthusiasm I was hoping for I guess it's going to have to do. An awkward silence descends which eventually I have to break.

"You will be okay, won't you?"

"I'm sure I shall survive, Maddy." The sarcastic edge to his response is obvious. "You just look after yourself."

"I will," I say as I smile, hoping to reassure him. "I just need a bit of space to get some things sorted out."

"Understood." He looks at me strangely, then adds, "but you will call me if you need anything, anything at all, won't you?" I nod, and the feeling of relief this decision has given me tells me it was the right thing to do and allows me to pick at the salad in front of me, much to Dan's approval.

When I walk back to my car I see the word *Slut* has been written in the dust across the boot and bonnet.

Nice.

"Tag?" Dan questions but I shake my head, he wouldn't be that petty, besides I know he wants to get me onside, not annoy me further. As I clean it off, using a tissue dragged from the depths of my bag, I indicate across to Mike's place. There's only one person I suspect. Dan is all for going over there but I say no, I'm not about to take the bait and although my middle finger is itching to rise in that direction I won't dignify this childishness with a reaction.

We go our separate ways a short while later, and even though it is my decision I hate saying goodbye, holding on to him for far longer than is strictly necessary, my spirits dropping when eventually I reluctantly let go but deep down I know I'm doing what's needed. I have a basic plan that requires me to stay focused. Do what I have to do, get Tag to go home and then get back on track with this relationship. And with a plan as watertight as that, what could possibly go wrong?

Well, the first thing that does is that I run into Letitia. I pop into the village shop and there she is, her long dark hair pulled back in to a jaunty ponytail that bounces as she clip-clops around in her high heels, and she pounces on me the moment she spots me.

"Oh wow! I'm glad I've seen you, it'll save me a call later. Friday at eight, alright?"

"Alright for what?" I'm bewildered as to what she is talking about.

"For you to come round and meet Tim of course, your blind date," she clarifies and she does some sort of weird shimmy thing with her shoulders at that point and appears to be terribly excited about the whole thing. *Tim?* I had forgotten every word about it and honestly can't think of any more horrific way to spend an evening. I'm on the verge of telling her about Dan and cancelling the 'date' but something stops me, an evil little something that can't help but cause mischief, and this opportunity, a golden one at that, is, after all, being handed to me on a plate.

"Sorry, I'd forgotten all about that. Yes, absolutely, that would be fine, thanks." As she positively preens at my enthusiasm, I continue, "Actually I saw Ben, in Hartleigh, just the other day."

"I doubt that very much. Why would he need to go to that dreary little town when his offices are in the city?"

Why indeed, Letitia?

"Maybe I was mistaken then; maybe someone else has the same blue jacket."

235

"Oh I don't think so! That was bespoke, Savile Row you know."

I do know, Letitia.

But I shrug, conscious I should remain all laid back with the seeds I am planting.

"Perhaps it was just a similar jacket then, I didn't see him to speak to. I was in the pub on Market Square and I saw him out of the window."

"Where was he going?" I can feel her, her weight on my line, well and truly hooked and unable to resist asking.

"To The Cromwell, I daresay they were going to a meeting."

"Yes, of course," and she's nodding her head as if that will strengthen the lack of conviction I hear in her words. "He wasn't alone then?" Any feeble grasping at the tendrils of hope this question contains are dispelled as I say,

"No." I leave it at that but do actually feel bad as I see her face fall, the doubt and insecurity I have caused obvious. I've given her something to think about, but now question if I should have done, because for the first time I feel a little twist of discomfort for my nemesis and wonder if perhaps Diane was right about her after all. However, I'm still irked by the fact I let the Mehew situation go unexposed and sensing an opening to reveal a wrong being done, I've jumped right in. I mean, I'd want to know, wouldn't you? "Do you need me to bring anything on Friday?" I say, which shakes her out of her thoughts, and she pastes on that smile again and says no, I needn't bring anything. But the smile doesn't reach her eyes and I see the concern I've raised etched there instead. I was merely hoping to get the chance to watch Ben squirm a little on Friday but now I'm rather wishing I hadn't brought the subject up.

On Thursday Mike is in the gym when I get there, which I could do without. He glowers at me, his face sullen and although I ignore him his anger affects the atmosphere, and my mood. I hope he goes back to work and his strict routine soon. However, it's not just him that's affecting me. My background here has tarnished the way I feel about the place now and I decide I'm going to have to change gyms. I'll start looking for a new one after the weekend. This decision only serves to make me grumpier, my session failing to give me the usual post exercise buzz.

I see Dan, briefly, just as I'm leaving the gym; he's not going in he tells me, he was just passing and by some happy chance saw my car, which is thankfully graffiti free today. We chat for a short while sitting in the front seat of my car, the moment only ruined by Mike walking past and giving us a filthy look.

Thankfully, however, there is no sign of Tag popping up anywhere in my life and I start to allow myself the briefest daydream that he did, in fact, believe what I said and has decided to have nothing to do with the De Havilland display. But the minute I think that I dismiss it from my mind – that is exactly what he wants me to think. I know he will be lulling me into a false sense of security so I keep alert, and then find myself checking around so often I must look like I have some sort of nervous tick and that will not do at all. I don't want him to see I'm affected in any way by his presence so I take deep breaths and force myself to at least give the outward appearance of being relaxed.

I've got Dan, mostly, out of the way so there's less chance of Tag getting to him which solves one problem. Although on the nights without Dan I've been strangely lonely, despite our lengthy phone chats. I've also been half-hoping Cat would put in an appearance, however it seems my hour of need is not desperate enough as there's no sign of him and I simply get through the hours anxious for the weekend to roll round so I can get all of this over with.

At long last it's the end of the week and I wake with a start. After days of relative inactivity, I now feel like I have a lot to do and I set off in a great burst of energy but find myself unexpectedly halted in front of Sidney's. It's barely got light so far today, but I stand, oblivious to the icy drizzle that's falling, the ash cloud sky setting the tone for the news I read in the window.

Closed due to death.

It's brutal in its brevity. A handwritten scrawl on a scrappy piece of paper stuck to the inside of the door with a ragged length of tape and little love. I haven't called in over the last couple of days so have no idea when this happened, but I'm inexplicably saddened by it even though I barely knew him. I may be jumping to an assumption that it's Sidney of course, I guess it could be he who's been bereaved but I believe if it was he wouldn't have even bothered with the sign, he'd have merely not opened. I wonder who did put the notice up, and I peer through the window to see the ghostly outline of the counter and sweet stand in the shadows, but no sign of anyone. The town won't see his like again, that I do know, and if this place ever reopens it will no doubt have been sanitised and changed beyond all recognition, which is probably just as well. I think back to my last visit, the only time Sidney ever spoke to me and the fact he did so because he noticed something was wrong. I wish now I'd made more of the opportunity. I get back in my car, close my eyes and try to recreate the memories the shop interior sparked, then I shake my head and wonder why I'm doing that. It hardly recalls a happy time.

Putting this setback behind me, because I can't afford to dwell on it right now, I get on with my day and keep a careful lookout as I do, purely so I'm as prepared as I can be for Tag's next appearance. I know he'll only surface when he wants to but time is getting short so if it's going to happen it's going to be soon.

I'm tense when I see Mike walking across to the leisure centre as I drive into the car park. I consider leaving but something in me rails against giving in so I proceed as usual. He does nothing more than give me the evils, and reminding myself that I'm the one who hurt him I put up with it, knowing a change of gyms will put all this behind me.

Conversely I'm missing seeing Dan, although realise that's my own fault as he's only heeding my request and keeping away but I am surprised when Steve, on a break between clients, comments on his absence.

"Where's your boyfriend gone then? You two haven't had a tiff already?"

I'm about to retort that he isn't my boyfriend but stop myself. I hadn't thought about him in those terms and I'm not sure what he is yet although it seems those here have put two and two together.

"He's working, but he'll be back." He puts a hand on my shoulder and gives it a little squeeze.

"I'm happy for you, Maddy."

"Thanks." I feel unexpectedly emotional and turn away, not wanting him to clock my reaction. But the thought has been planted in my mind and I realise how much I do want to be able to call Dan my boyfriend. I want that, and him and everything that goes with it.

I'm still distracted by my charitable thoughts towards Steve when I leave the gym a while later, but I'm jerked back to reality when I see Tag leaning up against my car. There's a sinking feeling deep in the pit of my stomach but knowing I have no option other than to see this through when he says, "Follow me," I do.

We drive back to the Market Square, and go into the same pub, and the same booth. He orders a pint for himself and a diet coke for me, but no food. He comes to join me but I haven't forgotten what happened the last time and, not wanting things to escalate between us, when he tries to pick up where he left off and sit next to me I tell him this is business and indicate the bench opposite. He pauses for a moment, I think a little surprised by my stand, and I wait patiently until he sees sense. He's serious when it comes to work and I know he won't jeopardise that by making an unnecessary fuss, and it gives me some time to collect myself.

Once he sits he takes a quick sip from his pint and doesn't waste any time in getting to the point. "So when are you hitting the House?" There's going to be no dissuading him, I know that, so I come clean.

"Sunday morning, 0300 hours." There's no one around who could possibly overhear but I keep my voice low anyway and there's a satisfied smile on his lips as he acknowledges the fact he was right all along.

"I'm coming with you."

"No you're not." His eyes widen at my immediate response but I'm adamant, there is no way he is taking this over, there are certain things I will not do and I need to make it very clear that I am in charge here. My thinking is that the more positive and determined I am, the more he will believe I am totally on board with him being involved at all. I can see he's about to argue and I hold up one hand. "I'm running this show, Tag, and this is the way it's going to work. We will travel separately. I will be leaving my car in the layby outside Danewright village. You will have to leave yours somewhere else as I don't want them parked up together." I look at him, raising my eyebrows in question.

"That's fine, I've found a gateway the other side of the estate." I nod, satisfied.

"We each make our way up to the House and we'll meet in the woods behind the car park to the rear. If you line up the horse chestnut tree at the end with the entrance to the walled garden, we'll find each other directly behind there.

"It's a full moon. There's a chance of showers early in the evening but then the temperature is dropping and the sky should be clear."

"Noted," he murmurs.

"If one of us gets caught, there's no ratting out the other, obviously."

"Obviously," he repeats, a little too sarcastically for my liking.

"And if you're late, I will go ahead without you."

"I wouldn't expect anythin' else." He grins at me in a way I choose to ignore. "Do you have a plan of entry?" His forearms rest on the table between us, his hands linked together. There's a pulse running through the glass in front of me, a slight tremor across the surface of the liquid and I realise it's the relentless beat of his leg jittering under the table. Unlike the Tag I remember, he's jumpy, and I wonder why.

"Of course. You?" He nods. "Do you want to share?" I lean forward in anticipation.

"No chance." I'm disappointed, but not surprised, I'd have liked a heads up but it was probably asking too much. Tag and I had always had different methods of approach and I dread to think what he has come up with. But there is no way I'm going to give him any of

241

my details so it's only to be expected he feels the same. I've already decided to play it by ear on the night anyway, and I'll be quite prepared to go along with his plan if it helps cement my cooperation in his mind. I need him to be totally happy with everything in the hope he'll then be satisfied and leave me alone, and I try to convince myself I'm not being completely naïve.

"This is great, isn't it?" His words bring me out of my brief reverie.

"What?"

"This," and he waves a hand casually between the two of us, "us, working together again." *No, it's really not*, I think, but not wishing to antagonise him say,

"Yep, I guess it is." But I'm dismissive, I don't want to get into conversation, I don't want to be friends with him so I drain my drink then excuse myself with a visit to the ladies after which, with our business being finished, I intend on walking straight out. I'm being deliberately cool and standoffish, sending a clear message for him to keep his distance.

However, when I come out of the cubicle he's waiting. Leaning up against the counter top opposite, his arms are crossed, his face serious.

"You can't be in here," I say.

"Why not, there's no one else likely to come in."

That was a true enough though concerning thought, his presence making an already small room claustrophobic as I mutter, "What do you want?" and move across to the one basin he's not blocking to wash my hands.

"I would have thought that was obvious." I don't react as I reach for a paper towel the other side of him and feel his hands on my waist as I do. I try to pull away, to not make anything of it as I drop the scrunched up towel into the bin, but he stands and pulls me closer so we're face to face. He turns, pushing me

242

so my back is to the wall and as he moves nearer I can feel the heat of him through my clothes, his hardness pressing into me, his body fitting to mine. His head is tilted, and as I feel his lips soft against my collarbone then trailing across my skin it's as though the years have been swept away. Mist-like delirium takes over and I gasp as my once-upon-a-time obsession's hot kisses send molten messages firing through my body, and my hands come up to his face, my fingers tangling through his hair as his lips find mine. His tongue is ardent and seeking as his hand slips into the waistband of my trousers. And I'm lost. I didn't want him to touch me and this is why, this animalistic response I have to him, that I've always had and I'm tumbling back in time to a place where our loving was fierce and fevered, where torrid nights melded into carnal days. "You are mine," he murmurs against my lips, his hand crushing my breast through my shirt as he reaches for the button on my trousers. And again I'm taken back to when I ached to be around him, to when I couldn't get enough of him, to when I longed for him to say those words. But that was then, and it has been too hard and taken too long to break free to go back there now. A pair of kind eyes, soft and grey appear in my mind. *No! I'm not yours*, I think, and brought back into the moment, back into the reality of my situation, of everything I could lose, I react and push his hand away.

"No!" I say.

"Oh come on," he says, his voice rough, his lips hard against mine again, his insistence growing. I wrap both hands into his hair, and gripping tightly I pull his head away from me.

"I said, no!" And with space between us I plant both hands on his chest and push him hard, quite prepared to take further action should it be necessary. He takes a step backwards and stands glaring at me; his breathing is heavy and I can sense the fury in him, his clenched fists at his sides as he battles for control.

I take a deep calming breath before saying, "I am no longer yours, Tag."

"Coulda fooled me," is his cocky response at my shameful rising to him, "You just din't wanna do it in 'ere. Too down an' dirty for yer now."

"I don't want to do it anywhere with you, Tag."

"Yeah, well we'll see about that." The threatening undercurrent is not lost on me but I don't dignify it with a response, my only interest for the moment being to get out of here.

"I'm leaving," I say as I fling open the door.

"Wait for me," he calls, and as I walk straight through the bar I can feel him directly behind me. I'm confused and flustered by my reaction to him and just want to get away, but once out on the street he's at my side and, as if we're some loving young couple whiling away an afternoon with a relaxing drink before a carefree walk about town, he slings an arm around my shoulder and draws me to him, his normal persona back in place. I'm surprised but then less so as I look up and see Dan and know it's all for show. He's leaning up against the railings that run alongside the town hall, and just as I wonder what he's doing there I realise the answer's obvious, he's seen our cars parked side by side in the Market Square. I glance up, see the grin adorning Tag's face as if he's scored some kind of victory and can't bear to look at the hurt on Dan's.

As I try to move away Tag pulls me closer, planting a kiss on my temple as a goodbye. Then he allows me to go, drawing his arm away as if separating is his idea before calling out a cheery goodbye as he climbs into his car and leaves.

I'm left standing by mine, although I still have things to do before I get to go home. First I have to face

Dan who, now I'm alone, strides over. I can hardly raise my eyes to look at him, ashamed at my reaction to Tag, at how quick I was to fall back into his arms, at how close I'd come to surrendering. My guilt is running as deep as if I had.

It's spitting with rain and he's standing in front of me. I look up, hating to see the pain on his face as he no doubt registers the discomfort on mine, but there's something else there and it's barely contained as he says, "What the fuck are you playing at?"

"I'm playing at nothing. *That* wasn't what it looked like," I respond, defensively in the face of his anger.

"Really? So you haven't been having a jolly old time of it with your ex in the pub then?"

"No, I haven't. We were…," and I peter out, I can't tell him of my plans, of how Tag and I are involved, so end, "we were just talking, that's all." Which sounds as unconvincing out loud as it did in my head.

"Is that why you wanted me to keep away? I thought it was so you could get this job done but did you just want to take up with your old flame for a bit?" I don't appreciate the accusation and am irritated that he's not listening, but it's the guilt that makes me snap.

"But that's the point, isn't it? You haven't kept away. If you'd done as I asked, we wouldn't be having this row." My voice is raised, there are others in the Square that can hear us but his is no quieter when he responds.

"I've done my best, Maddy, and if it was only about the work that would be fine but it's him, I don't trust him and I can't protect you at a distance."

"I don't need protecting, not from Tag. I know him."

"You know nothing. He wants you, plain and simple." He looks away, his jaw clenching and unclenching as he wrestles with what to say next. He looks back at me, his voice quieter now. "I know it's early days, but I thought we had something."

"We did… we do," I hastily correct myself, "please, Dan, give me some space to sort this out." His exhale is an expression of frustration.

"Sunday?" he says, this one word loaded with finality.

"Sunday," and I hope I'll be able to stick to that. He gazes at me a moment before reaching a conclusion on how to proceed.

"And you'll keep away from him?" I want to argue his right to ask this of me, although I can hardly blame him, but it's only going to exacerbate the situation so I choose my battle. He's deadly serious so I say what I need to in order to bring this to a close.

"Okay," I lie, and hate myself as I do. Because it's not, it's not okay at all. He's not wrong, Tag does want me, I know that, but I equally know that I'm determined that today is where it ends. I feel bad enough for what has already occurred between us and it's going no further because for the first time I'm experiencing a feeling that I've not felt before. I know Dan is enough, and I know that he is all I want.

But then he walks away, hands deep in the pockets of his coat, and I feel bereft. I could have done with a hug, a kiss goodbye, a kind word, but this treatment is exactly what I deserve and he makes me feel it, every step.

With a sigh I head off across the Square and around the corner to the offices of Watson & Grove. I say hello to Helen as I enter and ask if Cubby is free. She calls through to him then tells me to go right in.

He's frowning, his brow furrowed with concern and as I enter his office he's already coming across the room to greet me. "Is everything alright, Madeleine?"

246

I know he would have called me later, if he hadn't seen me, to check I was all set for the weekend.

"Everything's fine. I was in town so thought I'd drop in and let you know I'm ready." His expression softens and he exhales.

"That's fine, for one moment I thought you had a problem."

"Not at all," I reply, and I sound so positive I almost convince myself.

"Dan's out, I'm afraid, he's off seeing a client."

"I didn't come here to see him." My reply sounds curt, even to my ears and, judging by his response, to Cubby's too.

"Okay," he says, and he holds his hands up defensively as he draws this one word out in that way that gives me the distinct feeling he knows more than I think he does, but I don't want to dwell on that so get to the purpose of my visit.

"There is one small thing you could help me with?" He looks at me sharply.

"What?"

"Could I have access to the safe please? I need to borrow something." I try to keep it light, nonchalant, and as though I don't have a care in the world. I meet his piercing gaze and don't look away for a second. There's a long pause while he considers the implications of my request and then he says,

"Should I ask?"

"I'd rather you didn't." I accompany that with a shake of my head as he reaches for the keys.

Chapter 24

I leave the office; the rain is no worse but I wrap my coat around my body against the cold wind. As I turn the corner back towards the Market Square I find myself in the direct path of Ben Pritchard, and he is not alone. We spot each other at the same time, but other than loosen his arm from around the waist of the woman with the tumbling blonde hair he does nothing to divert from the trajectory we are on. We meet almost directly in front of the imposing entrance to The Cromwell.

"Maddy, fancy bumping into you," he exclaims, as if he's actually pleased to see me.

"My offices are only around the corner," and I indicate over my shoulder with my thumb, "but I thought yours were in the city?"

"They are, we're..." and he glances at his companion, "we're here for a meeting," and he gesticulates towards the hotel.

"Of course, I have heard that there is a dreadful lack of places to meet in the city." I give a wry smile and turn to look most pointedly at his friend, and she smiles rather nervously at me as I finish, "I don't think we've met?"

"Um, Maddy this is, erm, Purity, my secretary." Ben clears his throat as I reach out to shake her hand, while curbing my smile. Undoubtedly misnamed, she's pretty in a painted face sort of way, the makeup is layered thickly but it doesn't disguise the fact I doubt she's yet made it into her third decade. More surprising though is what she considers to be appropriate office apparel. With stripper heels ideally suited to swinging round a pole at a nightclub and a skirt little more than a belt, her top plunges so daringly low that an edge of lace is all that's sparing the blushes of her nipples.

"I bet he's a hard taskmaster isn't he?" I smile at her, "keeps you at it day and night, no doubt." She looks awkward, as if she doesn't know how to respond, or given that she hasn't uttered a sound so far perhaps she is actually mute, and she looks at Ben for reassurance. I look at him too.

"Oh I think I'm pretty fair, Maddy," he says.

"I'm sure you are, well I must be off, things to do." I can sense his relief that I'm going and delight in delivering my parting shot; "it's been lovely meeting you, Purity, and I shall look forward to seeing you later, Ben, when I believe I'm meeting another of your work colleagues." His smile is as forced as mine is wide as I walk away, and I glance back once to see them disappearing through the hotel doors, but as I approach my car my discomfort for Letitia turns into a rush of sympathy. For all she has materially, she has absolutely nothing at all by way of a solid marriage with a faithful partner, and all at once I can understand what Diane had meant about her lacking self-esteem and feeling insecure. Once upon a time Letitia had been that secretary.

Wasn't it Oscar Wilde who'd said that when a man marries his mistress he creates a vacancy? I bet Letitia has suspected for a while, how could you not, in fact how could you ever feel comfortable in a relationship that started the way theirs did?

I sit for a moment in my car and ponder on what she would do if she were to be given proof of his infidelity. Mr Mehew's cavalier treatment of his wife still rankles with me and I'd taken no action there but this time I am in a different position. Putting my dislike for Letitia to one side, I decide that although I think she is weak and one of those wives who'll turn a blind eye for the sake of house and lifestyle, I feel I should give her the chance to prove me wrong and take charge of her future. So I get back out of the car and go to book a room at the hotel. With it hardly being the type of place that charges by the hour I am still reeling at the cost of it for a night when I am eventually driving out of Hartleigh. Ben was certainly splashing out some serious lolly on the tight-lipped Purity, which might well mean that Letitia's days are numbered anyway.

But although what I plan to do might give her the leverage she needs to secure her future, I wouldn't lay a bet on whether she'll choose to use it.

On my journey home my thoughts wander, and in an attempt to keep them away from the sadness I felt when Dan walked away from me, I allow them to drift back to my earlier encounter with Tag. I'm embarrassed by my lack of self-control with him but concerned at the anger he showed then so carefully covered up. I'd not seen this in my previous life with him, at least not directed at me, but then again I'd never said no to him before either.

I knock on the door of the Pritchards' place shortly after eight to be greeted by two flat-coated retrievers and an anxious Letitia, and find I'm the first to arrive.

"Hi," she says in greeting. *What?* No *wow!* This is not the Letitia I know and detest, and that bothers me. She assures me Ben will be home any minute, but I am nowhere near as worried by his absence as I am at having to make small talk with her until someone else arrives. The dogs take an avid interest in giving me a good sniff as Letitia leads me through to her massive kitchen, which has an island in the middle of it that I suspect covers roughly the same area as my entire kitchen. I ask if I can do anything to help, and as she is just finishing slicing some bread she asks if I could get the platter from the fridge in the utility. The dogs follow me out to what is obviously the area they sleep in and I take the opportunity to have a look around it. I retrieve the largest plate I've ever seen from the fridge, take it back into the kitchen and put it on the island. Taking a seat on a high bar stool on the far side to Letitia, I watch as she reaches for a glass for me. I see hers is already in use and I wonder how long ago she started. Fortunately, she has only just handed me my glass of red when we hear tyres on the gravel drive and Ben bowls in through the back door moments later, followed by another man with product-packed hair and a precisely-manicured beard.

"Sorry I'm late, darling, work can be such a bore," he says, and as he leans in to peck Letitia on the cheek I notice he's in the same clothes as earlier and wonder if he's washed the delectable Purity off himself. My question is answered moments later when he crosses to me and does the two-kiss thing in welcome. He smells body wash fresh from the shower, and I glance at Letitia. She's staring at him and from the look on her face this has not gone unnoticed with her either. He turns swiftly away from me and says, "Tim, you've met my wife before haven't you?"

Tim nods and says, "Of course I have. Letitia, it's lovely to see you again, and thank you for inviting me round." He smiles. "I'm sorry I was a little late, I got to the village but then couldn't find your place."

"I told you to head for the biggest house, Tim, or didn't you believe me?" Ben's laugh is loud as he slaps Tim on the back and without allowing him to reply he carries on, "and here is the purpose of you coming round to Letitia's matchmaking evening, this is Maddy." I inwardly cringe and see a flash of something I can't quite fathom cross Tim's face as he reaches for my hand and we shake briefly.

"Nice to meet you, Tim," I say, and I watch him for a moment as his attention goes back to Ben who asks him what he wants to drink. I smile to myself as I recognise the nervousness of someone else living a lie. Though how Ben and Letitia can't see it I don't know. My one concern in coming here this evening had been the possibility of meeting someone who might be attracted to me when in fact because of Dan, and excluding my disgraceful display with Tag earlier, I now consider myself unavailable. As that was the reason for the evening, I would therefore be here under false pretences. However, that worry is washed away as I watch the way Tim's eyes follow Ben around the room and know immediately that his interests are not going to lie with me. It's a relief because I can now focus on my task for the evening.

"I'm surprised you got lost, Tim, seeing as you both came straight from work," Letitia says, "I thought you would have followed Ben here anyway." She's probing. I like that. Her suspicion is growing roots.

"Oh, no," Tim says as his eyes flick towards Ben, "Ben wasn't in the office this afternoon," and he stops abruptly, as if realising he's said something perhaps he shouldn't. Letitia turns sharply towards Ben as Tim tries again. "He was out at a meeting." But having nothing to add to this rather feeble sounding excuse for an explanation, he reaches for his drink instead and takes a large gulp.

"I saw him actually, Letitia," I offer, grinning inwardly at having the opportunity, "I met him just going into The Cromwell for it. Didn't I, Ben?" I look over at him and he nods then uses the contents of the glass in his hand as a tool to prevent him having to reply immediately.

"That's right, we had a quick chat about this evening, didn't we?" he says when his mouth is free. I ignore the question and before Letitia turns to look at him his eyes flash a warning in my direction, then as soon as her back is to me I exaggerate the drawing of my finger and thumb zip-like across my lips as if I'm about to heed it. I glance over at Tim, whose facial expression is showing his bewilderment at what is going on around him, and at that point I push the platter covered with all sorts of tasty looking things, as well as olives, in his direction.

"You alright there, Tim? Here, have a nibble." He reaches out for a smoked salmon topped something or other and having impeccable manners is quick to tell Letitia how delicious it is. This distracts her from Ben for a moment and for a little while the conversation flows perfectly normally, and I play my part as I think about the hotel receipt currently nestling in my pocket and wonder how I'm going execute my plan for the evening.

I'll give him one thing, Ben is a good host and only too happy to refill everyone's glass just as often as he does his own. Tim only has the one as he's driving but mine and Letitia's he keeps returning to, and before I know it I'm giggling and having a jolly old time of it. Ben has moved closer to me now and as I'm feeling warm, and more than a little fuzzy, from all the alcohol I'm amazed he's still wearing his blue checked jacket. He's chatting, laughing, telling a joke and as he fills my glass again he's close, far too close, and he leans into me and unobserved by the others he runs his hand down my back until it's resting right where it shouldn't be. I ignore this, behaving as though it is perfectly acceptable and as he gets to the punchline and we laugh I'm louder than I should be, and as I go to bat him away as if he is just too funny for words, I've forgotten my glass is in that hand, ditz that I am, and moments later he has red wine dripping down the front of his jacket, and soaking into his shirt...clumsy of me, I know, but at least he's removed his hand from my backside.

I gasp, my free hand coming up to my mouth in horror at what I've done and amid profuse apologies I offer to clean up the spillage, to pay for the dry cleaning. I feel a fool but that's all brushed aside, of course, as these things are in polite company and then his jacket is on the side, his shirt sponged down and it's back to the business of drinking. And now I have done what was needed, I slow down on that.

I try to get the conversation back on track as I ask what everyone is doing over the weekend.

"I have to work tomorrow, it's a busy day for us," says Tim, and Ben confirms that he'll be in the office as well.

"I'm off to a horse show," says Letitia and from the way she's smiling I can see she's looking forward to it.

"I didn't realise you had your own horse," I say.

"I don't but at the stables I go to you can hire one of theirs for the day, so a few of us get together and they then fill a lorry and get the horses there and back. It's a lot of fun."

"Letitia does love to keep herself busy, don't you, darling," Ben chipped in and it doesn't surprise me, anything to keep her thoughts away from what was going on in her life, I imagine.

"So what do you do with the dogs then? I presume you can't leave them in all day?"

"Oh Mrs Tompkins comes round and lets them out," she says as she waves her hand vaguely in the direction of Mrs Tompkins's cottage next door, "and they'll get walked early and late so they'll be fine."

"That's handy then, having her on your doorstep."

"It is indeed, now come on, everyone, please eat up," and with Letitia's change of direction we all concentrate on the food for a while.

The evening winds up a little later; it's still reasonably early but as everyone has a busy day tomorrow it suits us all.

Amongst all the alcohol and chatter the supposed purpose of the evening seems to have passed Letitia by, a result of her mind being elsewhere no doubt, so I'm glad to escape without her asking any probing questions about whether or not I want to see Tim again. We all say our goodbyes at the door, our breath visible in the air of what is already a chilly night. Although Tim offers me a lift home, I make the excuse that I could do with the walk to clear my head. I thrust my hands into my pockets and hunch my shoulders up against the cold as I walk off up the drive. I can hear Tim getting into his car behind me and he's soon following me out, raising his hand and smiling as he passes. I feel it's unlikely we shall be meeting again.

Despite earlier appearances I am more than capable of holding my liquor, so there is not much head clearing to do, but I use the walk to wind down and calm my thoughts so that by the time I get home I have a quick run through of all my plans for the next day and then go to bed.

It's only when I'm lying there that I realise Dan hasn't called this evening, and I wonder if this is it, if the fade away starts here. After what happened today I could hardly blame him but it saddens me. We didn't exactly kiss and make up after our row and I contemplate calling him for a chat but, still embarrassed, end up sending him a quick goodnight text and get one a short while later wishing me sweet dreams. As he's not here, those are unlikely and the loneliness I feel in his absence only accentuates how much I miss and want to be with him.

Chapter 25

Unsurprisingly I don't have a good night, only falling into a restful slumber approaching the time when I should have been getting up and therefore I oversleep, which I hate doing. I try to get back on track by telling myself I don't have that much to do during the day and I will have plenty of time to prepare for the long night ahead of me. But it's more than purely the oversleeping that's making me rattled. It was this business with Tag. I'm not convinced I'm going to manage to pull off what I was planning. It's a tricky job anyway and I know Tag's involvement is only likely to jeopardise my reputation, future employment, and any possible relationship with Dan but I can't see any other way out. I could come clean to Cubby and Dan but I don't want my past to catch up with what I hope is going to be my future and I specifically don't want Dan to know anything about my murky background. Somehow I have to satisfy Tag and get him to go back to the life he is more familiar with and I can't allow myself to think about the fact he may not be happy to leave. That is an outcome I simply can't contemplate.

I have a whole day to get through before the main event though, and first I have to tackle the second, and final, phase of what I have come to call Operation Free Letitia, because I didn't manage to complete my task last night.

My stomach churns as I force down breakfast, but I know I'm going to need every calorie today so there's no skimping. I then take a couple of jars of homemade jam, homemade that is by someone other than me, out of the cupboard and checking I have all I need I leave the cottage.

There's no sign of Diane as I pass her place, and other than greeting a few people I see with cheery hellos I don't stop to talk to anyone. It's late morning by the time I get to Mrs Tompkins's house. She is a stalwart of the village and is always called Mrs Tompkins. I assume she has a first name but even if I knew it I would never consider using it. There's not a committee she's not on nor a role she is not wanting to fill, and she is worth her weight in gold for the amount she does to keep village events ticking along.

Tomorrow it is the Harvest Service at the church, which will be followed by a fundraising auction where locals pay quite extraordinary amounts of money for pots of jam and pickles, quite often buying back the exact same produce they donated in the first place. It's a mad world but this is what passes for entertainment in the countryside. This comment may come across as a little scathing, but that is not my intention. I've only recently realised how much all this means to me, this country living. Ironically it's come to me like some epiphany right at the point when it could all be taken away, because if people find out about me I don't think I could stay. Anyway my point is that I know Mrs Tompkins is collecting for the Harvest Service and this is my in.

As I walk up the path towards her front door, I look in the window and find I can see straight through the sitting room, open plan dining room and right out into the garden because of the French doors. I ring the bell, but as I expect I hear a shout from behind the house telling me to go round the back. Mrs Tompkins is an avid gardener and this is where she is usually to be found. I'm not sure how old she is but she's best described as wiry. Cut short, her predominantly white hair is in stark contrast to her weathered and constantly tanned face. She's slightly built, not much over five feet tall, physically capable and mentally astute. Today she is filling a wheelbarrow with produce she has grown, and as I first catch sight of her she is halfway up her long garden doing battle with a particularly large marrow as she wrestles it into the barrow to join the other veg she has gathered.

I lift my pots of jam in the air so she can see what I'm there for, and in a voice that easily carries across the distance, because she was once a school teacher, she tells me to put them in the box inside on the kitchen table. Walking through the utility room that contains several litter trays resulting in a gritty floor and a decidedly feral smell, I quickly make my way over to deposit my jars in the already half full box, then I look around. There are cats on every surface which distracts me for a moment but then I see that right by the door there is a row of hooks with sets of keys on every one. *Tut, tut,* I think, *people make life so easy for the likes of me.* One cat jumps down from the work surface and winds its way around my legs in a figure of eight motion. I know Mrs Tomkins is the go-to person for all sorts of pet duties, and to give her her due the keys are not actually labelled but, by a simple process of elimination, I take a wild stab in the dark and guess that the key attached to the keyring sporting a flat-coated retriever might just be the one I require. But this doesn't give me everything I need, there is still the alarm to manage. Below the keys is an address book and I open it up at P for Pritchard. Sure enough there is an entry, with a phone number that I know is wrong. I make a mental note of the last four digits, go to the front door which I put on the latch but then push closed, and picking up the cat, which I hope is going to be as amenable when handled as it was when rubbing up against me, I return to the back door. I give the cat an obvious cuddle as if to make clear that this is what has delayed me before putting it carefully on the ground. I see Mrs Tompkins watching me from further up the garden than she was before, and instead of shouting goodbye I do so by lifting my hand in the air which she responds to in the same manner before turning back to whatever it is she is doing.

Moments later I'm walking up the drive to the Pritchards' place. The cars are all gone but just to be sure I ring the front door bell. No one overlooks this house and it's surrounded by an outer ring of trees to maintain privacy but I'm prepared, obviously, and should anyone see me coming or going, the thank-you card for the previous night's hospitality I have in my back pocket gives me the reason to be there. Checking that no one is around I go to the side of the house, open the door and holding my breath, because this is where it could all go horribly wrong. I punch the four digits into the alarm and let out the breath when I see it is disarmed.

The dogs have risen from their beds at my entry and I make a quick fuss of them while at the same time checking round the utility room, and then the kitchen. I spot Ben's jacket still lying on the worktop, and pulling the hotel receipt out of my pocket I cross the room and push it into one of his before retracing my steps, resetting the alarm, saying a quick goodbye to the dogs, for some weird reason, and closing and locking the door. I doubt a minute has passed since I was standing at the front door, but my heart is beating rapidly and I don't exhale again until I'm pushing the thank-you card through the letterbox and am easily able to explain away my actions, should I need to.

I return to Mrs Tompkins's house fully aware that this is the tricky part, the one for which I require a bit of luck. I was hoping to intercept someone else delivering produce and offer to take it in for them but as there is no one around I opt for Plan B. I walk back towards the front door and look, as inconspicuously as possible, through the window again. I breathe a sigh of relief when I spot Mrs Tomkins still out in her garden although note with some alarm that she is now much nearer the house.

Checking again that no one's watching, I push open the door and nip along the passageway towards the kitchen on my tippy-toes. As I reach up to hang the Pritchards' key back on its hook, I see Mrs Tompkins pass the kitchen window on her way to the back door. I turn tail and run back the way I came, silently flicking the door off the latch and softly pulling it closed behind me. Moments later I'm out of sight of the house and sauntering back through the village as though I haven't a care in the world. However, my nerves are jangling with all the adrenaline that has been surging through me, and knowing I need to calm down and restore my energy levels I'm delighted when I see Diane coming out of the shop and she invites me for lunch.

Diane notices me cuddling Cat when he jumps onto my lap, and smiles knowingly but doesn't say a word. After our night together I take the therapy he seems happy to dole out, his purrs rumbling against my thighs as I stroke him.

She sits across from me, having served up bowls of suspiciously bright green and therefore undeniably healthy, she tells me, soup, before she asks, "So how are things going with delectable Dan?" I smile weakly at her description of him.

"It's become complicated."

"How so?" I wonder if I should have ventured down this path but given that she knows about my 'other life' I guess as long as I'm careful it won't do any harm.

"I've had a problem with one of the guys at the gym," I explain.

"Oh?"

"It seems he had developed feelings for me. Not that he ever showed that, but he didn't take it well when I finished with him and he's caused problems since, been aggressive, that sort of thing."

"That's tiresome, still it's early days, I'm sure he'll calm down." I love how practical she is and I nod, realising that he hadn't done anything other than throw dirty looks at me for the last couple of days so perhaps he has already. She watches me carefully. "Is there something else?" she asks, her tone enquiring.

"My ex turned up this week." I've never actually told her of my background, other than the fact I had an ex, and although the vast sum of money I carried in cash must have raised some suspicions, she's not to know that I've been hiding in plain sight from him all this time.

"Oh that's unfortunate." The understatement makes me smile.

"Indeed."

"So, how did it go with him?"

"Awkwardly. My relationship with him was... tricky. To be honest it wasn't really over when I left and he's... well—" I pause to try and think how best to explain, deciding it is just easier to cut to the chase— "well, he got a bit fresh with me yesterday." I look away, feigning interest in a snag on the sleeve of my jumper.

"Really! And how did you react to that?"

"Badly. I mean from his point of view well, but from Dan's I hardly covered myself in glory."

"You're still attracted to him?" I nod.

"I always will be, he's that sort. He's like a drug to me and equally no good. It's why I left." Not entirely true but it fits with what Diane knows about me.

"I see, and where was Dan in all this?"

"Around, which meant we rowed about it, and haven't really made up, but he shouldn't have been there as I told him to keep away because I needed some space while I try and sort this mess out." This comes out in a garbled rush and confusion wrinkles her brow, unsurprisingly.

"Why?"

I can see from her point of view it would make sense for Dan to be close by to show Tag I wasn't available, but it's not that straightforward and all I can manage by way of feeble explanation is, "Ah, well that's complicated too."

Diane is full of reassuring and terribly wise noises about keeping my distance from Tag, and I assure her I will and hate myself for lying so blatantly to her.

The soup doesn't do its usual trick so I try to rest by reaching for my book; however, when I've read the same paragraph for the umpteenth time I put the television on instead and stare blankly at the screen. I'm not as calm as I usually am before a job but I know the gnawing I feel in my stomach has more to do with my nerves about Tag than it does over what I'm about to do. I run through my notes again and prepare everything that I'm going to need that night. I know my timings, I know what I have to do and I know I am ready. However, there are still several hours between now and when my plans become action so I'm pleased to receive a call from a friend.

"Food?"

"Food."

I get there first and order the drinks. I decide on cider for him, bourbon for me. *Just the one*, I tell myself, *it'll take the edge off*. Chris arrives as I'm getting seated.

"I thought I was quick off the mark," he comments as he takes his seat opposite, "what are you drinking?" He frowns as he looks at my glass.

"Bourbon."

"Straight?"

"Yup." He smiles.

"I was not expecting that."

"Well I do like to be able to surprise you now and then." Kourtney is crossing the room towards us.

"Is there any point in me askin' if you want to look at a menu?" Chris and I glance at each other and laugh.

"Not really, we'll have the usual," I say, "don't rush off though, how are things going?" I feel out of touch, like it's been an age since I've spoken to her although it was only Tuesday. However, I was hardly at my best then.

"Yeah, great, thanks. How are you? You were in a bit of a state the other morning, okay now?"

"Yeah I'm absolutely fine, I had a bad start to the day that's all," I say, and I change the subject quickly as I notice Chris is looking at me with interest. "How's the driving going?"

"Got another lesson tomorrow." She's bursting with excitement and I'm delighted for her. "Chris and I are meetin' in the week so he can show me how to keep my records as well, aren't we?" She looks at Chris who nods in agreement; there's a grin on his face and I can tell he's proud of her and I am too. "I'd best get on and put your order in, I'll be back in a bit," and she turns and heads off to the bar. I watch her for a moment as she joins Josh and he adds the order to the till. Their backs are towards us and as they chat I see his arm come around her, his hand on her waist, as he briefly hugs her closer. Her head turns towards him, I see the look she gives him and I know all is well in Kourtney's world.

"It looks like everything is on the up for her at the moment, doesn't it?" I murmur.

"It does indeed. I'm pleased for her; Josh is a good bloke." I completely agree, they'll make a great team. Chris sits back and studies me for a moment. I can feel his eyes on me so turn to meet them. 'So what's going on with you? You seem a bit tense."

"Do I?" Feigning innocence, I smile, "just a few things on with work that's all."

"Ah ha." It's like he doesn't believe me at all and I pick up my drink and down it in one. His eyes widen.

"It's alright, I'm just having the one," I explain, "I have something on later."

"Is it a romantic assignation with this new boyfriend of yours?" And he grins in that knowing way of his.

"News travels fast, I can't believe she told you." Not that there was any reason why Diane shouldn't of course.

"Don't worry, we weren't gossiping, she just happened to mention in passing there might be someone." Kourtney is walking towards us bearing our plates of food.

"That was quick," I say.

"Yeah, it's almost like chef saw you walk in and knew what you would be having," and she laughs. As soon as we're alone again I start eating. My stomach is feeling like clouds of butterflies have taken flight in there and I need to get something into it to steady it down again.

"Hungry?" comes the amused remark from Chris.

"Always," is my mumbled response, then I take a breath and sit back realising I need to slow down a bit. I glance round. We are in early tonight and there are only a couple of other tables taken so far though I notice there are more people in the bar.

And I stop.

And do a double take.

A chill runs through me as I see Tag taking the first sip out of a pint just handed to him by Josh.

What the hell is he doing here?

I pick up our glasses and say I'm getting refills. My head is buzzing with white noise as I try to quell the panic Tag's presence has created in me, so when Chris responds I don't hear him but just get up and go. Tag is already halfway down his pint and sees me approach via the mirror behind the bar. There's a buzz of conversation, and sliding in next to him as I wait for Josh to finish serving someone else I keep my voice as low as possible as I say,

"Checking up on me?"

"Not at all. I felt like some company an' I'm sure there are people in 'ere I could chat to. Who's the bloke you're with?"

"A friend."

"You and your friends, Red, though this one does look old enough to be your dad." I ignore his comment. Josh is free now and I ask for the same again for Chris and a coke for me.

"I don't want you talking to anyone in here," I mutter.

"Well that's a bit antisocial," he starts and I glare at him. "Alrigh', I won't, as long as you keep your end of the bargain. I'm just lettin' you know how easy it would be, that's all."

"Speaking of bargains, shouldn't you be preparing for later?" I hiss at Tag, aware that Josh is eyeing him with some suspicion.

"Shouldn't you?" is his retort and then he downs the rest of his pint.

265

"I am ready."

"Of course you are, I'll see you later then," and he winks at me, turns and walks out.

He's playing me, messing with my head, I know that and I wish I could simply brush it off as if it meant nothing, but him showing up here has rattled me. I hope he didn't notice but I suspect he did, he knows me too well.

Josh places both drinks in front of me and says, "You okay, Maddy, you look a bit pale?" I can hear the concern in his voice and respond,

"Yeah, yeah I'm fine," but this has thrown me and I'm distracted as I go back to our table. Tag had come to check up on me, but was it more than that? Had he come to cause trouble? He'd intimated how easy it would be and he couldn't have known I was going to be here, it was pure chance I was. I disliked the thought of him being in my village because after taking such care to avoid anyone here finding out anything about me, and I'd hate for it to come out now, but him doing this just showed how little he was to be trusted.

I sit, then with a rush of understanding I realise that there is absolutely nothing I can do to stop him. Whatever happens tonight Tag could come back here at any time, and talk to anyone. Initially a panicky feeling rises in me at this realisation, particularly as that includes the possibility of him telling Dan as well. However, as I mull over my options that first reaction soon changes to calm resolution. I take a moment and make a considered decision to alter my priorities and not worry about people finding out, or about what they might say. I will simply have to deal with their judgement when it comes and put my trust in the friends I have made here. I can't bring myself to think about how it will affect Dan and me, or even if there will be a Dan and me after all this so I'm dodging that one. I'll face all that another day. This feels like a radical change in my thinking and once I acknowledge Tag's actions are out of my control, things in my mind are simplified considerably and I know, with some relief, that what I need to do now is the right thing. That might just slow him down a bit, and as I think through my new direction I'm deep in my thoughts and of course Chris picks up on the change in me.

"A friend of yours?" he asks, as casual as you like.

"Not really," I reply, brought back into the real world by his words, "well, once, perhaps." I stare down at my plate of food and find I've lost my appetite. To keep up appearances I take a mouthful of steak but it becomes a hard lump in my mouth that I struggle to break down and swallow so I give up, pushing my plate away. I see concern on Chris's face.

"That's not like you." I don't want him to probe any further so I deflect attention onto something else.

"How's the book coming?"

"Slowly, but fine." I suspect he knows exactly what I'm doing but he plays along anyway.

"What is the glorious Gabriella up to at the moment?"

"Actually she's got herself in a spot of bother."

"Really? How is she going to get out of it?" He shrugs his shoulders.

"That's not quite clear, I'm working on it up here," and he taps the side of his head, "I'm ever hopeful the solution will present itself before I have to write it tomorrow. I'm sure there must be a way out of her predicament." He smiles as I nod.

"Do you already know the ending?"

"More or less."

"And will it be a happy one?"

"This is contemporary fiction, Madeleine, not romance, happy ever afters are not guaranteed. But I can tell you one thing." I fix my attention on him, willing this to be good news.

"What's that?"

"Everything will work out exactly the way it's meant to."

I sigh as I sit back in my seat and wonder if that philosophy of his holds true in real life, and if so what that means for me.

We leave together a short while later and part once outside. I start to walk back home then stop and turn back to watch Chris disappearing into the distance up the street. Once he is out of sight I walk up towards the shop and go into the telephone box at its corner. I don't know if this is going to be too late, or if anyone will take any notice but I make the call anyway, anonymously. It wouldn't take a lot to find out where it came from and most likely from whom but by the time that has been done it won't much matter anymore. The end game is already in play.

Chapter 26

It's three the next morning, and I'm warm though my breath comes out as white clouds, frozen on the icy air. I hear it, behind me, and to the left. The snap of a twig underfoot and a sharp intake of breath at the indiscretion. He's here, just as I knew he would be, but I allow myself a small smile of satisfaction knowing he'll be cursing his mistake. I have no intention of making this easy for him so leave him to come and find me. I still, and although my heart is pounding, blood pumping in my ears until I'm sure he'll be able to hear it too, I concentrate on making myself small and silent. I am one step ahead of him and plan on keeping it that way.

It rained earlier but now the sky is clear and with the moon on its way towards becoming full a ghostly pall is thrown over everything. I'm in the shadows and he passes so close I could have touched him but I wait until he has crept past me and is crouched, waiting, before whispering, "Good morning." I see him start then he turns his head and draws back level with me. I can sense the excitement in him, the addictive thrill of doing something bad that I remember him loving.

"Thought you'd stood me up," he says.

"No I'm just less conspicuous than you are what with all that crashing about in the woods."

"Give over, I wasn't that bad." I see he has a package strapped to his back which makes my heart sink but I'm intent on pressing ahead with my plan in the hope he will go along with it. This uncertainty is far from ideal for me but there was no way I was going to share my information with him any earlier and as it turns out he wouldn't have listened anyway. Fool that he is.

"I want you to keep low and do exactly what I do," I say, "I've found an in…"

"No," he interrupts, "I've planned my route, you're the one going to be doing the following." He's close to me, I can feel the energy radiating from him and something about it unsettles me. I try again.

"Tag, I've put weeks of planning into this, listen to me." But he's determined.

"Remember what's at stake, Red, we're doing this my way." What's at stake here is his threat to tell the village, and Dan, all about me. What he doesn't know is my change of heart on that. However, as I'm not sure if the plans I have put in place are going to come to fruition I need to keep all options open, and that seems to mean for the time being going along with him.

Tag was the foolhardy one. Whereas my plans have always been modest, erring on the side of caution, of taking the safe option, the less audacious route, Tag would be wanting to show off. This time looks like being no exception.

However, I want, no, I need him to be happy with my participation so I shrug and ask him to give me a clue.

"We're going up," and he directs both index fingers towards the star sprinkled sky. As he does that his face gets caught in the silvery light of the moon and what I see alarms me.

We're hidden enough for this not to cause a problem so I pull out my small torch, flick it on and shine it directly at his face. His pupils are dilated as you'd expect but under the bright light they don't constrict, not at all, not even a millimetre and I realise he is high. Things have changed indeed.

"What are you on?" I demand.

"Nothing."

"Liar, you're putting us both at risk. What are you on?" I repeat, a little more fiercely.

"Okay, okay, I've taken a little something to heighten my awareness, that's all, something to give me the edge. It's nothing for you to worry about."

"Oh give me strength, you were always warning me about taking stuff, and now here you are as high as a kite. You bloody idiot!" I can't believe he's been so stupid. He's not listening to me at all, has gone against my preferred option of entry point, and now this. I can't help but feel he's on some glory-seeking mission.

And now I wonder if I've misjudged the situation. Earlier, when retrieving what I needed from my hidey hole, my hand had closed around the knife I used to carry. I hadn't, not since moving here, but I'd considered bringing it with me this evening, worried that after my disgraceful behaviour with Tag I was going to have a problem with him and might need some additional protection. I'd considered it and decided against it. This was my new life and I didn't want to retrace the steps of someone I had once been. Now I wish I'd made a different decision.

"It'll be fine, Red, come on, let's get going," he says, and he takes off, out of the trees. I'm furious with him, and he knows it but I'm going to have to put that to one side for now and deal with the job in front of us as well as trying to handle him.

I race to catch him up. There's a brief open area to cross then it's easy enough to keep to the dark shadows of the gardens as we follow the walls round until we reach the back of the House. At this point I grab Tag's shoulder and pull him back. I check my watch and know it's time for the security guard to make his rounds. The House is currently unoccupied and there are only two guards on duty overnight. In my opinion that is not enough. They are only checking the outside, and only once every hour. They alternate in doing a circuit of the house while the other keeps an eye on the screens, and that's it. As we are about to prove, a lot can happen in an hour. I already know that in my report back to Watson & Grove I will be bringing this up as an issue. I personally think the guards should have dogs with them too. Men have no capability to pick up on the presence of intruders like a dog can. I whisper to Tag about the guard and at least on this point he listens to me, nods and settles down. The guard makes his pass a couple of minutes or so later. He could be out for a nice walk in the country the way he ambles past, not a care in the world.

Tag is itching to get going the moment he's gone but I make him wait a couple more minutes, and then we're off again and I'm only just able to keep up. As soon as Tag said we were going up I knew where we would have to be headed, the black fire escape that snakes down the rear of the property. A health and safety addition that was as unobtrusively attached to one end of the building as was possible and provides a safe escape route to all floors. It stretches up as far the roof because the row of skylights provide exit opportunities for all the rooms on that floor. We reach it with no cause for alarm and I note another suggestion for my report, action activated security lights. There are some on the front and at the end where the coffee shop is but none here. If there had been we would have been lit up like actors on a West End stage by now and finding life considerably less comfortable. As it is we scale the zig-zagging flights of steps on silent feet and stay hidden in the shadow cast by the House itself with relative ease.

At the top we drop over the parapet and into the valley created between that and where the roof begins to slope upwards to create the third floor. Tag is in front of me and I follow, assuming he knows where he's going. I hope he is planning on going through one of the skylights but suspect he has a more acrobatic entry in mind.

My suspicions prove right.

He leads the way right around the edge of the building and then across and over a flat roofed section until we come to the atrium window that tops the library. I can't believe he thinks this is a good idea, my main concern being that he is going to make me look like a total amateur and ruin my reputation all in one night if we get caught. After all, he must be winging this, as it's not as if he could have come up here at any point to check out if this entry point is even viable.

I crouch down beside him, delighted that at least here we are completely hidden from view. I decide to watch and not involve myself in finding a way in, still hoping he will fail and come round to my way of thinking.

The atrium is of an old fashioned design as it is made up of panes of glass inside frames of wood rather than being of any type of sealed unit design. The wood is rough, worn and flaking in places, an area in need of maintenance that I imagine is easy to overlook, being where it is, and this is more fodder for my report. I watch Tag as he takes out his knife and runs it around the edge of one pane. As he then eases the knife in further and levers it I see the frame move ever so slightly and independently from its neighbour. It's hinged along the top edge but catching along the lower one and Tag returns to this area using the knife again along the crack. I know he's hoping to slide whatever catch there is to one side, and it crosses my mind that I have no idea if this window is alarmed or not. I guess we're about to find out as on his next pass Tag's knife runs smoothly and I know the catch has shifted. Tag eases the knife under again and this time the window lifts free. He wedges the fingers of one hand under it as soon as the gap is big enough and puts the knife to one side. Using two hands he lifts the window up and rests it back on its hinges. The hole it creates is easily big enough for a man to fit through and Tag looks over at me, a big grin on his stupid face.

He removes the bag he's been carrying and places it on the roof beside him. I only realise once he's done this that he's wearing a full body harness and I know what's coming next. Opening up the bag, I recognise the rappelling gear I've seen him use before. This is going to be a straightforward drop so I see him set up for a fast rope descent using only a dual hook anchor.

"Are you using ascenders to get back up?" I ask and he shakes his head.

"No, I've brought a ladder. Can you set it up once I'm down?"

I'm surprised, he has actually put some thought into this, and I say, "Will do." I watch as he edges himself over the window frame; this is the tricky bit but once he's over he will be on the floor of the library in a matter of seconds. I lean over the hole and sure enough when I check the rope it's slack so I pull it back up. Tempting as it might be to not lower the ladder and leave him to be found by security in the morning instead, I know that's not going to help me achieve the outcome I want so I reach for the second bag and take out the ladder.

Made of Kevlar webbing and aluminium rods for hand and foot holds, it's a handy bit of kit, I'll give him that. It attaches to the edge of the window with the same dual hook anchor and I lower it down into the darkness hoping Tag has done the maths on whether it's going to be long enough. Leaving him to haul

274

himself back up when he's ready, I set about packing the rope back into its bag so that we can get going as quickly as possible. The sooner I can get away from here the better.

I shiver. There's a frost forming and a breeze up here that's adding a significant wind chill factor. I'm wearing several thin layers of thermal clothing and while I've been active they have been sufficient and the cold has gone unnoticed but now, as I've been still for a few minutes, the biting cold is beginning to tell and I can feel my body temperature falling.

I hear his breathing as he nears the top of the ladder. Climbing up one of these things takes strength and stamina and even though he's fit he's labouring under the effort. Eventually his hands reach the top and grasping the edge of the frame he heaves himself out and onto the flat roof. He rolls over onto his back, taking in lungfuls of air as he recovers, and as he does I pull up and pack away the ladder and close up the window section.

I look back towards Tag; he's already sitting up, his recovery no doubt helped by whatever it is he has taken, and I say we should go.

"Hang on a minute," he says, and I can hear the eagerness in his voice, "let me show you the treasure." He's grinning like a kid that's got top prize in the lucky dip as he reaches into his pocket and I'm dreading to see what comes out, wondering how much he's taken. But then I'm surprised because he's actually only got the main necklace from the display, exactly as he said he would, and he gazes at it now slung across his palm. Even in the dimmer light of the moon I can see the diamonds shimmer and sparkle, the sapphires glisten as black as night as the loops and swirls of this main piece fill his hand.

He's buzzing, I can tell. Success, the ultimate high. He gets to his feet and I tell him to put the necklace back in his pocket and we'll get off this roof and away from here.

"Killjoy," he calls me, and he's probably right though I prefer to think of it as saving my own skin. We can celebrate later, I say, trying to encourage some movement from him. But he's not listening, not anymore, he's just talking to me, at me. Rapid fire.

"Look at this, Red, look at this," he's repeating and he's holding his hand out to me, showing me something I've already seen. "This is just the beginning for you and me." *There is no you and me*, is what I'm thinking, but I keep that to myself. "We could go big time, major league hauls, jewellery heists, bank vaults, deposit boxes." The man is talking nonsense and I know he's high and peaking with the added adrenaline of what he's just achieved but right now, right at this moment this is causing me a problem. He's spinning around and grabs me trying to drag me with him as if we're about to leap into some weird roof-based dance routine directly out of *Mary Poppins*. I pull away and he goads me.

"Come on, Red, live a little." He's worrying me but what he does next makes my blood run cold.

He leaps up onto the top of the parapet, his arms outstretched, the necklace dangling precariously from one hand and says, "I dare you. Come on." He holds his other hand out to me and I just stare at it in disbelief. "Go on, you know you want to." He always loved to challenge me and in my previous life I'd never have let him down but this is ridiculous, on so many levels. He's in full view, he's jeopardising everything I've worked for and he's inches away from a sheer drop he's not going to bounce back from.

"Stop buggering around, Tag, get down," I order, although as all of what we're saying to one another is in muted tones not much above a whisper I know I'm lacking any force behind my demands.

"When did you stop being fun?" He's mocking me, but I'm not rising to it.

"This is not fun. Get down. You're gonna get hurt." I'm aware of my voice getting louder but that's the least of my problems. I don't want to call for help, because that might make the situation worse, but I'm starting to think that if one of the guards overhears by chance I might get some assistance in getting this lunatic down.

"Shhhh…" His finger is to his lips. "Keep your voice down, Red, someone might overhear." He's taking the piss by speaking in an exaggerated whisper and I've had enough. I don't know what else to do so decide to leave him to it and hope that when he sees me walk away he'll give up and follow. It's a weak plan but the only one I can come up with. I pick up his equipment, the rope bag and the foldaway ladder and sling them onto my back. My intention is clear as without acknowledging him further I walk off the flat section of roof and back into the gulley that runs alongside the parapet he is still on. This does involve me initially having to pass closer to him, and for a moment I think he thinks I am about to take up his challenge, but I make it clear what I think as I ignore him and carry on walking. I'm surprised therefore to hear him drop down behind me without any further aggravation but breathe a sigh of relief that he's seen sense.

"You're no fun," he grumbles, and I hate the fact he's making me feel old and sensible.

"This is no time for having fun, Tag," I hiss over my shoulder at him, "this is serious, this is business. And put the necklace away."

I hear a zip being opened, an incoherent muttering at my nagging but I'm past caring and only want to get out of here.

We're back at the corner with the fire escape and I hand back all Tag's equipment before peering over to check all is clear, then we begin our descent and in what seems like only a couple of minutes later we're running past the horse chestnut tree and into the woods.

We're far from the House now, deep among the trees and safe from any possible watching eyes, and I know I need to change direction to get back to my car, so I put my hand out and placing it on his forearm bring him to a halt.

"Time to split, Tag."

"What?" He seems surprised.

"I need to head in that direction," I say, and I jerk my thumb to my right.

"No," is his only response that I bite back against quickly.

"What do you mean no, I've done as you asked and you've got what you wanted. It's time for us both to return to our other lives."

"I don't want you to go." This would have sounded plaintive if it wasn't for his tone.

"Well I have to, bye, Tag," and I turn to walk off. But he takes hold of my arm and spins me back around.

"You left me once, you just tried to leave me on that fuckin' roof, and now you're doin' it again." His words are spat out, emphasised with a finger pointed right in my face but I lean in towards him giving as good as I get.

"And you told me that if I'd wanted to go you would have let me, but that seems to be proving unlikely." He stalls for a moment and I take that as my cue to go but as I turn he grabs me.

"No." His tone is fiercer now as he pulls me towards him, his hand so tight it's hurting me, his fingers digging into my flesh. "You're not doin' this again, not this time."

"Tag! You're hurting me!" I try to pull free, try to drag my arm out from his grasp but he's too strong, and he knows it. "Let me go!"

"Go on then." And as he releases me with one hand his other, clenched in a fist, connects with my jaw, hard. I'm knocked off my feet, and land sprawled in the dirt. I struggle to sit up, my head spinning and there's the iron taste of blood in my mouth. When I bring my hand up I find my lip's split, blood wetting my fingers. I gingerly feel my teeth with my tongue while cradling my throbbing jaw and look up at him. He looms, a menacing shadow, distorted by the silhouettes of trees, against the lighter shade of the night sky. I feel an icy chill of fear slither down my spine as the man I knew succumbs to the ragged demons in his mind and becomes someone I no longer recognise.

He pauses for only a second and then he's on me. His weight pins me down as I fight to push him off with my hands, clawing and scratching at him as I heave my body under his in an attempt to get away. His open-handed slap across my face stings as it connects and leaves me dazed and with my senses lost in the immediate lull after he grabs my wrists and holds them tight together, roughly grinding them into the ground above my head.

His heavy breathing rasps next to my ear as he warns me to be quiet. I can't move now, or fight back and I feel him pull my trousers down along with my pants, the material scraping roughly against my skin and I become rigid, forcing my legs together.

"Please don't," I plead, my last ditch appeal barely more than a whisper.

"I own you, bitch, and I'll beat you black and fuckin' blue if you don't let me." He pushes his leg in between mine, his fingers digging into my thighs to prise them apart, and I know there is nothing I can do to save myself.

It hurts when he forces himself inside, and I hear myself whimper as tears come and his voice growls close by my ear, "It ain't like you've never done this before, you filthy slut."

I close my eyes tight shut but feel the tears squeeze out of them and wet my cheeks. Gritting my teeth, I turn my head away, to distance myself. All I see on the inside of my eyelids is my old bedroom wall, the dark patch where a boy band poster was stuck. He's right, I have done this before, only not in the way he means. However this time I'm all grown up and I know the score. I close right down just as I used to way back then in an attempt to block out what was happening.

"You are mine, you dirty slut, and don't you ever fuckin' forget it," he hisses in my ear and with each agonising thrust come another insult. "I know you fuckin' love this, you fuckin' whore. You think you can leave me? You bitch, think again, you fuckin' slag..." and on, and on, and on.

I will it to be over and tune out his abuse. *This is one moment*, I repeat in my head, *just one moment, and I won't let it be who I am.*

His weight is constricting me, crushing my chest, my breathing rapid and panicky and I slow it, purposefully taking deeper steadier breaths, concentrating purely on the physical action of inhaling and exhaling. White noise builds in my head until the vile words spewing out in my direction are muffled as though I am under water, as though I am floating as if in another world and no longer part of this one.

I think of my happy place, of my home, of safety, of cuddles on the sofa and of the one who stayed and who only wants to protect me. More tears come though they're not for this vicious act but for fear that I may have lost the one for ever.

He grunts and stills at last and I lie quiet beneath him, and hope the worst is over. He releases my hands and gets up, telling me to do the same as he turns away to straighten his clothes. I struggle to get to my feet. I brush what dirt I can from my body and shakily reach down to pull up my underwear and trousers. I wipe away the wet on my face with the back of my hands, the grit rough on skin already sore from the bruising below. The skin below my nose is itchy from where my nose has bled, the blood drying and sticky and as I touch my swollen lip tenderly my breathing catches in my throat. My heartbeat is racing but while I want to get away I fear running now, that option has gone as I'm not sure I'd be able to get far enough before he caught me and I don't know what he'd do to me if he did. After this he might be capable of anything.

"Let me go," I say, my voice quiet, "I won't say anything."

He looks over at me and without even seeming to consider what I said, says, "No chance, you're comin' with me," and in case I look like putting up a fight he grabs my wrist and walks off, dragging me along with him.

"Tag, please," I say, but get no response. Everything has gone wrong and while I seriously don't want to be heading in this direction I'm not deliberately trying to be obstructive. However, he's moving too fast and in my weakened state I'm struggling to keep up with him but he ignores me and his grip remains tight as he drags me along.

It's about the same distance as it would have been to my car but it's been a long night and with my energy level at such a low ebb I find the journey difficult and am relieved when we eventually get to the boundary wall.

Once we've climbed over it he takes hold of my wrist again and I turn to see his car parked in the gateway opposite. The night is silent and I'm anxious. My plan has not worked and now I know I cannot get in Tag's car, there will be no hope for me if I do. I pause, wondering what my chances of running now would be. But he forces me to move again, jerking me forward and across the road as I try to remember how far it is to the nearest house. I think it's a good mile and know he'd be upon me well before I made it there but for the lack of any other option I think I'm going to have to give it a go. I think about the likelihood of a passing car coming to my aid and dismiss that thought. It's still too early but even as I'm thinking that I hear it, a car, coming at speed, then I realise the sound is from both directions, and it's closing in fast. My spirits lift at the opportunity to flag down some help, and as I look for the opportune moment we've only just reached the other side and Tag's still getting his keys out of his pocket when they're upon us, but instead of passing they slow and as Tag's attention is drawn to them he looks at me and shouts, "Did you do this?"

Exhausted and confused, I look at the vehicles now drawing to a stop and blocking us in, and at that moment one flicks on its lights and they spin, the strobing blue and red brightening up the night. My relief is almost tangible, although I don't let on.

I check back with Tag, concerned at what I see there and it's my turn to hold on to him. Taking his arm, I say, "Don't." He looks at me and I shake my head. "Don't run. They'll hurt you."

"Like you care." Policemen are climbing out of their cars.

"I don't want you to get hurt. You should have let me go when you had the chance, I told you I wouldn't have said anything then."

He looks at me curiously and it occurs to me that he doesn't realise that what he did to me was wrong. Then he smiles as he says, "Oh sweetheart, you have no idea." I don't understand what he means but the moment when escape was still an option playing through his mind is gone. A policeman approaches and pushes Tag up against the side of the car, another does the same to me and handcuffs are put on as we're arrested for theft, cautioned and told we're being taken in for further questioning.

I stay quiet, relieved they responded to the anonymous call they received earlier and then I see him. Dan. He walks across from the other side of the road and stands between the two police cars. I'm initially confused as to why he's here, but then realise. Of course the police would have made contact with Watson & Grove, and Dan has come to see the results of my night's work. The fact I'm here shows that part of my plan hasn't worked out so well but at least the police, and Dan, have taken the tip-off seriously.

I can hear Tag remonstrating as he's being forced into the back of one of the cars but I block that out. My focus is on Dan now. He wouldn't have been expecting me to be here and there's a look of profound disappointment on his face that I am. As I'm led towards the back door of one of the cars I pass him, and never taking my eyes from his I see the flash of anger

283

as my face is illuminated by the headlights and he sees the state of it. But he says and does nothing.

I stop, resisting the policeman's efforts to keep me moving, and I gaze at Dan. His face is impassive like this is only business and I know I have lost him. I'm on the brink and tears well in my eyes as I say to him, "Make sure you check in with Arthur Ramsey first thing."

But why should he listen to a word I say?

Chapter 27

There's blood under my nails, darkening as time passes, and dirt ingrained in the creases of my skin as I examine my hands which won't stop shaking.

I try and breathe through my mouth because it smells of piss in here, piss and blood and vomit. A stench no amount of bleach can overcome. The walls are dirty yellow, tiled at the bottom with gloss paint higher up, presumably so they are easy to clean, only it looks like no one's bothered as they're stained, and I don't like to think with what. I shiver, chilled in clothing that due to the exertions of the night I've sweated in more than once, and now cooling my tired body is struggling to maintain temperature. I'm sitting, uncomfortable and sore, on a solid bunk and I tuck my grubby hands in between my knees to avoid touching anything as I wait, hoping someone comes to get me soon. I'm right opposite the door and every now and then the flap in the steel has dropped down and a pair of eyes have peered in at me then moved on.

I'm desperately tired but can't close my eyes. If I do I relive the earlier violence and I've enough reminders anyway. There are abrasions on the skin of my hands and wrists, my back and bottom are grazed raw in places, made so from the detritus on the ground. My face and lip are tender, I ache with the bruises that are developing and although I'm trying to ignore it I fear I'm bleeding.

I've said nothing, as yet, not about all that.

I've been questioned but I have no idea how much trouble I'm in and when, or if, they are going to let me go.

I've always taken my work seriously, treating each job as though I were a real thief while at the same time I've known that the police are aware of my activities and therefore if I get caught I'm not going to be in any danger of serious charges. But now someone else is involved and I'm not confident I have that protection any longer.

A duty solicitor had sat with me while I was being questioned and advised me to say nothing. He was thin, his suit hanging on his frame like he'd recently lost a lot of weight and I wondered if he was ill. His ashen face with deep grooves carved in arcs around his mouth and the dark circles under his eyes suggested he was, and I felt sorry for him having to turn out for a fool like me when he could probably have done with being in bed. I didn't say much, just explained who I was and what I was doing there. Those are my instructions from Cubby, should I ever get caught. Although I know I wouldn't have done if it hadn't been for Tag but I'm too exhausted to be irritated by him now. I was at the House on legitimate business and I knew Watson & Grove would back me up on that. Of course the same couldn't be said of my connection to Tag and I was deliberately vague in my answers to those questions.

They asked me if there was anything else I needed to tell them, and I said there wasn't.

They asked me this more than once, and I think they know.

Given the state of me it's not surprising they have their suspicions but they asked no more and I was left to talk to the solicitor. He didn't say much. I asked if Tag was close by and he said yes, but not for long. He told me that as Tag was only released from prison three months ago and was still on parole he would be returned to serve the rest of his sentence. I should have guessed. That was why Tag had smiled at me. He'd known he was going back and the threat of my accusation held no sway with him. I'm surprisingly hurt by the lies he told. He'd served two years so all that talk about having moved on to bigger and better things was sheer fabrication. He had no bigger network, no fence capable of taking on higher quality merchandise. I imagined his old crew would have faded away without their leader and he was merely living on past glories and I suspect aiming to take me home with him to get back something of what he had before.

Sitting in this cell has given me much needed thinking time and I've never felt so alone, not since the day I turned eighteen and gazed down on those filthy sheets at that emaciated body of a wasted life and known that I truly was. But just like at that point I've had another moment of clarity. I'd always thought that it was my life I was running from, not him. I didn't see the red flags when I was younger, I didn't realise their significance, their warning that I should go and too late it has become clear that it was him I was fleeing all along. It has always been him. Blinded when I was younger by a man who knew so much, who appeared so strong. I see him now for what he is, a predator.

I know rape is not about sex but about the power a man can exact over a woman and it saddens me that Tag felt it was the only option left open to him. However, I'm not entirely convinced he even realised he was doing wrong and this worries me more.

I try to get my thoughts in order about how to proceed. I feel safer knowing he is locked away and that he will remain so for the foreseeable future. But I hate the thought of having to take this further, of court, of intrusive questions about what happened, of examinations into my private life, which will not stand up well under scrutiny. But I'm reminded of when he arrived and how it was only then that I knew the life I wanted to be living. In order to keep that I need to protect my anonymity in the press and once that decision is made, I know what I have to do.

The next time the flap in the door is lowered I say I need to talk to someone, I say I need to see a doctor.

The rape accusation is taken seriously immediately and I'm transferred to the sexual assault referral centre at the nearby hospital. I'm cared for by lovely people and examined by professionals. Evidence is gathered, tests are done. Swabs and photos and bloods all taken, along with my statement. I'm counselled about my options and I take all this in only partially, preferring instead to switch off and stare beyond the walls that surround me.

Eventually I get to leave and I say I can get myself home, with no idea of how I plan to do that.

I walk outside and stand for a moment breathing in the fresh air, with not much clue as to what I do next, but then I allow myself a brief smile of relief because he's waiting for me. I hadn't thought for one moment that anyone would come but there he is. Standing at the kerb, leaning up against his car with his arms folded. I put up my hand in greeting and he uncrosses his arms and legs and pushes himself off the vehicle. When I reach him I'm wrapped in the biggest hug and I try not to cry.

I don't want to leave the safety of his arms but eventually I have to, and while I appreciate him being there, when I get in the car I acknowledge that a part of me, a really deep down desperate part of me, can't help feeling a little disappointed that it is Cubby that has come, and not Dan.

Although what else should I have expected? After keeping Dan at arm's length for what feels like forever I've been caught at the scene of a crime after spending time cavorting on the rooftops of Danewright House with someone Dan knows to be my ex, the same someone he'd asked me to keep away from. I expect him to be giving me a wide berth from now on.

"Home?" Cubby asks, "I guess you could do with some rest."

"Actually could you take me back to my car, it's just outside Danewright village." He nods. I feel we need a debrief. There is much we have to discuss, much that requires sorting out but I don't seem to have the energy to summon the words. We travel in silence and Cubby appears content to leave it like this. I wonder if he is mad with me, I don't think I could bear that.

Cubby pulls his car into the layby in front of mine and we sit for a moment. I still assume he knows nothing of my relationship with Dan so I hope he just takes it as professional interest when I ask where he is.

"He's at the House. We were both there earlier, there's… stuff to sort out. He asked me to come and get you." That confirms it then, I think, he's keeping well clear. I know he can sense my concern as he tries to allay my fears, "He's in charge now, Maddy, it's his responsibility to lead on sorting this out. Don't worry, we've spoken with Arthur Ramsey and everyone is happy with what you've done. No one expected you to come across a real life burglary in progress but you did all you could and the necklace is safe.

"We're more concerned with you, with what you've been through." I can sense him treading carefully and his unease at potentially saying the wrong thing and he ends, "How about we get together over the next day or so and put your report together? Okay?"

I nod but stay silent. I know what he's doing, he wants to make sure we're all telling the same story. I'm aware if the police start probing into my relationship with Tag things could get messy. If they come to the conclusion that I was colluding with him in any way, life could become extremely difficult and it's going to be tricky to explain how I was where I was and did what I did, without raising at least the suspicion of collusion. I've already thought it all through and while still in the cell resigned myself to the fact that after this it is unlikely my past is going to remain just that for very much longer.

However, I remain hopeful because anything Tag reveals about our history will also land him in further trouble and if it gets to court, who are they likely to believe when it comes down to the he said/she said stuff?

I get out of the car and Cubby makes sure mine starts before he drives off. I reach into the back seat for the coat I took off the previous evening and put it on before making a turn in the road and heading home. Despite the coat the car feels cold, and I shiver as I turn the heating full on.

Chapter 28

It's just as well he's locked away because you want to rip his head off. However, instead of getting the satisfaction of doing so you're here brooding over a black coffee in the hospital canteen and trying to quell the anger that boils through your veins.

She wanted you to keep your distance but you've done everything you can to stay in touch, to keep checking in with her.

Because there was no way you were going to leave her on her own.

Not with him around.

And yet, when it mattered most, right at the point when she needed help, you were not there for her and you can't imagine what she must be thinking about that.

You hated seeing them together in the Market Square. Every second of that gut-wrenching encounter is indelibly etched in your mind. Seeing the two cars parked, and waiting for them to appear. The shame written on her face, the triumph all over his. She couldn't look at you and you wish you'd wiped that smirk right off his and given him something else to think about, but she would not have tolerated that. You rowed and she'd told you to give her space to work this out and you've tried to respect her request. But it hurts, still, the pain of seeing them together cutting like a knife through your soul and you can't bear to think of his filthy hands on her.

And that was then...

You had already planned to be close by last night. From the details she'd shared you knew what time she was going to attempt the break in and you were going to circle the estate on the lookout for the car, his car. Because although you asked her to stay away from him you knew she wouldn't. You don't understand the hold he has over her but it's definite and there's been a faraway look in her eye like it's out of her control, like she has no other choice, and you detest every bone in his evil body.

But then she surprised you because she called the police, anonymously, of course, but it could only have been her, and as they had already been briefed on what was taking place they'd called you for clarification and you'd relished the opportunity to take some action against him.

However, the shock of seeing her climb over that boundary wall with him was something else. You nearly confronted them there and then but held back long enough to see her reluctance at crossing to the car, which came as something of a relief.

You stayed out of the way while the police did their job, knowing you'd need them onside in the future, but then she came towards you, stood in the headlights and you saw the damage, you saw what he had done to her. You felt the tightness in your chest, your constricted breathing, the longing to hold her tight, all of it overwhelming.

And that was then...

After the longest night imaginable you've been a step behind her all day.

You had to straighten things out at the House, which went smoothly because even after everything she pointed you in the right direction. The Trustees gathered and were eventually satisfied. The security guards were completely unaware of what had gone down.

You'd sent Cubby ahead but then followed on to the police station as soon as you could get away. You were *told you'd already missed her then had to sit down heavily on hearing where she'd gone.*

And you'd followed her there.

Naturally they were discreet but you know, you know…

And this is now…

Hatred coils in your gut, visceral and black like angry snakes roiling around each other and you'd give anything, anything, for five minutes alone with him.

Cubby has already picked her up, she's probably home by now, and you wonder if she is disappointed in you, if she thinks you failed her because you damn well know you did and you doubt she'll forgive.

How can she when you won't ever be able to forgive yourself?

You push the untouched coffee away, the sickening twist in the pit of your stomach only deepening as you get up to leave.

Chapter 29

As I approach Crowbridge I see a small black car coming towards me, learner plates stuck on in warning and one of those triangular roof signs advertising the driving school. We draw closer and I smile when I see Kourtney's determined little face peering out of the windscreen, her brow furrowed with the ferocity of her concentration.

While I feel as though nothing will ever be the same again, here in my village, all appears unchanged. I turn down past the pub and raise my hand in greeting to Josh, who's arrived for the start of his shift. Mrs Tompkins is hurrying towards the church pushing her barrow loaded with produce for the service. Further on I see Diane out in her garden, Joe is there as well, and she flags me down. She is saying something I can't hear over her shoulder to Joe, and I wind the window down as she approaches but lean my elbow on the sill so as to cup my chin in my hand and cover the worst of the bruising, and the split lip.

"Morning, are you only just coming home, you dirty stop out?" she says, then laughs before adding wistfully, "I'm so envious." She has clearly not had a proper look at me or she'd see the state I'm in and the rather strange choice of clothing I made for the romantic tryst she thinks I've been having. There's something else agitating her though and she wastes not a moment before she tells me, "You're not going to believe what's happened."

"What has happened, Diane?" I say trying to show enthusiasm in the hope she spits it out quickly. She's not generally a gossip so this must be important.

"Letitia has thrown Ben out! Can you believe it?" With all that's been going on in the last twenty-four hours I had completely forgotten about my meddling. I am genuinely surprised and my eyebrows must show this as I need say nothing more for Diane to continue, "He got home from work last night to find all his belongings out on the front lawn and her inside with the doors locked and bolted. There was one hell of a row by all accounts, she was yelling out of a top window at him then he got back in his car and drove off."

"Did he take all his stuff with him?"

"Of course not, you'd barely fit an overnight bag in that stupid roller-skate of a midlife crisis he drives around in. No, apparently he's got a van round there right now loading it all up." Letitia had proved me wrong after all, and I am pleased my judgement of her had been misplaced.

I give a brief smile though as I feel my lip splitting again I change the subject by saying, "Why have you got Joe working for you on a Sunday?"

"He's come for his dinner actually, but wanted to plant some spring bulbs out first. He says he's got some for you as well."

"Lovely, what sort?" I hear her ask him and she tells me daffodils and tulips.

I'll be back.

A wave of sadness threatens to engulf me once again.

I'm transported instantly to a beautifully warm and sunny day when Dan made me laugh with his suspect knowledge of the meaning of flowers and, distracted by my thoughts, I miss Diane asking if I want to stop for something to eat. She repeats herself and I say no, thank you, I have so much to do. She looks at me as if for the first time as if something has alerted her to my state, and she asks me if I'm alright in that way people do when they can see you're not. I tell her I am, which I know she doesn't believe, but I'll fill her in another time, I can't deal with doing so right now.

For the last few hours all I've wanted to do was get home, strip off and stand under a hot shower but now I'm here I see the horses are close to the back wall of my garden and I'm distracted into going to see them instead. They wander over, vaguely interested but not enough to stop them picking at the grass as they come. The brown one is still chewing as he brings his nose up to investigate my outstretched hand. I can hear the chomping of his teeth as they grind together and I smile at the way his top lip moves independently to nuzzle and check out my hand for any possible treats. I don't know why, I've never given them anything, Joe told me I shouldn't, not without the owner's permission. I stroke my hand down his nose and he's happy to put up with my fussing for a while then moves off. The grey one can't bring himself to leave off grazing for even a moment to greet me but I'm happy to watch him instead for a few minutes.

Wrapping my coat tightly around myself, I go and sit on the bench seat under the kitchen window and breathe in the peace and quiet while I try and make sense of all that's happened.

I haven't cried yet, not properly. I can't even think of Dan, and of everything I've lost, that might break me completely and I block all thoughts of him from my mind. I will have to deal with them another day. But when I think of Tag tears spring unbidden and I'm not sure if they are for him, or me. His life had only gone downhill in recent years, his increased drug use no doubt playing its part in that and despite what he'd done to me I couldn't help but feel bad for having left him, like I was in some way responsible.

I wonder what he'd gone through at the hands of the police, and at what point he'd found out that he hadn't just pulled off the greatest theft of his life…

Because there was no way I was ever going to risk losing that necklace.

My meeting with Tag had not been my first visit to the House that night. At one o'clock I'd left my car in the layby outside the village of Danewright, climbed over the fortunately low perimeter wall of the estate and hiked the nearly one mile to the House through the woods. I'd skirted round to the rear and made my modest entry via an unalarmed toilet window near the kitchen which put me right in the heart of the servants' quarters.

It had only taken a moment to get my bearings and I'd set off steadily along the dark passages I recalled from the plans I'd pored over.

The layout was simple though I was held up for a while when I found my expected route was blocked by a door that hadn't been on the floor plans. I double checked, running through the plans I could see as clearly as photographs in my mind, but I was as sure as I could be that I was on the right route to finding the librarian's access. I paused, knowing that beyond the library entrance there had already been a door and I wondered if that had simply been extended forward. The door wasn't locked and my theory turned out to be correct as I found myself in a long but quite narrow storage room. There was no window in there so I switched on my torch to look around. The walls both sides and at the far end were racked, the shelves piled high with catering goods. Heaps of tablecloths and serviettes were alongside large pans and crates of cutlery, stacked up plates, bowls, teacups and saucers, enough to feed a small army, or much more likely here a large wedding party.

However, there was no obvious sign of the entrance I was after. I knew it had to be on my left and I looked through the shelving along that wall to see if I could see it. Sure enough about halfway along I could see a line running down the wall and a couple of feet later another one.

A door, of sorts.

If I could manage to reach it.

The shelves in front of it were where the linen was housed and I could see that the wooden shelving came in sections, which I hoped I was not about to find were bolted to the wall, or floor, or indeed anywhere. I'd pulled at one end of the section that stood in my way and it shifted, a fraction. It was all the encouragement I'd needed. It would probably have been an easier job had I removed the piles of cloth filling the shelves but that would also have taken longer and I had somewhere to be, so I'd wrapped my hands around the upright struts, braced myself and half lifted, half dragged the whole structure towards me, or at least one end of it. It moved towards me in a semi-circle away from the wall, its other end the pivotal point. As soon as there was enough of a gap to get through I stopped and stepped behind the shelving. The thing that I was hoping would get me into the library was as unrecognisable as a door as it was possible to be, and I hoped I hadn't made a terrible mistake in thinking this was my way in. It was narrower than your average door and flush with the wall, apart from a small scooped out section large enough to fit your fingers in about halfway down, otherwise there was nothing to distinguish it from the rest of the wall.

I'd pushed it.

Nothing.

I'd pushed it harder.

Still nothing.

I'd shone my torch round the line in the wall but there appeared to be no catch, nothing to press, no hidden lever. I thought for a moment and imagined the room that I thought this opened up into. My favourite choice for this hidden passage had been in the corner. I realised I had been indiscriminate with my pushing and when I thought about it the door would have to be hinged in some way. Most likely on the edge away from the corner, otherwise the shelving on the other wall would prevent it from opening. And it would be heavy, it was filled with books on one side after all. I crossed my fingers and hoped no one had decided to seal up the entrance for any reason and I put my shoulder into it, my whole weight all on the right hand side and I gave it everything I had.

Which turned out to be more than was needed.

As soon as the door started moving it slid open easily, as if it were on runners, and I nearly fell into the library. Gathering myself I'd grabbed for my torch to turn it off, then taken a moment, and a deep breath before making my way across the library, which was bathed in silvery muted tones shining in through the atrium.

The collection was displayed in three specially made cabinets currently lined up to face the public walkway, which was separated from the display by sections of thick rope looped between upright stands like the sort deployed to keep the queue in its place outside a nightclub. By day discreet security guards stood watch over the jewels but by night they were left to fend for themselves. After all there was only one way into the library and that door was locked and watched over by a camera, which was in turn monitored by the security men in their Portacabin.

I'd moved in front of the dark wood display cabinets. They were built for purpose, that being the easy movement of this collection so that it could be taken anywhere, and with minimal effort opened back up for display. The cabinets were on wheels and had several drawers with covers that lifted up and covered the collection but while the jewels were on display these covers were removed and stored elsewhere. Therefore, what I was here for was laid out on the bespoke display area on top. Every item of this collection had its specific place. There were feminine shaped moulds for the necklaces to grace, cases for the bracelets and hooks for earrings, all designed to show off each item in its full glory. If one piece went missing the gap would be spotted immediately and I could only imagine the hullabaloo this night's activities were going to cause in the morning.

My object of interest was right in the centre of the middle cabinet, it being the most valuable item in the display. I'd admired it for a moment, the stones glistening and beautiful even in the ghostly light. It was made up of loops and layers and when I'd lifted it there was a surprising amount of weight to it.

I'd taken the replacement I'd brought with me, the item I'd borrowed from Cubby's safe, out of my pocket and put the real necklace in there instead and then I'd hung the imposter in its place. It was no replica of the original but it was a fair imitation and I believed good enough to fool someone who hadn't done their homework properly. Especially if they were in a rush. I'd taken one last look around to check nothing was out of order and then I'd left the way I'd come, putting everything back exactly as I'd found it.

I'd travelled the mile back to my car as quickly as I could and when I'd got there I'd taken a padded envelope from the boot, placed the necklace into it and sealed it up. It was addressed to Mr Arthur Ramsey, Chair of the Trustees, who lives at Rose Cottage, Danewright. I'd jogged silently into the village, knowing exactly where he lived. I knew he was there and I knew he'd wake up to a nice surprise on his doormat in the morning. There were no streetlights and I'd not seen a single person before posting the package through his door. As I'd returned to my car I was as certain as I could be that I'd come and gone entirely unobserved.

It was by then two-thirty and I needed to get a move on to make my appointment at three.

Tag had lost his freedom for nothing more than a decent imitation of a fancy necklace, all glass and paste, smoke and mirrors. I didn't feel bad for cheating him, after all I'd originally told him the jewels were fake, that time in the pub. He hadn't noticed but the replacement necklace wasn't even that similar to the real one. I'd taken a chance there but relied on the fact that he'd never been one for the detail in the past and he wouldn't have prepared as I had done and researched what he was there to take. For him a necklace is a necklace, it's the challenge that is the goal.

Eventually succumbing to the cold, I go inside and run a bath. I scrub every inch of skin until it's pink in an attempt to remove the filth I feel I'm coated with but I can do little about that which makes me feel dirty inside.

Overcome by inertia, I'm at a loss as to what to do after. Food and sleep seem like the order of the day but I end up sitting on my sofa and staring at nothing.

There is silence here, absolute silence, and I find peace in that.

But then I hear it, the approach of unexpected company in the soft roll of tyres over earth. The slam of a door, confirming the threat to my solitude. The squeak of my front gate as familiar as the metallic rattle of the catch as it swings closed and the crunch of gravel under unknown feet that tells me I will have to move.

There's a knock on my door, and I stand before it. Other than the future I don't know what's on the other side but I take a deep breath, and open it.

THE END

Thank you for reading. If you are able to leave a few words as a review on the mighty Amazon, Goodreads or any place of your choosing, then you will feel the warmth of my thanks in the form of a virtual hug. It really does matter as it helps inform other readers as to whether they should pick up this book, or not.

Now follows the beginning of the first novel in The Grayson Trilogy, the romantic and suspenseful, *A Single Step*.

<u>Chapter 1</u>

"Tell me about the kickboxing. How did you get into it?" A surprising first question that I'd neither expected nor prepared for. I met the cool blue of Cavendish's eyes, determined not to look away or show I'd been shaken, in an attempt to present good body language, just as the situation required.

"I took up kickboxing for exercise, mostly...but also to relieve stress a couple of years ago," I replied, a little bewildered.

"Stress?" He looked at me sharply as his brow furrowed, deepening the frown lines already forming between his eyes. Damn, I thought, my heart sinking, I've screwed up already – why did I mention that? He's not going to want someone working for him with stress problems. I was annoyed with myself for bringing it up, although it could have been worse I argued; I could have launched right in and told him all about my anger issues as well. I tried to explain in an attempt to mitigate.

"I'd had a bad couple of years and found this type of exercise more than anything else provided an outlet. It always succeeded in making me calmer and more relaxed so I stuck with it."

"Hmm...I can see how that would work," he nodded thoughtfully as though understanding, which was encouraging. "So, do I take it you prefer solitary sports to team games?"

"Yes." I could feel my anxiety rising as I couldn't think of anything to add to this rather blunt response.

"Okay, your instructor has indicated you're pretty good and I believe you've competed on behalf of your club a few times?"

He's spoken to my instructor?

"Yes, that's correct," I replied, not at all sure where he was going with this.

"You've also learnt self-defence, I see. Do you enjoy that?"

"Yes I do, and although fortunately I haven't had to use it in a real-life situation, I think I'm quite proficient if the need ever did arise."

"Excellent. Your instructor used the words, er..." He opened the envelope file on his lap on which he'd rested the rather sketchy copy of my CV and flicked back and forth between the surprisingly large number of sheets it contained. I took a deep breath in an attempt to relax and looked towards the far end of the room where there were four floor-to-ceiling windows which afforded a view onto a well-manicured lawn and immaculately tended flowerbeds, though these were currently not very flowery.

I'd been nervous coming to attend an interview anyway and had already been thrown on my arrival by finding that I was going to be interviewed by Lord Henry Cavendish himself, instead of Mr Trent, who was the estate manager. I'd then been further surprised when shown to the office by the butler, Forster, to find Cavendish – for that was how he introduced himself to me – was considerably younger than I was expecting. The title, I guessed, had mentally added at least twenty years but he was only in his mid-thirties; tall and attractive with a friendly, open face and dark hair, short at the sides and slightly longer on top, combed forward.

We sat in his large office on a couple of settees, of which there were several in the room, and I wondered when so much seating would ever be needed. Ours were set at right angles to each other around a large coffee table and in front of an unlit fireplace. The mantelpiece was stone, limestone I thought, creamy yellowy-brown, the same as the Manor and the wall that enclosed the estate. A tray of refreshments had been delivered by a young woman while I was waiting for Cavendish to find my file amongst the mountain of paperwork on his desk. She was slim and wore smart black trousers, a white fitted shirt and flat shoes. Her brown hair was tied in a high ponytail which swung as she walked. As she'd come across the room she'd given me a friendly smile which I'd tried to reciprocate, though mine had felt weak in response, betraying my anxiety. Carrying a large tray, she'd deposited it on the coffee table in front of me, whispered for me to help myself then quickly left the room. Looking at the cup of coffee in front of me now I could see a skin starting to form on the top as it cooled.

I started as Cavendish suddenly came upon what he had been looking for. "Ah yes, here it is – he used the words 'committed' and 'quite brutal' about your self-defence techniques." Cavendish looked back up at me, appearing to be highly delighted with this.

I could feel myself blushing. "Ah, yes...I caught him with a lucky punch one day, and he took some time to get over it."

"Oh, that's very good. Okay, I think that's all I wanted to ask you. Do you have any questions?" What? I thought with some alarm. Is that it?

"Well..." I replied, nonplussed, "I'm a little surprised by the direction this interview has taken. I was expecting some questions about my experience with horses, that sort of thing."

He looked at me in surprise, and then went on to explain: "Oh! I'm sorry, I'm not used to doing this. Trent usually handles all employee issues for me. I should maybe have explained at the outset that we've already carried out a fully comprehensive background search, including references on you, your experience, etcetera, so there's nothing else I really need to ask. I've got it all here in my file." He shuffled through the pile of papers on his lap before pulling out a sheet which he then scanned down. "I've got details here of each riding school, livery yard or farm you worked at after school and during weekends and holidays in each of the places you lived, I believe swapping your work for lessons and riding experience?" As he looked up I confirmed my agreement with this. "And you then settled in Crowbridge and worked at the local riding school in your free time," and then hesitating, he finished quietly, "...until four years ago." He stopped as I tensed, exposing my unease as to what he might say next, and meeting his eyes I could see his discomfort. Realising my arms had unconsciously wrapped themselves around my body I looked away, reluctantly releasing them and forcibly placing my hands back in my lap. He didn't acknowledge my behaviour in any way, for which I was grateful, but cleared his throat before carrying on steadily, "We've taken references from all these places and they all say the same things. You're conscientious and knowledgeable and while you haven't had your own horses to look after you've often had sole responsibility for other people's horses.

"We're not looking for an instructor, Mrs Grayson, the children can already ride, although they will be spending time at the stables during their holidays which you would have to be prepared for and manage. Would you be all right with that?"

He was looking at me keenly and I nodded, partly with relief that the awkward moment had passed, but also as it seemed to be the right thing to do, although in all honesty I didn't know how all right I would be with that. However, I did know I wanted this job and having been surprised to have got as far as an interview I really didn't want to mess it up now.

The advert for the position had originally arrived through my letterbox on my birthday in January, anonymously, delivered as if it were a gift – it was my only one. It was quite short, torn from a magazine, advertising for a stable manager/groom to look after the family horses for the Melton Manor estate which, being some way away, I was not familiar with. A cottage came with the position and pets were allowed – I wouldn't have considered applying otherwise.

My interest had been immediately piqued and although I now doubted I'd have enough recent experience to be successful in getting the job, horses had once been my passion. They had provided the stability I'd craved during the unsettled years I'd faced growing up and were the recipients of the love I had to give in lieu of anyone else; I'd ridden and worked with them obsessively, as is common with many girls. But then unlike most, who tended to move on once boys came on the scene, I'd continued working at a local yard in my free time, always intending one day to have a horse of my own. That, however, was not to be.

I'd thought about the advert for quite a while considering the position. The fact that it had even raised my interest told me something and I came to the conclusion that as horses had provided the balm I'd needed to soothe my soul during turbulent years before, perhaps they could provide that relief for me again.

I'd also mulled over who had put it through my letterbox in the first place, dismissing most of the names I came up with and leaving me with one suspect. My still viciously raw feelings towards her and the thought that her motivation for doing this was to get me to move away almost made me tear it up. In the end, however, so as not to spite myself, I'd written a CV, attached it to an email as requested, and sent it together with a covering letter. And now here I was.

OTHER BOOKS BY GEORGIA ROSE

<u>Acknowledgements</u>

They say it takes a village to bring up a child and it seems the same adage applies when releasing a book out into the world. So I must say what feels like a rather inadequate thank you to all those who have helped me along the way.

I have a super set of six beta (test) readers: Debra Cartledge, Claire Millington, Andrew Moore, Sarah Postins, Kathy Sapsed and Katherine Winters. These unfortunate individuals are exposed to my work at a horribly rough stage as I like early feedback and I thank them for their candour and for telling me what they really thought, it informs my way forward.

After testing the waters with The Joker, to see if and how we could work together I was delighted that my editor, Mark Barry, agreed to take this project on as well. I have not made it easy for him as the manuscript has been back and forth to him three times and I know he is a busy man. I thank him for his words of wisdom and warning, and for telling me when mine are 'fundamentally unreadable' but most especially I thank him for his friendship and for the bucketloads of enthusiasm he has shown for this book. May it find many readers that feel the same way!

There are countless punctuation and grammar rules and I consider myself truly blessed, and mightily relieved, to have met Julia Gibbs who knows them all! A great big thank you goes to her for her diligence in proof reading my work so that the final product is as polished as it can be. Any errors that remain are mine and mine alone.

I feel fortunate to have been introduced to the wonderfully patient Simon Emery who has designed this fabulous cover. He managed to come up with a selection of terrific ideas from the mangled mess of my thoughts on the subject and I thank him for his expertise. I am delighted with the end result.

There's an extra thank you to Amanda Stock for spotting an issue at the eleventh hour that I'm thrilled could be resolved before I hit the publish button!

My thanks as always goes to the incredibly generous online community. Surprisingly, finding all of you has been one of the most enjoyable aspects of becoming an independent author and I thank you for your friendship, knowledge and support.

My family, of course, have to put up with the actual process of me trying to get a book out and while my grown up children have now managed to escape most of that, my husband has not. So, Russell, thank you for your patience, for your support and for coping with my absence as I continue to try and juggle far too many things as always.

Contact details

Thank you for reading this far. I'm always interested to hear from readers with any feedback, thoughts or observations they are willing to make. If you'd like to get in touch, or you want to hear about what's coming next you can do so through my website at www.georgiarosebooks.com where you will also have the opportunity to follow my blog or sign up to my newsletter. Alternatively you can email me at info@georgiarosebooks.com for a chat or to ask to go on my newsletter list; follow me on Twitter @GeorgiaRoseBook; find me on Facebook where I am georgia.rose.books or 'like' my Georgia Rose Author page. I look forward to hearing from you.

Finally, if you have enjoyed reading this, please tell ~~someone~~ *everyone* you know and, whatever you think of it, if you are able to, would you please consider leaving a review? Of whatever rating! You might not think your opinion matters, but I can assure you it does. It helps the book gain visibility and it informs other readers whether or not to purchase it, so if you could take a minute or two to leave a few words on Amazon and/or Goodreads that would be hugely appreciated.

Now, if you're sitting there holding a beautiful paperback in your hand and you're thinking that request doesn't include me... well please think again. It doesn't matter how or where you bought your paperback Amazon and Goodreads will still accept a review from you.

Thank you.

www.ingramcontent.com/pod-product-compliance
Lightning Source LLC
Chambersburg PA
CBHW031216120726
47905CB00002B/360